ALMA

BARONESS ALMA JOHANNA VON EHRENFELS
Née Koenig, Pseudonym Johannes Herdan,
Alma Johanna Koenig
Born: August 18, 1887 in Prague
Deported: May 27, 1942 (Minsk Ghetto)
Missing since 1942

So you say she has returned, Alma Johanna, from a long trip, you say; Alma Johanna is back. I saw a light in her apartment. A shimmer of light came through the kitchen curtains, through the window in the corridor. The bathroom is in back. Kitchen and bathroom were seldom separate in these old houses. Alma Johanna—it has been thirty years since then—they took her away when she was having breakfast (O. said), simply took her from her breakfast in the summer, in the early summer. No, it was winter, a cold, gray, winter morning. Johanna is in the bathroom. (There's a knock at the door.) Listen, footsteps. No, Anna was standing outside, the old woman. Or couldn't Giovanna finish her breakfast? She hadn't finished it (once in May), the pot of coffee, the rolls (actually there weren't any), bread, awful, gummy, expensive bread. She placed the wartime bread, the winter bread on her plate with trembling fingers, but they were probably not trembling with the cold in those unheated rooms with the high windows and the old stoves. There had been nothing all winter that Alma Johanna could have used to warm her soul. Knit mittens, knit socks, winter aid for Giovanna's trembling fingers. Who would have wanted to cover Giovanna's fingers in those days? Who had the courage to wrap their hands around Alma's frozen fingers? There was a war going on, and everyone had something to be afraid of. (Everyone?) Everyone. Even the janitor, the block warden, the watchman nods and points upstairs with his thumb, with his index finger. Everyone walks past Alma's door with its brass plate brightly polished, scrubbed clean. Who bothers to scrub things clean in these brown times? Don't you know? Don't talk so loud. Who wants to hear those things after all these years? Nobody wants to hear where they took Alma, during

5

breakfast at five. A poet usually lingers over breakfast in the morning, with a notebook on her lap and the lamp—or was it a candle—in front of her. (Did they really have candles in those dark days?) It was winter, even if it was early summer, and in the cold hours of morning (of murdering?), with the laboriously scrounged, gummy, wartime bread between her teeth and her notes before her in her lap—to have written a book, to have planted a tree, to have given birth to a child (you accomplished only one of those things, Giovanna)—sitting at breakfast. (Were you lying down?) Were you on your knees, Giovanna, and did you pray half the night? To whom would you pray in the winter? Unheated rooms, much too high for war, much too dark for peace; with curtains and wallpaper that were much too stained. You spent your whole life in Vienna, in this city, your whole life in Austria, in this country, your whole life as a stranger among the people.

My Lord, what are you talking about? Neighbor, what are you talking about? You've been watching too much television. You've let yourself be brainwashed. You saw a film from that time. Sure, the war was going on, but the fashions, but the hats, but the music. (That was forbidden, stupid woman!) You heard music on the radio, listened to the news on the radio, received an important message on the radio. Be careful, Alma Viva. The stairs will not creak softly. (Boots do not squeak in the city.) No stairs, no steps creak—in the city stairs reverberate (and so do corridors with pounding foot-steps) beneath the tread of the troops.

When I wake up at night, I always turn the light on in my sleep—I light the candle. During this blackout no light escapes into the night through the cracks, through the windows. And I pick up a notebook and write down the dream, the word, the thought, the fantastic dream image, the incomprehensible word. I make notes and lie down again on the bed, my resting place, my couch. (In the camp, did you say?) Which is it, bed or camp? I mean pillows. The bed sheets are tattered in this war. I make notes and close the booklet, the notebook, lonely in my bare, plundered rooms. (Plundered?) Oh, now and then you handed out something of value and politely said "You're welcome," and were courteous. You hid and you walked through the streets afraid, o Alma, Giovanna, Regina!

With her hair pinned up, her soul startled, while the siren sang, she followed the footsteps, went to the cellar. They made room. She said, "Excuse me," begged their pardon, remained steadfast. That's the expression; in all these things she remained *steadfast*. Breakfast! Just who would have had breakfast one last time? Who thought about breakfast in the tunnel, in the mountain, when they went into the mountain with bag and baggage and immediately fainted because of the lack of oxygen, because of the closeness of the many people, near the mothers, the sleeping (sleeping?) children. We thought of the heroes. (Really? did we think?) And didn't my son die, too, and didn't I wear the cross, the Mother's Cross around my neck? Neighbor woman, you never had six children, three at the most, so that they could be slaughtered all the faster. My good woman, have you gone crazy? A criminal, a ne'er-do-well, as he proved to be, was sent to the camp for rehabilitation. Now you remain silent, you're quiet and unwilling, you refuse to give information. Sister-in-law, if you had only remained silent, refused back then, having married into the family, having gotten pregnant, yes, pregnant, the way you did! But who still wants to talk about it these days, with all

7

this abundance, with all the beautiful things, with all the beautiful colors, with all this beautiful stuff? When people are already talking about a third car, they don't talk about the ones who have nothing to say. "But back then, those were the days," he says, "when I fired my slingshot from the garden and hit the Jew's daughter in the cherry tree. Think of it, a stone with my slingshot! And the Jewish girl looked startled, didn't know what hit her, sitting in the cher-cher-cherry tree, the Jewish girl in the cherry tree, the Jewish girl during the war." Hit her with your slingshot, you say? The trees are no longer standing, the victims no longer walk. They built an apartment house in the Jew's old garden. (Or do you have something against that?) Back then a Bohemian tailor bought it. He's no longer alive, either. She sold the ground for a lot of money. Children were not permitted to play in the garden after that, still aren't, even now, only the poodle. And the tailor's widow had the walnut tree cut down because of the tax. And the way she broke the apricot tree, broke off the main branch, hanging from it with her face contorted! What a spectacle! After the war, the Jew's son visited us once more, very secretly. Yes, those were the days. "If I had hit her, the Jewish girl in the tree," he says, "think of the trouble it would have caused my father. He had just gone bankrupt. Great! Zing! The stone whizzed across the hedge where the concrete playground is now. A barber had just acquired the ground-floor apartment for a large fee. He was the owner of the two poodles that were permitted to play in the garden. Zing, over the hedge and into the cherry tree, where it hit the Jewish girl right in the neck." The Jewish girl is gone, my youth is gone, forever, gone forever. Moved away, Alma Giovanna. It says *Sold* on the door plate, *Confis-*

cated above the little plaque that was rubbed clean by hardworking hands. (Rubbed his hands? The Bohemian tailor rubbed his hands? And we?) And what about us?

She was always there, that good soul, Anna: Anna the cook, Anna the servant, a companion to her mother, Pepi, old Pepi, her mother's companion, old, half-blind Anna, she (with the characteristic article). Trembling, Anna, the half-blind woman, dips her red hands into the dirty rinse water. She cleans everything so well, she makes everything so clean. "How do you do that," I ask Anna, "when you really can't see well enough?"

"I feel with my fingers. I simply feel along the dishes with the tips of my fingers, to see if they are clean and smooth. That works wonderfully well."

Where was Anna when it was still dark on that morning in the late autumn, in the winter? No, it was the early summer. The rooms with their high ceilings were unheated. For days the atmosphere had been eerie on the streets, in the alleys, in the marketplaces of Vienna. For days, for weeks, for months there had been the endless freight trains, the long columns, the vehicles, the sealed freight cars. Where was Anna, her mother's blind, half-blind kitchen servant (blinded?), a nation blinded? Where was the aging maid servant? Yes, Anna, I refer to Anna. They say she came by at the time. They say she gave warning. They say she scurried by at five in the morning. "Child, what are you still doing here?" Anna supposedly said.

"Let me be, Anna. I haven't hurt anyone. Are you crazy?"

Anna was already dead by then. Besides that, she wasn't blind, but deaf. At least she was hard of hearing, completely deaf in one ear.

The doorbells in the old houses out in the country,

actually villas with at most one family per floor—the privy councilor lived there. There was an old bell on a cord (with the cord? strangled?), a bell on a cord. On the pole a little bell rings, reminds us of monastery gates and similar places, an iron pole. The cord is pulled cautiously, the bell rings in the vestibule, a door opens. (Does it open?) The steps are mottled, mottled stone, mottled and glistening, not the kind of patterns they have in Vienna, or perhaps they are, if we are reminded of Roman villas, Carnuntum, Petronell, Anima Alma. (*Ancora viva*?) That was much later. Carnuntum was after the war and has nothing at all to do with Giovanna. That was another woman, and again and again we have these stereotypical, these typical repetitions of words. Otherwise there's nothing new. Oh yes there is, a renter. An older lady? It's hard to say. She's not really an old woman, but she's unapproachable. She lives next door, reminds me of somebody. I've seen her someplace before. That's right, you know, the poet on the fourth floor, on the left. It was during the war.

Just why are you whispering? Am I deaf? Who whispers to the deaf? To the mute, with voices, at most there is the whispering of doves, early in the morning at four, at five, when the others are still asleep in their beds. The doves whisper up high under the eaves: Where is Alma? I wouldn't call it whispering. By the way, she doesn't feed the doves, she's not one of those, old, but lonely. (Is that supposed to be a contradiction?) Yes, of course, a different type. Somehow it's peculiar to find such a renter in that house. Which house are you talking about, anyway? The one across the street? That's been gone for a long time. Of course, a renter without dependents; she washes her stockings daily, violently, and her other things twice a week. Yes, yes, unbelievable, the back room, with the corridor window, admittedly small, and with the unmistakable scent of the old, ornate rooms where old maids live in Vienna.

You say, the new woman is elderly and looks so peculiar? How so? Can't anyone explain that to me? What excites you, the similarity? And she has returned, she's back, and I'm supposed to believe that such a thing can happen? Should we change? What for? Weren't we all in danger? Didn't we all experience the nightly false —and then no longer false alarms, warnings, and the hiding from the air raids? Now I've had enough of that topic. And you also know she didn't go along anymore at the end, perhaps because we made it clear to her that we didn't want her. But what difference does it make? She sat up there alone, and out of pride she didn't tremble. That's all.

Proud decisions, back then. Just who could decide so quickly? It was hard enough, having nothing in common with them, robbed of any natural historical development and not good enough for the critics, and hardly mentioned in literary history. It was because of her youth. It was because of her childhood. It was because of her maturity.

Hidden up in the attic, living as a submarine—because form is not an idea but a thing (criticism can say a thing or two about that)—the poet has things in front of him, objects, realities, not ideas. He lives very concretely as a submarine in Vienna, and doesn't walk around too much, and doesn't drink too much liquid, and gives a friendly person something of value now and then, so that he can betray us all the more easily. But bourgeois criticism does not like it at all, because form arises from the content, and if we do not like the content, we smash the form, and thus we write about the officially accepted art that covers up all unpleasant contents with a hypocritical veil.

So Alma was alone and yet in the best of company. And nothing has changed about that to this very day. That's the way it was, yes, that's even the way it could have been.

After all, consider what we read, consider what we wrote, what then remained as—they call it *sunken cultural heritage*—which then haunts our vocabulary. We couldn't have known, we say, and we think that the others after us don't want to know. And because it was not honestly overcome but half-heartedly covered up, there was simply a chasm there, between the artists and historical reality, and sometimes reality caught up with the artists or called them home.

"Silence is complicity," said the deaf woman, the old woman, the woman up in the attic.

It's so hard for us not to be blind, Anna, not to be deaf, Anna. At five in the morning a poet crouched on bended knees with her notebook. She watched, she prayed, she wrote during the night. She was never silent.

HELENE AND ELISE

ELISE RICHTER
Austrian phoneticist
First female Austrian college teacher
Born: March 2, 1865 in Vienna
Deported: October 9, 1942 (Terezin Ghetto)
Missing since 1944

HELENE RICHTER
Sister of Elise
Austrian Anglicist
Wrote about English Romanticism
and about the history of the Burgtheater
Born: August 4, 1861 in Vienna
Deported: October 9, 1942 (Terezin Ghetto)
Missing since 1944

"In the beginning," she said, "everything was quite different. In the beginning there was something else."

"How was it?"

"In the beginning everything was quite different."

"Tell us, tell us."

"In the beginning Franca came to see us."

"Oh, please, tell us something unprinted, unpublished, something short, a novel or at least a story."

"Once she came to see us with a friend."

"So, how was it?"

"In the beginning," Helene said, "in the beginning you still weren't here yet."

"Where was I?" asked Elise.

"In me," her father said. "You were still in me before you were in her. Then you grew and got big."

"How big?"

"Well, that big, just that big."

"When did it begin? How did it begin?"

"It began on the coast, on some coast or other."

"Tell us, tell us."

"It was after the planet had cooled down, after the interplay of physical life forms, after the development of favorable conditions for life."

"Tell us, tell us."

"Yes, the differentiation, the sense organs, the habits that delegate to the hands activities that differ from those performed by the feet. Yes, oh yes. Take Dalmatia, later a synonym for Illyria. The Adriatic coast. Think of the Roman intervention, 299 B.C., and how it ends in the ninth century, after the suppression of the Pannonian-Illyrian revolt. The establishment of the province and what came in between, and what that means: *intervention*. Think who is served by it and against whom it is directed. Suppression of the rebels. Thrown to the ground, to the ground, an entire people, if you can imagine it, the turncoats, the collaborators—those foreign words—the followers and fellow-travelers who deliver others up to the knife before and after the suppression of the insurrection. The beautiful coast, the settlement of the colonists, the establishment of cities, the trade routes, the highways and the superficial Romanization of the hinterland. The division of the empire, the invasion of the Slavs and the Avars in the sixth and seventh centuries. The cities that belonged to the Byzantine exarchate of Ravenna—Zadar, Trogir, Split, Dubrovnik, Kotor."

"Tell us, tell us."

"And the Croatian kings, and the competitor Venice that sought bases for its trade with the Levant region, you see. And later the Hungarians intervened, and Bosnians and Serbs, and then Venice emerged as victor after all. But the insurrectionists are still not broken in my story. Think of the force—it should actually be called *movement*—necessary to bring a few rebels together like that, after six centuries of intervention. Yes, when there was already a synonym for *the people*, when it had gone so far that the people had almost been assimilated, they rebelled, a small number revolted, perhaps a bit too late, a few centuries too late. History had passed them by."

"Which history?"

"Well, yours and mine. But Venice had hardly settled there when the Turks were at their gates. They made a brief guest appearance, then Venice remained victorious. But no, the Peace Treaty of Campoformio was signed and Venice lost its Adriatic empire. When Dalmatia was given to Austria, it soon became a pillar of the government. And then all at once there is another

18

insurrection, or at least a movement. Some of the people, city dwellers, want autonomy and lean toward Italy. The others, peasants and workers, want to be Southern Slavs. Perhaps they are. Perhaps there is a differentiation among the people with the same name. Well, anyway, then came the defense laws and the revolts and the crushing of the revolts."

"Was he already alive then? Were we already alive then?"

"We were alive," said Elise.

"We were alive," said Helene. "We are witnesses of the story. Our brief existence is testimony in this story or in that one."

"Then there has to be an end, but you haven't even started yet. Why Dalmatia?"

"Because of the sharply divided strips of coast, because of the Adriatic Sea, because of the islands that lie parallel to the coast. Because of the alternation between dinaric, striated limestone ridges and partially bog-laden strips of marl schist mixed with sandstone, because of the bathing resorts, because of tourism, because of Spalato, oh yes, because of Split. In the beginning, the rabbi of Spalato sent his son Adolfo to study medicine in the capital city. His name was Giovanni Amadeo. His son was just eighteen, and he was to become the first Italian philologist and the first Italian linguist. I forgot to say that from 1809 to 1813 the Napoleonic annexation to Italy occurred, and although Split definitively belonged Austria, it belonged to the kingdom with Dubrovnik and part of Albania."

"That's precisely what I meant, Dalmatia."

"In the beginning a rabbi from Split sends his son north to study medicine in the capital. At the end, two sisters are sitting on a train bound for Terezin, telling a

19

story. But that's not the end. And something lies in between, and something comes afterward, and again and again there are these emerging and disappearing threads of history."

"Marburg, for example. Mama's villa and the little wooden summer-house that Mama gave him for his birthday, and the dog that begged for the cookies. My sister had these bows in her hair, and she really wanted to put on other stockings, and Mademoiselle didn't know what to do. 'Chérie,' I said while standing in front of the locked door, 'don't lock yourself in. I've brought you a croissant. Please, please open the door.' And our first ride in a car, the honking of the horn. Everyone congregated, really, my cousin Hans, there was room for everyone. A shiny automobile. Why didn't Papa ever talk about it? Oh, Marburg, Mama's home town. Then he wrote that he had sold Mama's house to save us. Just think, he sold it to save us. That was in 1917."

"Oh, what do you know?"

"What do you know?"

"That was in Zurich, according to their aunt. But the aunt is from another thread of the story. In 1918 the rabbi's son had already been dead for thirteen years and the sisters Elise and Helene were established in their careers. Helene published three volumes of English romanticism. Then came the characterizations of actors, and in 1918 *Unser Burgtheater* appeared."

"And Elise?"

"Numerous essays, and especially the book in honor of Adolfo, the son of the rabbi from Split. That's how it was back then, and we must not forget it."

"It will be forgotten. It will be forgotten along with us," says Helene. "Yes, possibly with us."

"But the books?"

20

"Burned, but not all of them."

"And Adolfo, the Italian philologist?"

"He remained in Vienna for almost fifty years, and then went to Florence to die. An Austrian Italian and a connecting link to modern Germanic scholarship."

"And didn't he ever speak?"

"In 1902 he spoke in the upper chamber of parliament. In 1902 an old man stands up and speaks during a meeting of the senate. He speaks with carefully chosen words, in a somewhat old-fashioned Italian, in a somewhat old-fashioned German. An old gentleman speaks in the senate, with his hair combed back, shoulder-length, with eyes that were once fiery, an old man with fiery eyes, with fiery hair, with a fiery voice, fiery. An old gentleman in the senate. With a handlebar mustache, a narrow nose, wide lapels, a white shirt, a black tie. An old man raises his voice. A senator in the senate, not a man of the people, a professor, *honoris causa*. At the age of twenty-six he wrote his most definitive works, composed his most definitive sentences, spoke his most definitive words. At the age of sixty-six he decides to lift up his voice in the senate, a voice from the nineteenth century. It sounds old-fashioned; the vocabulary the professor employs is outdated. He speaks in favor of tolerance without knowing that it is a tolerance for the sons of the senators. He speaks in favor of an Italian university in Triest. Floating along in this old-fashioned voice of the nineteenth century there is much tolerance for the whole world, much culture from the whole world. In this old voice, the voice of romanticism is raised once more, and the reception is extremely cool."

"Is that so important?"

"It's his story. We're indebted to him for the European atmosphere of the linguistic-philological studies written during the second half of the previous century and during the first years of our own."

"And the Slavs?"

"He believed in friendly relations between the two groups who were concerned only with the welfare of their homeland or of the people."

"And what is Franca's role in this story?"

"Nothing, other than the fact that she came to Vienna a hundred and twenty years after Adolfo, the rabbi's son, to the Vienna that existed after we died," said Elise.

"To the Vienna that existed after we lived," murmured Helene.

"What is left? Which way does the wind blow, the nasty wind of Vienna, in the variously tempered streets of the capital?"

"There are no philological studies, there is no research concerning the relationships between the ethnic groups. People have grown accustomed to explaining their actions more on the basis of their thoughts than on the basis of their needs. Profit has remained the only motivating force in Vienna. And not the profit that the thinking mind takes from its striving for knowledge—and that fact is reflected in the minds of these people."

"So how can I establish a relationship between Franca and Adolfo? Franca, who has never heard of Adolfo, who hasn't even seen his picture in the university cloister. Franca, the painter, the painter's daughter."

"Where was Franca's home? Dalmatia?"

"No, the Dolomites, that is, her father's home."

"Was he an Italian?"

"No, an Austrian, a Tyrolean. The old gentleman didn't understand that the senate no longer reigned, nor was he spared a year later from witnessing the bloody confrontations between Italian and German students in

Innsbruck. The old gentleman, a prominent philologist, the founder of a scholarly discipline, didn't understand anything."

"Look here. This is the automobile. It's very similar to a coach. It was black. The spokes, the rubber tires, the outstretched fenders. Hans and little Fritz on the running-board."

"Was little Fritz a neighbor's child?"

"That's Hans, my cousin. Uncle Hans at the steering wheel. Papa behind him. They had the automobile sent from England. The steering wheel was on the right side. A beautiful day. My sister sat in front next to Uncle Hans. That's me in the corner. The top was down with Mama entirely in the open air. I think I remember Mama leaning back and laughing. The frame of the windshield cuts her face in two, but I recognize her by her cheekbones and her hat. We were wearing beautiful, large hats for the drive in Marburg, shortly before the end of the war or not long afterward."

"How was it?" she asked.

"The way it was," they responded.

"Once Franca came to see us. Once she visited us with a friend. She took off her coat. She let her coat slide into my hands. It was already late. She came to our place with a friend."

"Once, it was already late, she came to our place with a friend whose name we didn't understand, the way it can sometimes happen with introductions. Only when the two of them were gone, that is, a few days later, did we find the address and surname of our guest in the address book. Klaus was amazed. He said, 'She isn't the daughter of T., is she?' And she was."

"The daughter of a French woman and a German-speaking resident of the Dolomites."

"She, the daughter of a French woman and a border-land dweller. Formed by her mother's problems, shaped by her father's problems, and she didn't suspect a thing. One day her father set his paintings on fire."

"My father has many problems," she said. "Mother once had to stop him from committing suicide," she said. She was a child, a young girl from Milan. The young woman from Milan who had many relatives in the Dolomites said it.

"I don't know them. I've never been there."

"I go there every year for a few weeks."

"My father has so many siblings in him's house," she said.

"She said, 'in him's house,' and had no idea what she was saying."

"Many of them are poor. My father wanted to burn the paintings in the garden. We were able to save some of them, but most of them were singed or charred. He sits for days in his studio..."

"She said, 'He sits in his studio.'"

"...and can't paint any more. He hates everything he painted before."

"Even the frescoes?" asked Elise.

"Even the frescoes. Especially the frescoes."

"He hates the frescoes that made him famous," said the painter. "T.'s daughter was at our place," the painter said. "Her father wants to commit suicide. Her father hasn't made the transition from the mountains to the plains."

"He acted against his own convictions, sold out. He made concessions. He lost his power. Suicide was only the hope of finding himself again. He has to destroy what he created because the market put an end to his development. His paintings catered to the market. He

24

sacrificed his development to the salons and so-called good taste, and she had a part in it, too. She helped him. She introduced him to it. She decided against her family. But at what price? Don't you see what happens to people who sell out to the market, who make concessions, who create the art demanded by the reigning critics? He burns his paintings for empty husks, for money, for nothing."

"But the fresco! But the fresco!"

"Yes, there you could still see the development that he made in the beginning, but the denial was also there. It was weak, powerless, because he lost the form with the content."

"And if he makes no concessions? And if he makes no compromises?"

"Then all he has left is suicide or political asylum."

"And it isn't true that the writers drag themselves to their execution. It isn't true that these texts are an excuse for their execution. It's pure fabrication that some of these people will become cannon fodder in the search for bias. It is completely out of the question that one particular author already knows everything, because one particular author is nothing to get excited about. On the contrary, the fact is, we need no cannon fodder. The real truth is that the jury acts according to its best judgment and conviction. The actual truth is, you have nothing to report. And doesn't your acquiescence indicate that you are in agreement with the conditions? Doesn't it? It isn't true that we publicly execute you. You don't deserve that much attention. It isn't true that we're amusing ourselves here at your expense. Be happy that you're permitted to read. Be happy that you're alive at all. She was always so touchy. The Illyrians have always been so touchy. These minorities and fringe groups have always been far too touchy. Is it our fault that there was already a synonym for the Illyrians? Is it our fault that there is already a synonym for the authors? What you say isn't true at all. Everything is really quite different.

"This idea of making everyone equal. Who is supposed to do the menial work if all people are equal? You understand that, don't you? And in general, what will happen to the best sellers, the stars, if everyone publishes? You understand that, don't you?"

"And how do I make a connection between menial labor and writing?"

"In your mind, my dear, in your consciousness. It mirrors your situation. You can do it in your mind, can't you?"

"I can pave the way to breakfast with lectors like you," says the publisher.

"I can build a concrete road to dinner with critics like you," says the editor-in-chief.

"Indeed."

"You know," Elise writes, "when I sit here this way and act as if I conform, he believes it. A woman can always learn something from someone who thinks that. Recently, H. from the radio station called me on the telephone. He says he wants to get acquainted with me. And I showed him the plays, or shouldn't I have? But he thought they were quite terrible. He said I had disregarded all the rules of drama. Then I just kept still and listened. Or shouldn't I have done that? And the way I stood there, at our embassy in Paris. I mean, I do represent my country as a writer, or don't I? And the secretary turns her back on me and simply says, 'You introduced yourself to Jankoditsch in the elevator.' And this Kandoditsch was once a foreign minister, and now he has fallen. Now he's a kind of building manager. Let me tell you, when I saw that man Schankoditsch, I thought, a person comes here and is given a somewhat festive reception, but then what? That's what I thought. And then I was in that little attic room, and on Maundy Thursday I had to move to the students' quarters for no reason, because Mr. Schrankowitsch's guests were staying through Easter. And next door to me was the music student, a young girl who plays the violin. She brought a long dress with her because she thought they might ask her to give a concert at the cultural institute. Surely a young thing like her can think such a thing, can't she?"

"After all, such things do happen," said Helene.

"Yes, such things happen," said Elise.

"Go on, go on."

"So the secretary turns her back on me and says, 'I have to get in there. Move a little bit. I have to get into that cabinet.' And everything was so grimy. That anteroom and the waiting room. I had to look up the area codes myself, and the young violinist was finally supposed to introduce herself to Schimankowitsch."

"Well, how does he look?"

"Terrible. His state of consciousness is mirrored in his face. He raved at the cleaning women. The only person in the entire building, the cleaning woman, of course, and the culture-apartment manager was yelling. I had hoped to be able to write in peace there. I mean, the ministry had granted me three weeks. And then when the student misplaced the key on Maundy Thursday, I was totally cut off from the outside world. Fortunately I noticed it and walked around the building all day, leaving notes for my husband. And then by chance I see these two people coming toward me, on Maundy Thursday, my husband and the child. And the secretary was very nice to the student. She looked for Kankoditsch along the entire street because she didn't know his address. It's another department in the ministry. And she asked every concierge, and when she found Kankoditsch's apartment around noon, his wife opened the door. And she curses and yells, and then he comes and curses and yells. And all she could do was beg their pardon again and again, just beg their pardon again and again, until she was finally allowed to speak and could explain that she had misplaced the key and had to get in because the plane was leaving soon. Then he yelled again and finally gave her the key."

"The writers, those grumblers. Elise is dust and ashes, Helene is dust and ashes. Essays, writings, research. And we only want to explore those tendencies, but you already know what I mean: the trend in literature. We need a fluent narrative, I think, one from which the audience gets something, something decent, not too much commentary, not too much ridicule. I mean, you can't do that."

"So, what else was there about Franca?"

"She left the house, she rented a room, she traveled north, she went to Vienna. Franca attends the Academy of Art. She has no typewriter at her disposal. Bacon and pickled pig's feet are piled on the academy typewriters. Franca, the painter's daughter, becomes a painter and tries to distance herself from her father. She's in the right place for that, in Vienna. Franca created her first lithograph in Vienna; she prepared the stone, and she rolled the paint into it. Franca waits for a friend. She can't stand it in Vienna, and she hurriedly returns to Milan. Franca, the daughter of the mountain-valley dweller and the French woman, doesn't make the transition from the metropolis to the blasé province."

"How can a story be made from this material, one that flows, one that is fleeting and hasn't been printed? Suitable to be read aloud, appropriate for discussion, for selection? Appropriate for bitter competition? (It isn't true that the author must remain completely calm. It isn't true that the author has no notification at all. It isn't true that the judges accepted this invitation for entirely different reasons, each one for a different, compelling, dripping reason.) How can such a mass of unintelligible details be brought together to form a whole? How can a story be created from unintelligible personal remarks, without any purpose or point? Where is the beginning of this story? What about this form? How can you claim that the painter has sold out when he sells his paintings? And besides, the gallery bears no small share of the responsibility. Why are you trying to convince us he has to burn his paintings, that whole pile of trash? Because of the form? For the sake of the form? Because the content determines the form?"

"Not every subject justifies its form, Gentlemen."

"And even if we must admit that this man's work has very compelling subjects as long as they are not situated in his own country, we must nevertheless inform you, dear readers, that this man's work is not at all in accordance with the form produced these days. We believe he simply can't draw. You see, in the past, writers didn't make their living with their work either. In the past they had money. Hasn't that occurred to you? And if we, the critics, are not wealthy, then our painters should be, our writers should be, so that we have something to hold on to."

"If you don't have somebody lobbying for you, you never get on television," says the clown. "Yes, that's the way it is. You can't do anything about it."

"In the beginning everything was quite different. In the beginning there was something else. In the beginning there were swirling, glowing masses of vapor. In the beginning," she said, "in the beginning."

"Tell us, oh, please tell us! Something unprinted, unpublished, something short, simple, a novel or at least a story. Tell us how it was. How was it? Tell us."

"In the beginning, after the clouds of vapor, the progressive cooling of the planet, the interplay of physical forms of movement became more and more important. And finally there were favorable prerequisites for living protoplasm," Helene murmured.

"These bases for the formation of structures, the cell, this organic world," answered Elise. "Species that became identifiable as plants and animals, and finally the most complete development as nature achieved consciousness of itself."

"The general enmity toward foreigners in Vienna," said Elise.

"The comments about the Italian roller-skaters," said Helene. "That's mean," she continued.

"I can't think of anything else," Elise says. "The possibilities, the thwarted possibilities out in the country," Elise says.

"The time that passes until you finally understand why *out in the country* is called the Götz quote. Oh, culture! Fiction!" shouted Helene. "We can't imagine it, we library dwellers, we recipients of handouts, we employers of servants."

"The pneumatic mail is here," Elise says.

"Yesterday I read three postcards from Adolfo again. National Library, manuscript collection," whispers Helene.

"The history of Israel," the reporter says. "These

people who have come together from the most diverse societies. At the table in the mess hall are the Jews from Latin America. They're leftists, of course, and they say, 'We're going to join the Arabs and build a modern state.' And there are the orthodox Jews from the East, who don't want that. The natives, the Jews who were born in Israel, they say, 'Arabs? They understand only the language of violence.' And they're not so wrong, but in a different way than they think. And they hardly arrive in the country, and then with a lot of trouble and propagandistic display they have their teeth straightened and are ill. In short, after receiving those few hundred dollars—that's the currency, Yankees, you know—they enjoy all the social benefits, which are enormous, of course. No, nobody who can adapt has to starve, but nobody can adapt. And of course the only ones who can leave for a big weekend are those who can immediately pay fifty percent of the cost in taxes, even when they receive the ticket for the flight as a gift. All that is calculated carefully, otherwise it wouldn't matter. 'I shall have the ticket sent to me,' I say, and that's the end of it. And the others are angry, of course, and they say, 'How are we going to do it?' And they feel like they're in the concentration camp again. And those atrocious contrasts, where they all fight like cats and dogs. They all say, 'Let's hope war comes again soon. Then we'll all be one people, heart and soul,'" says the reporter.

"It's always been that way. I've read the Old Testament often enough," said Helene. "When the people murmured, God always sent the plagues."

"Or war," said Elise. "Then there was peace."

"And the dark-skinned Yemenites are embraced by the American Jews. To be sure, nobody wants to

31

immigrate from over there. They just want to keep saying 'Next year in Jerusalem.' I like that," says the veterinary student from Tel Aviv. "You don't have to hide my coat. If I don't want to sleep with you anymore, I won't come again in spite of the coat."

"And why do they discriminate against the people from the Soviet Union?" Elise asks. "They will soon be in the minority anyway, because the Arabs are multiplying like rabbits, and the Jews have hardly any children."

"The consistency of a story means remaining the same throughout the narrative. It means the suspension of time during the course of the story, which is an impossibility. So there can be no consistency, unless the things I recount occur simultaneously. Simultaneity in the unfolding of a story is an impossible thing," says the reporter. "When I tell a story, I change. I'm not the same as I was, and therefore the story is not the same at the end as it was in the beginning. Do you understand?"

"Yes," says the technician, "I understand. One image after another. Cut. One image after another. Cut. The temporal succession of language. The linguistic chain is a continuum, the emergence of what has come into being through differentiation."

"What's that?" asks the assistant.

"He was so tormented. He had his hands full, trying to resist the pressure from above. And when he qualifies as a university lecturer, what is more urgent for him than applying immediately for the position that should actually go to the professor? The pressure to which he was subjected from above, he passed on to those below him."

"From what you said, it seemed to be just the opposite. And why does it happen to me in particular? Why me?"

"Everyone who gets caught asks that," said Helene.

"I don't understand things like that anymore. I think that if it's meant to be, it will catch up with you. There is no exception for a particular individual."

"I see," says Helene.

"So there is no consistency in this story."

"No, there's no consistency in the story because it is a creation of man. History is man's creation and is therefore mutable. At least it can be recounted," said Helene.

"So tell us now! Tell us, tell us the story."

"How can I, if I'm standing here reading? A reading match, a competition, a contest, a challenge."

"Time," says Elise. "Hanging up the receiver, the clicking on the other end of the line, and the reaction to it. By the time you dial the number to return the call, get connected, and ask for the person you want to talk to, he has left the room, gone down three flights of stairs, crossed the courtyard, passed the monuments erected by the nations, the delegations, and the visitors, and has left the place where they were executed, the memorial, the death camp. Our connection couldn't be made. Between the clicking in my telephone receiver and my renewed dialing, time passed, time that runs its course differently for this person and for that one. And then," says Elise, "everything is irretrievably gone, irreversible."

"With no turning back," Helene murmurs.

"I'm not the same, a human being is not the same. No, the unity doesn't exist any more. As soon as I recognize that the boundaries are blurred, that nothing is isolated, and see interaction in this general motion, see that truth is great, to be sure, but stratified and diverse, no consistent narrative exists for me," Elise said.

"*Tout se tient*," Helene answered. "Time is a sub-

33

stantial factor in a story. One must include it, but not present it except through language. But without it history isn't possible, this story isn't possible."

"'I love you,' says the man on the television screen. 'Thank you,' says the woman on the screen. One image after another. Cut. One image after another. Cut. Segments, separate parts of a continuum, a semiotic chain. Is there such a thing?" Elise asks.

"If you identify the story as a semiotic corpus, view it as a conventional sequence of symbols, the lack of solidarity among the women is a symbol. Do you understand?"

"For what, or of what?" Elise asked.

"Of their oppression. As with painters, writers, employees, wage earners, dependents in general, as with the victims in this story, in history."

"Are you familiar with the Dolomites?"

"Only on the basis of passing through them, the spas, those groups of mountains, those southern limestone Alps between Rienz and Eisack, Etsch and Piave."

"The acquittal," said Elise. "The acquittal of the four watch officers. The ones who taught the escapee a lesson. It was in all the papers. The honorable court that casts sidelong glances at the mass media, and the mass media that cast sidelong glances at something else."

"At wage slips," the journalist laughs, "with balance and objectivity, viewing everything that is wrong objectively and without polemics. As is appropriate for the media. Not too long. Don't forget the lead, and be especially careful to get out of there before press time and before Friday. On Saturday not even a dog is interested. Not even a cock crows on Saturday. On Saturday everyone breaks off their hunger strike, even in St. Stephen's Cathedral. On Saturday all the editorial

34

offices, all the newspaper offices are closed and the front pages are locked up."

"On Saturday I'm at my ranch," says the weapons expert. "But it isn't all that easy to break off a hunger strike. The best thing is to let the cardinal talk you out of it. That will sell a lot of newspapers."

"But he won't even receive me," says the school girl, the duped hunger striker.

"Just leave that to me," says the expert.

"You tricked me," says the cardinal.

"We tricked you," laughs the journalist. "We tricked everyone, and everything went out over the teletype all the way to Los Angeles and San Francisco. Then we laid everything aside and left for our ranch."

"Until Monday. There will be reports again then. They come over the teletype. There will be a night report again. Run it before seven o'clock and don't forget to make coffee. Read the perforated tape, run the press, keep your mouth shut and look modest when they tell dirty jokes, and don't wear pants into the parliament building. Yes, our ladies have to know what to do," says the department head, not without pride.

"Three guards armed with rubber truncheons—the fourth just happened to walk by—gave it to a prisoner. It was pure self-defense, and the judge understood that, too. To be sure, one of them had previously been convicted of child abuse, but in the first place it was only his stepson, and then a good slap never hurt anyone. The judge doesn't have time—get it out quickly over the teletype—to ask the guards (cut), what they were doing in the cell (cut). Haven't we become decent people? And we haven't spared ourselves. Our fathers didn't spare us."

"What were you doing in the correction cell—yesterday?" sneers the guard, a true man of the people, a people's man.

"Real patriotism, public punishment of children, prisoners, and demonstrators, the citizens, the civilians, the fact that they are being crippled (confirmed by medical officials)—these are also symbols in our semiotic chain, in our differentiated story, in our movement and its equivalent, power (or might), acts of violence by officials against civilians."

"Get rid of that stuff quickly, put it in the trash. Who's going to believe it?"

"I've already heard about it," says Elise.

"It's sharply on the rise of late," says Helene.

"Those who were not alive at the time have no right to judge," says the reporter. He is a disabled veteran, but he came home just the way he went out, that is to say, without any ability to think.

"Was he there when they cleansed the hinterland of civilians and rabble?"—investigate the meaning of the word *cleanse*—asked the author, who often calls for cleansing (for example, among the teachers, among those who are entitled to educate, the wearers of colored vests). "If you are against military build-up, perhaps because you have a son, I can only tell you that your son is better off in the army than with the civilians. Yes, indeed."

"The glorification of violence by officials. Look at the pictures. Stare at the tube and watch how these people are openly mistreated by officials on the street. And nobody says anything, because they believe they will be spared something."

"Yes, this continual whining," says the editor. "Society is always to blame. You and I have him on our conscience, my dear colleague."

36

"Ha, ha! Just like the old days in the trenches. It was like this:...," his colleague responds.

"He came back from the war without any ability to think. He didn't know what he was doing when he was cleansing the hinterland of Jews, civilians, and other rabble. He uttered no opinion as he struck the little girl's head with a rock."

"Don't start generalizing again," said Helene.

"Sometimes you have to generalize in order to set up a thesis," Elise answers.

"Hypothesis," Helene corrects her.

"He promptly joined the right party after the war, promptly took the right position after the war, promptly (while still acting in an official capacity, [editor's note]) forgot everything, because a human being has no ability to think. At most he has an imagination. Suspending time with the imagination, clinging to the image of the official and the mistreated civilian—is lethal," said Elise.

"That's why it has to go into the stove. Nobody will see it there."

"And no old-fashioned voice from the previous century is raised in the parliament building. No voice is raised for the other nations involved. No voice speaks somewhat antiquatedly and with carefully chosen words. No Jew from Split, no authentic Italian from Austria stands there with eyes that once burned, *honoris causa*, and speaks in the senate, and speaks against this senate's enmity toward foreigners. From Split, for Triest, spoken in Vienna."

"But what about the Slavs? What about the slaves?"

"You know, all that talk about the blue-eyed, blond Aryans, is nothing but a pipe dream," says the professor. "Basically, what you're giving us is nothing but a description of the Slavs. Try to make that clear to them!"

"Nonsense, I'm no Nazi," said the Nazi on the right bench in the right party with the right club pressure. "It's nonsense! But the extremists, but the demonstrators, but the civilians—you must take a closer look at them."

"Suspending time by activating the imagination, having the present in front of you continually and relegating nothing to the past—how could a person continue to live that way? Think about what lies before us. Think about what we have behind us. There's only enough for our own people when we have an arm ripped out, when we have a leg amputated. They say there are doctors who act on the basis of civil law. Hands are not chopped off, but amputated."

"But not here."

"It can still happen."

"And all of that is supposed to go into your story? No wonder, when you have such a small publishing house."

"And Franca?"

"She went to Mexico."

"And her father, the painter?"

"He wants to burn his paintings, the ones that are recognized by the critics, famous among his colleagues, valued by collectors. Then just look at art history, an endless series of revolution and restoration, with the classical artists as living corpses high up on the chart. The avant-garde (cut) and the rear guard (cut), but reality falls somewhere in between."

"And I?" Elise asks.

"And I?" Helene asks.

"And I?" those who have nothing more to lose ask each day.

38

"You're standing in a large, beautiful nude study, of course," laughs the director of the gallery. "You're well known to the police. It's important for us not to demand that art find solutions anymore. It's important for us not to require art to bring about changes. It's important to free art from the necessity of reflecting attitudes. To demand solutions and changes from art is to require more than it can give. To demand art from art is to demand more than art can give." (Cut.) "It's a matter of attitude." (Cut.) "It's a matter of stance." (Cut.) "It's a matter of the practical situation." (Cut.)

"Get to the point. Don't waste time in the Dolomites, in Dalmatia, in the Styrian forests."

"All right, let's go to Minsk. Let's go to Terezin. This time it really was Helene. This time it really was Elise. Elise and Helene traveling to Minsk. No time for cultivated conversation, no time for cultivated thoughts, precipitously, hastily, on their way, at night, early in the morning. After a lateral twist, the walls bent inward and burst. In the kitchen they crumbled away. A hiss from the elevator door, a cloud, white, maybe gas, maybe dust. (Never fear, we haven't gotten to that point yet.)"

"I take my sister by the hand. I take my daughter by the hand. We're calm. We didn't scream. We're disciplined. The whole city was extremely disciplined. We left the house at dawn, wearing only the most necessary clothing. We're the final form that has been produced through additional differentiation, from innumerable classes, orders, families, genera, and species, in which the nervous system reaches its most complete development, the final vertebrate animal in which nature has achieved consciousness of itself. So I take my sister, my daughter by the hand. I say, 'God is with us.'"

"Amen," says Elise.

"Amen," says Helene. "What else can I say?" she continues.

"Yes, what else can she say?" Elise murmurs.

"I still have some time left. I still have a few minutes—a relative factor, comparable to the color white. I still have this imprecise period to fill with my droning voice. How else could I render my voice in this peculiar competition?"

"How did it begin?"

"With the specialization of the hand, which means with tools, and that in turn means man's transforming impact on nature."

"Ecology again! Ten years ago I didn't know the word," the department head croaks.

"Man has managed to make his mark on nature. And all that with his hands."

"Of course," says the reporter (cut).

"Of course," says the cameraman (finally).

"So it may have begun everywhere. I just can't describe everything simultaneously."

"I hesitate. I'm marked, marked by death. Everybody is marked by death. The whispering in the corridors, on stairs, and in hallways. The whispering behind closed doors, keeping quiet about illness."

"Suddenly all roads lead to Minsk," says Helene.

"But in reality she doesn't know they are going to Minsk, that they are going to Terezin. In reality an old woman is simply abducted. Of course, she goes voluntarily. She responded to the summons voluntarily. It began with these uncommendable exceptions, but there are extremists everywhere. You must not take them seriously. You also have to understand the police. It began with the disturbances at the university. The old gentleman was very frightened, the old gentleman was very bitter. Yes, those billy clubs! Yes, those boots! Yes, those police dogs. But the others can't be ignored either. The others are in for it, too, but the others are squeamish."

"Is it our fault that the others are so squeamish? Is it our fault that the minorities are so squeamish?"

"So the apartment is vacated. For days now friends and neighbors have not been permitted to ask how their mother is doing. For weeks now there has been this secrecy about the diagnosis. Their mother really hadn't felt good for years, but she was used to being brave. She was a reserved person. First there had been her appendix. It had almost been too late already. Actually it was too late, and she survived it nevertheless."

Yes, back then, Helene thinks.

Back then, Elise thinks.

"Did they think that?   The journey goes on to Minsk, to Terezin, or to another of the numerous camps." (Cut).

"Stop. Stop."

"Why stop? Thirty, thirty-five years later, that's precisely the right time to begin talking about it. Man developed through differentiation. Not only individually, from an egg cell to the most complicated organism. No, man also developed through historical differentiation. Elise didn't say that; Helene didn't say that. But she could have read it. Why not?"

"Yes, why not?" asks the judge, an excellent, unerring author. "Even I could have read that somewhere. That was a long time ago. But now, to include it in such a story—I find that to be in rather poor taste. I find that to be quite naïve. Almost opportunistic. Yes, and it's also terribly late in coming. That's already over and done with here. Not a soul is interested in it any more.

41

We have delicately abbreviated the theory. We have decisively simplified our publishing program. We have become a bit more realistic." (Cut.)

"If time continues to flow inexorably, if we bring man into the story, if we begin this journey to Minsk or to someplace else, during these last moments, during these last minutes, on these last pages of my story, in these last minutes, we want to try to recognize when it began and why we're doing it."

"It began when I went to school for the first time," said Elise.

"Had to go to school," Helene corrected her. "The old teacher," she continued, "so strict."

"We were educated at home," said Elise. "We had to walk past the boys, run the gauntlet, between rows of club-wielders. After bathing. The red, swollen, burnt bodies were driven out into the snow."

"Like pieces of meat," said Mr. Kovac.

Like blue pieces of meat left lying in the snow, thought Elise. But it was not Elise.

"It's so peculiar that you call today and ask if she's going to sleep or come," Walter says. "How long has it been since you last called? My mother has been dead for a year and a half. I work with water-purification systems. The apartment has been sold; my sister has been paid off. There was so much to do back then. I had just returned from Germany. I informed everyone I could think of. I think you're the only one it happened to."

"Time, a substantial factor in a story. It can be incorporated but not portrayed. It can't be restored, brought back, reproduced, except through language. Without it, history and this story are not possible."

"It was my fault," said Elise.

"It was my fault," said Helene.

42

"We should have...," said Elise.

"The murmuring had been drowned out in the sobbing of prayers, in the stammering of the other travelers. It did not begin in Dalmatia."

"What are you saying there?" The judges notice at this point that a dialogue is taking place, as if language were not a matter of dialogue. "Hey, quit trying to explain your actions on the basis of your thinking. Explain them on the basis of your needs." (Cut.)

"We made such a long trip, and then to have to listen to that, to have to see that, to have to experience that. (These eternal self-indictments, a historical relic of many critics.) Was my presence necessary? Was my journey necessary? The powerful people."

"You hesitate, so you mean those who have power now, the ones who treat you as a civilian."

"Organs that carry things out, speech organs, organs of order. Speech organs and mind, together with the hands."

"You mean the systematic course of action that already exists (already exists in embryo), the one that sets certain activities in motion as the result of certain external stimuli? Forget the analogies, if you will."

"Material for the radio play I'm working on," says Elise.

"It wasn't Elise. Back then I was interested in the legal proceedings. I did not attend the trial. But there was the notice in the daily newspaper."

"No, we didn't have a trial."

"So what happened in the beginning? Say it. Tell us."

"She won't hold out much longer. To carry on to the end of a story, from the first page to the last, tense, concise, and snappy—that would be something for us."

"First there was the immediate usefulness of work, and later came this separation into rulers and subjects. But not everywhere. And in the end somebody has to assume the responsibility, the risk, the duties, the costs. But not everywhere. Sometimes there were compensating forces. Objective forces. Without polemics, really free and independent. Look at us, we, for example."

"You Austrian writers, for whom do you actually write?"

"It wasn't the way you think. It didn't happen as you might wish. Things don't turn out the way you expect them to. It was the unequal distribution resulting from the accumulation of what had been purchased. Means for the preservation of the work force paid for with the work force."

"Nothing but dialogue. Nothing more than foolish dialogues."

"I know, that was your great-grandfather. Half of the village belonged to him. Property owner, standard bearer, president of the workers' union. They don't understand how the owner of a house and a factory could be the president of the workers' union."

"That was during our time," Helene murmurs.

"Long before Minsk," whispers Elise.

"All right, the revolution in production methods."

"Do you think that doesn't produce a flaw in your story? This transition from the poetic to the theoretical text?"

"I don't think so, for language, this consequence of the use of the hands, this ordered continuum, this portion of an entire system of symbols—language contains everything, and everything always interacts with everything else. Poetics with linguistics and everything with whatever comes of it."

44

"I want you to know, on your journey to Minsk (cut) or Terezin (cut), that such things are not caused by fate (cut), but by improper distribution."

"Quite right," says the painter, who doesn't come to the train, of course, but doesn't burn his paintings out of remorse, but rather because he is freezing.

"Quite right," says the musician who just fell into the trap of the third black-marketeer.

"Quite right," say the painter, the musician, the writer, the worker, the employee.

"Wait, wait, wait, didn't time run out long ago?"

"Oh, the changes in movement—oh, the timelessly limitless existence—oh, the indestructibility that belongs to matter in motion by its very nature—oh, the language that belongs to the most highly differentiated being by its very nature. So, have we arrived at the hour zero again?"

"Yes, but if there is no difference between organic and inorganic elements, between spirit and matter, how can there be a difference between good and evil? Is everything really suspended in the time that permits the worlds to collapse, that lets our bodies decay? Then what about the conscious part of matter, the conscious part of the population, the conscious part of me?"

"Everything that strives toward a maximum," says Helene. "Everything that is present and constant in the world. Everything that is eternal. Dust and ashes, nothing."

"I am eternal," said Elise.

"Eternal," echoed Helene. "Indestructible, in a word, motion."

"In the beginning," she said, "there were whirling, glowing masses of vapor. With the progressive cooling of the planet, the interplay of physical forms of move-

45

ment became more and more important, and finally there were favorable conditions for living protoplasm. Yes, this basis for the formation of the structures of the entire organic world, these cells, these innumerable species that can be identified as plants and animals, and finally the most complete development as nature..." (cut) "...con-sciousness..." (cut) "...of itself." (Cut).

"So, I will shorten the whole thing a great deal," says the publisher.

"And this struggle that has gone on for millennia," Elise responds. "The differentiation, the hand, yes, this sensitive tool. Used for picking and climbing—oh, the trees of childhood—and finally production."

"It will become differentiated after we are gone," Helene whispers.

"When everything is stone cold," Elise answers.

"The planetary systems must collapse in the end. They are already calculating the amount of heat that will be produced in the process. Thus sequence is nothing more than the expansion of simultaneity," says somebody in the audience.

"How was it in the beginning?"

"In the beginning everything was quite different."

"Tell us. Something unprinted, unpublished, brief. Simply narrate a novel, or a story. Tell us, tell us."

"Where was I in the beginning?"

"In me," he said. "You were in me, before you were in her."

"And then?"

"Then you grew. And you got big. That big. Just like that."

(On October 9, 1942, at 8:25 p.m., the 45th Jewish convoy [the 13th daily convoy to Terezin] departed from Vienna's Aspang Station with 1322 people aboard.)

46

RESTITUTA

HELENE KAFKA
Sister Restituta
From the congregation of
Sisters of the Third Order
of St. Francis
Called Hartmann Sisters
Surgical nurse in the Mödling Hospital
near Vienna
Born: May 1, 1894 in Hussovitz-Brünn
Arrested: February 18, 1942
Condemned: October 30, 1942
Beheaded: March 3, 1943

Helene Kafka, Sister Restituta, dependent on herself alone, nurse.

What is the work of a nurse? How does the day pass for a nun whose profession is to care for the sick (a profession that is still acceptable) as a substitute for being a mother—a nun who gives service as a nurse?

What is Helene's story?

Helene as a child, Helene at one year of age, Helene after baptism, Helene at age five, Helene in the mountains picking flowers, Helene going to church, Helene at the edge of the forest. Helene running across a meadow, running rapidly down the hill, Helene on the little bench next to the brook, on the bridge. Helene and some neighbor children in the garden. Helene going for milk, carefully carrying the jug. The bucket is overturned, the milk spilled. Helene and the blue sweater that she knit herself. Helene holding a bouquet of heather—(and that's what it's called: *heather*).

Helene with a kettle and a pot tied to her waist in the woods, Helene picking huckleberries and blueberries in the summer. (Helene in the Helene Valley?) Helene in a white dress, Helene in silk, Helene in white. Strewing flowers for Corpus Christi (and that means: *heather*).

Helene at the age of five in the parish house in Witum. Her answers pleased the reverend. Helene in conversation (alone and with others), Helene with Brigitta. Helena with Brigitta at the May devotions in honor of the Virgin Mary. (*And the last shall be first, o-o, Ma-a-a-ry, help us!*) Helene kneeling up in front and remembering. Helene in front at the iron grating. Helene expressing her wish at a tender age. Helene in school. Helene at the age of twelve, at the age of thirteen, laughing in school. Helene praying. (Helene praying for forty hours.) Helene in the twentieth district. Helene in

51

the protection of the towers of Saint Brigitta's Cathedral. Helene being protected, Helene being consoled. Helene on the road of consolation, on the road of faithfulness, on the road of the hunters. (Helene praying for forty hours.) Helene walking across the cemetery. (My favorite walk?) Helene with flowers, this time marigolds, buttercups, yellow meadow flowers with a special gleam along the brook. Helene behind the house, Helene not running across the meadow, (Helene) not in the barn or in the hotbed. (Helene in the snow.) Helene not walking through snow and ice on the way to school.

Helene during the school excursion. Helene not with bare breasts by the stream. (The girls whisper, the teacher looks away.) Helene kneeling up in front and remembering. Helene in front of the food grating. (Helene in front of the iron grating.) Helene praying for forty hours. *Friedrich, Maria, Valerie, Helene, Anna, Sophie, and Albine.* Helene and the number seven. Helene in the middle. Helene, the middle child of seven. Helene in religion class, in history, in German. Helene hits the nail on the head. Helene at play. Helene imitating a nun. Helene called before the principal. Helene in front of the school teacher, the school director, the catechist on Sunday. Helene serious and taciturn. Helene as a child, female, in a world where men command ("... *into thy hands I commend...* ").

Helene, who was your father? Helene (Kafka), who was your mother? Honor thy father and thy mother, Helene. Keep the sabbath day holy, Helene. Helene, who is your master? (Seraphin). Leni, I called you.

"Helene, I am calling you," says her father.

"Helene, I am calling you," says the priest.

"Helene, I am calling you," says the master (a fine human being).

Helene was called. Le-ni! Le-ni! Le-ni! (*"Many are called, but few...."*) Helene during the day, Helene during the year. Helene in the year 1905 (first communion), Helene in Saint Brigitta's Cathedral. Helene on the day of confirmation, Helena with the priest's, with the bishop's, with the Lord's hand on her head in the apse. Helene a warrior of God. Helene, now a soldier of the Church. (Le-ni! Le-ni! Where are you?!)

We are telling the story of Helene, the solitary, lonely nun, the female monk. A woman, a female being in a world where men command (*"...into thy hands I commend..."*). Helene, she had the choice (still). Helene, given the choice, chose the better part. Leni (Helene), the novice, the nun, the female monk. Helene before the gates of the convent hospital, Helene in the year 1914. Helene in the *Hartmanngasse*. "I choose," said Helene, "my Lord among the highest, who is the most distant under the heavens. His name be praised (Amen). His protection is greater than that of my father (the court usher, the elevator operator, the shoemaker), is greater than that of the teacher, the priest, the ruler (a godless king), is greater than that of the bishop in his palace."

"I choose," said the girl Helene, the schoolgirl named Kafka, the nurse's aid, a child, a maiden (unmarried), a female monk, a female being. "I choose the name that I like."

"You owe it to me," said her mother, the nun, the head nun, the head woman, the female monk, the female human being.

"Yes, I owe it to you (I am a debtor), I give back my name (*restituo*), I give back my childhood (*restituo*), my youth (*restituo*), my girlhood (*restituo*)."—Helene, the female monk, the female human being, the woman gives back her name, her childhood, her life, her barefoot life: "My mother was a strict woman. We had to offer the morning prayer, the evening prayer *on our knees*. My mother was a cook, a female cook, a housekeeper, my father a shoemaker in Brünn, an elevator operator in Vienna, an office worker in Brünn."

Eleana, the child of the partisan and the cook. Eleana in day care, Eleana with her grandparents, Eleana with her wet nurse. Eleana grew too rapidly. Eleana with the baby-sitter. In the afternoon after school she tended the sheep, watched the goats, gave water to the cows (for the milk). In the evening she brought the milk home. Now that area is industrialized. Now there is prosperity in the area. We no longer recognize the area. (That also has a good side.) People there have forgotten how things used to be.

Given back, the barefoot hurrying (not lingering) across meadows, the waiting, the wading, the waddling, the joking. The child of poor parents, grandparents, great-grandparents, ancestors gives back. Helene gives back the name of the maiden. What has been given back? The life of a servant. Come. Won. Become. Weighed: Divided and weighed. Back came: Restituta, the bride of Christ, the nun. Back came the restored woman, the returned woman, the reborn woman, the sister in the Lord (Seraphin). Restituta, returned, not garlanded with dreams, not born in the leaves, not dewy like a poppy. Back came a little nun *risoluta*, Restituta, the alternative to motherhood, no choice and no torment (not for you, Restituta), liberated from service, but not from service to people, from the typical and natural service to others, not as they thought, not as they wanted, not as they planned.

Restituta, her honor: for the priest, for the bishop, for the catechist, for the teacher (that contentment, that

54

questioning), Restituta's honor restored in the Lord. She chose the Highest, because He was the most far removed under the heavens. (She was so unpolitical, she was so naïve, she was so carefree, she was so unrestrained, she was so power-hungry, she was so disobedient, she was so....) Accountable only to Him. (Answer me!) The returnee, given back, having entered the Order of Christian Love (and they had no love), entered and was of the Order of St. Francis, called Seraphicus (and for a hundred years they had planted the little twig, *unctuous as always*), entered and took the veil. Where else could she go? Not as they thought, not as they wanted, not as they chose. She entered, took the veil, covered her head. (Learn to enumerate the individual parts of the habit.)

In Tyrol, children say that nuns have their breasts cut off or tied down, that their growth is inhibited by pieces of linen and butter cookies—horrible propaganda, Amazon nonsense. But they do cut off the hair of the nuns, the female monks, the women—these first-class and second-class features (at least the pieces of linen, the butter cookies), rumors, lost cultural assets—which is why the dirty jokes about clerics seem especially repulsive to an enemy of the Church. Cover your head, Sister, and weep about yourself and your children, Helene Restituta, you heavenly bride (Amen). And she was a strong girl (a real Viennese child), healthy and taciturn. (She disguised herself, behaved herself, prayed, in short, she stuttered.) And then: *her will power, her steadfastness*. And growth could not be hindered, either way. And preserve us from the fires of hell and lead all those who need thy grace most. Amen. Morning prayer. Midday prayer. Evening prayer. Short fervent prayer. Prayer while putting on clothing. Prayers for every individual piece of the habit. (Back then things were still different. In those days they wore, in those days they dressed..., but the Holy Father doesn't want that. Everything is supposed to be more uniform, not: one of them with everything covered but the tip of her nose and the other one uncovered. It is all supposed to be more uniform.) Thus the difference between Benedictine and Franciscan piousness would also be legitimately established. That would go too far. To mention the individual prayers would go too far.

And they all had their story, and it was untypical and unnatural for the women to occupy themselves very much with public matters. And the rights that had been won were destroyed again by the Dollfuss regime. (In 1933 there were still thirty women in parliament. In 1938 there were no longer any.) But today, of course, all that is outdated, or isn't it? And they silently bore the burdens of the day, of the night, and they sat at the feet of the Lord (figuratively, of course), and listened and didn't think anything about it (figuratively), and all of them knew nothing, and they thought about it after all. Headband, collar, veil, habit, belt, cross. (Pins, rice starch, ironing board.)

What did the women think during vespers, while serving afternoon tea, supper, meals, snacks, with their brothers, their fathers in the field? While feeding the chickens, the pigs—in the garden, in the laundry, in the pantry? Did they think about their relatives, their friends in the field, on the field, while feeding the chickens, cows (if at all)? Did they think about the collection of clothing, blankets, leather, first-aid supplies. (About the wonderful parables of Mary and Martha?) *And at night she carried the sick or wounded (partisans) on her back, down through the forest into her cottage, and cared for them on a bed in a dug-out earthen cave behind the living-room closet.* (Amalie Jereb chose the better part).

She was a woman from the country, and as a girl she carried out milk that sloshed back and forth in kettles and pots. And in kettles that sloshed she loaded food for the pigs onto dossers and carts. And later in the war she often managed the whole farm alone. Men and brothers had been taken away from the fields, had been led off into the field, had gone into the field for.... She tamped down the hay and turned the grass and swept and brushed the threshing floor. She fertilized the field, she butchered on the sly and was always in danger like a man. She hardly went to church on Sunday anymore. Instead she diligently sent the children to school. They sank deep into the snow, and the clothes of the children from mountain farms constantly hung over the stove. And the village children laughed at the crumpled, knobby shoes, the damp socks, the ice-crusted felt pants, and they were much better in German.

And right after the invasion, people began to be hunted down in Brigittenau, too. People were driven together in the Karajan Street (not Jereb Street) elementary school, where they were tortured and mistreated and then sent to the concentration camp. But a memorial plaque would make no sense now, no sense at all.

The Slovenian names were Germanized, the Slovenian language forbidden in a person's own four walls, and the bishop issued an order. (But there is no point in mentioning that and the church flags with the Slovenian texts.) And there is simply no point at all to the Slovenian town signs.

Then the women went into the forest: not with kettles and pots, not with berry pickers and baskets. Because they were dispossessed. Their possessions had been destroyed, their relatives had been killed, had fallen

57

in battle (or they were fighting with the partisans). Then the women, who were now independent, you see, went into the forest.

She sang in the May devotions in honor of the Virgin Mary. Perhaps she had no voice. She attracted no attention. She had her father, who limped (perhaps)—perhaps he dragged his leg (an injury from the war)—and she feared the enemy and what they had taught her in school to fear as the enemy; and she feared evil, but inwardly nothing else as much as she feared people.

In their fear of people these women placed themselves under the protection of God and were (at least earlier) only conditionally subservient to the Church fathers. (I live for Christ.) And they placed themselves under the cloak of the church, and when that was too short.... (For me she is Helene Kafka and that's all!) But more about that later. (You would be amazed at how quickly the years pass, the days, the hours.) And she set herself aside, the restored person of the female gender, returned, reborn, one day resurrected, Restituta, *risoluta*, the female monk, the nun. (Her hair was very short.)

Perhaps when she looked in the mirror she saw the eyes of her ancestress, the chin of her aunt, the cheek of a forebear. Perhaps she sees in the mirror the peasant features of Bohemian ancestors, the countenance of a milk maid, the image of a mountain farmer's wife who spreads her laundry on the slope, not on the line (spreads the laundry on the grass with her bare feet), who is barefoot with ulcerated feet. And in the radiant blue there is the drone of the hostile—for the child friendly—planes. And the laundry and the grass and the bare feet of the Tyrolean mountain farmer's wife. And the plane turned away, and on the map black rings were drawn around the cities that had been taken, and it came closer and closer. The liberators came closer and closer in Poland. On top of her aunt's school atlas lay the mushroom book and the rhyming calendar and the cities with circles around them. The map was already quite black on the right side, that is, in the East. Those were beautiful, ice-cold, winter days in Tyrol. And could the nun Restituta perhaps see in her mirror the ranks of women who washed the wounds of their men, carried their weapons (performed courier service) in the peasant wars? (And the defeat of the peasants and the broken backbone of Germany.) Was a face from Bohemia perhaps visible in the mirror of the lonely nun Restituta? (Such things happen.)

Restituta, who gives you strength when you are completely alone and have nobody but yourself to rely on (men in the rear? an organization? traitors and gangs?), when you are responsible only to God—so who is the leader of this malicious mess?!—because He is the most distant under the heavens?

We see a face, alienated beneath the attire that women wore at the time the orders were established (people in the convent are obliged to wear the prescribed convent attire....), which in many respects developed from the worldly attire of the time. (Research needs to be done concerning the story of Brother Seraphicus of Christian Love). So down with the monks, down with human beings, down with St. Francis. How many women (a real native of Vienna), the history of the order (a real native of Vienna), where it exists (a real native of Vienna), the mother house (a real native of Vienna), the investiture, the preparation (postulancy), the probation (novitiate), the vow (profession). And how was the time spent? (Where, how long, under what conditions?) A real native of Vienna!

Simple and lonely (you finally become accustomed to it), even while in a group, she carries out the service of women (time-honored and handed down to us), waiting and nursing and watching: the bodies of the poor, the sick, and the dying. (Do you know what awaits you, my child? Yes, Reverend Mother.) In the name of love and for little reward. (Even earlier we had little.) In the name of love (Seraphin), I say only: Seraphin. (*She always said, "I'll become a martyr yet." "Yes," I said, "you look like a martyr." I must say, the Lord took her at her word.*) Who talks like that while changing the cloths, the sheets, the linen, while checking the instruments, while preparing, while cleaning, while swabbing, while wiping, when cutting the gauze, while injecting, while giving anesthetic, and while it is working? And the wiping cloth has been wrung out, the spittoon has been emptied, and one more catheter has been inserted (catheterize), and one more injection needle passed, and the bloody sponges removed. (She's not afraid of blood, I can tell you that.) She would have become a good midwife. The cellulose, the substitute and scarce goods of the time. (She's spreading insidious propaganda again, the nun, isn't she?) And the doctor, the doctors, the female doctor (none is mentioned) had probably gone home, gone home, home to the hearth or home to the Reich or home to Terezin. The staff, his personal nurse, his personal and life's (coquette?), a devil of a girl? With the cap and the red cross and the pin beneath her chin and the swastika armband. (It disappeared then. The woman from southern Tyrol wept as she took the picture of her *Führer* from the wall and the book, dark binding, and said, "Burn them." And her mother had the Mother's Cross, you know. She said, "My mother had six

60

children," and she said, "Where should I go? Just where should I go?" And the child said, "Aren't you happy? It's the liberators. They're coming to liberate us."

And the woman wrung her hands. She raised her hands high and danced and wept, "Where should I go with my children? My husband is in the war. The Americans are already in the main square. They'll be here soon.") Don't forget the swastika armband. During the retreat into the mountains, they were with the seven dwarfs, with us in Tyrol. They were quartered in my great-uncle's barrack, between gravel and camomile. They didn't dare expropriate. They didn't dare respond. They lay in deck chairs. (Ours? Theirs?) They enjoyed the mountain air. ("This air!") They laughed and chatted, and the uniform was dark green or appeared to be dark green, and the nurses had brown legs, and the child said, "Are you a devil of a girl?" "I'm a nurse." And the men in uniform were enemies. And the child knew: They are fleeing. And the child knew: Now you can't do anything more to us. And there is giggling and wheezing behind the barrack wall, and hardly are the first rays of the sun there, and in a flash, legs on the window sill, as a substitute for stockings, which was all horrible propaganda, of course, a clean girl, German to the core, yes, indeed, because no brother, no fiancé was stationed in France, in Norway. (Of course, it was called something else.) Just think of your aunt Herta's blue fox! So, white stockings rolled down, the saucy cap on her head, fastened with two bobby pins, and the dirty looks, and the giggling and wheezing behind the door.

But first there was the bowing and scraping nurse, the nun (the peasant woman), the woman from the Austrian convent to dispose of. We are the new people, not the shy people, the beautiful people. The medical

61

officer is ours: (So what?!) And that woman, that praying woman, the nun, the Norn with the non-German name, boiled needles for me yesterday, handed me sponges, assisted me, took down the medical history (the peasant face under the hood), looks like her grandmother (my grandmother). But we are the new people, not the shy people, the beautiful people. The world belongs to us, of course (what we leave of it). What, a bed for a woman like that? Rabble and riffraff! (Criminal law: Special court. Speedy trial.)

After sentences had been served there were arbitrary arrests in Germany (Chile, Argentina, Uruguay, Bolivia, and so forth). But we are the new people, not the shy people, the beautiful people. The world (still) belongs to us. It may have been that way. Can it have been like that? And it is written down. Everything is recorded. The trial documents are judicious; the archives are full. You must go there; you must pick up the book, pick up the document, pick up the index card. Everything is registered, even the machinations of the art dealer in the Commission for Degenerates that existed at the time, my dear colleague!

The doctor has a kitten purring in his chamber. The strict nun disturbs him (stout, with gall-bladder problems), the ponderous woman, too domineering, we always said. (Actually, I got along well with her.) And then she liked to cook, which a nun, of course, would not be permitted to do, a real native of Vienna. The doctor, an SS-man with a death's head (it was so black, a real death's head, I tell you)—he wanted to get rid of her. She has the impudence to suggest the other needle to me, the other scalpel, the stethoscope, the scissors, the clamps, the sutures. The clamps for the prisoner of war, for the prisoner, the clamp, the mask, caution—to let caution prevail. Rebellious and treacherous, the peasant nun, the beast, a praying cow (praying for the animals that are to be slaughtered). Just wait, we'll get rid of her, too. The incorruptible eyes (that's right, corrupted!), malicious, of course, to comfort weaklings, malingerers, front-line animals (if not to love them, oh Seraphin). A similarity with current deportment in barracks is purely coincidental. And that she walks erect, walks very straight with her head held high. (She will be a head shorter, soon.) Forward, help, lend a hand, quickly! Flying, with her veil fluttering, in white, until late at night.

Of course she did not deserve the death penalty. What do you want?! It was during the war. Indeed (a shake of the head), what was I supposed to do? (A shrug of the shoulders: close-up, pan shot). To execute a woman... (A shake of the head). Down on her knees. In front of the picture of Seraphin (Brother Francis). She had been Helene, was once called Leni, had chosen Restituta. Restituta at night in front of the tabernacle, down on her knees after finishing her work, down on her elbows, kneeling before the cross (not having knuckled under). "Why, oh Lord? The wounded in the hall, at night they scream for their mothers. So I am the mother of all of them. I served my brother, cared for and washed (sterilized) him: I was my brother's keeper, oh Lord."

Restituta, the nun, was too domineering (supposedly), too domineering for our priestlike obedience. She recited her prayers too loudly and clearly, enjoyed singing too much, played the organ too joyfully. She was too decent (actually, I got along with her very well), wanted to be the first. (Where? When? How often? Under what circumstances?) She was too carefree, too brash, too precise, too disobedient, too industrious. She was a real native of Vienna. I can only say: obedience, obedience.

Lonely and upright, sitting in the cell (wearing a nun's habit), writing. (It is 1940, November, December.) She has taken off the stiff clothing of her order. The carefully starched collar, the breast cloth, the headband, the veil of choice *(voile)*, the habit. (She memorized the names and designations of the individual parts of the habit.) She often performed the purification ritual, donned each piece with the prayer belonging to it on her lips, put it on, pinned it on (with pins). Now she has taken them off, oh Lord.

The lamps in the room, the cots, the lights, in the bright room, darkened, of course, to save light (let there be light), the gleaming, flashing implements, the blindingly white room (cut). A nun in white clothing (very simple) puts on her mask, spreads out the instruments, puts them in order. She takes the boiled instruments from the basin, the sterile instruments, the scoops, the (cut), takes from the pan the boiled, sterilized needles, the knives. (Why this effort? I ask you!) She goes to the light, she examines the instruments. (She sets the clock. She places the needles lying north to south.) Portray the conditions of resistance for women differently than for men. (Cut.)

In the room with the lamps, the cots, the lights. In the room of the gleaming steel. Hardly available at all, these metal products, these manufactured products that have been brought home, brought back—this world-wide steel shortage, the nationalized factories that have been returned to private industry, the rationing, the lack of orders, and the limitations on imports and exports, and the trade agreements, and the commitments to our allies,

64

and the savings, and the releases. Aren't we free? Aren't we loyal? (After all, they said it on television, too.)

The nun in white clothing (close-up), soft organ music in the background (not too domineering), the nun in white clothing, puts on the tulle mask, spreads out the instruments (pan shot of the instruments), goes to the light (a light shines in the darkness), examines the needles. (From north to south?)

Footsteps ring out in the corridor, feet drag on stairs and in hallways. The chief physician is approaching *with his entourage.* The door flies open, a personal physician, a personal servant, a body on the stretcher, on the cart (cut). The door flies open and there is a body for the personal physician, the personal servant (cut). The surgical nurse with calm fingers, with a calm gaze, with steady hands, receives the (cut) from the personal servant. A sick prisoner. (A Frenchman? A Russian? A Pole?) A dying Austrian, the son of his nation, from the prison (close-up, slowly fade).

I was arrested in 1936. Somebody was beaten to death in the police station. We protested against it. I lost my temper about it. In those days, a dead person was an isolated case. When the Nazis came, I really began to fight against it....

There was terrorism not only against antifascists, but against any resistance. To be a Czech with an accent and to have said something against the Germans.... Farm workers...foreign workers.... Others looked away filled with terror and fear. They took direct charge of the Nazi spy files, and that's why they had an easy time of it after the invasion. We didn't dare do anything about it. There were women, mothers of sons who saw a prisoner convoy and gave bread. (Recording. O-tone.)

He was to be prepared, he was to be cured, he was

to be operated on, (not) sent as a courier to (Nîmes)...
(cut).

Young girls participated in the resistance side by side with their fathers and brothers, married women with their husbands, and in many instances they remained united with them in horrible deaths....

Restituta bandaged the man on the stretcher, the flayed body, as if it were my father, my brother, united with my brother, as if it were the Highest, He being the most distant under heaven, among the men, lonely and thin on the stretcher, a corpse, a body, a new arrival (cut). Restituta, the nun in the peculiar habit. (A nun's hair is short.) We recognize the face that is framed by the head and forehead bands, with the slightly protruding cheekbones. The down on her face gleams in the light of the room; her eyebrows are slightly bushy. Does she resemble her father? Her brother? Her mother? The color of her eyes is indeterminable, her gaze warm and calm, in the top row of pictures (brown prints, like funeral pictures). *Peaceful the gaze of a sister, as if it were my sister, my mother,* thinks the body, the corpse, the future dead man (a living hero), the courier, who is being cured in order to die better. Restituta, a child of the people, Restituta from the line of convent women, Restituta, the untouched, the untouchable, the woman who returned. (Anabaptist?) Dips her gaze into his gaze, dips her hand into the jug, her hand into the basin under the cross, and makes a cross on the forehead of the atheist, the communist (the son of the people). Weep for yourself and your abandoned children, Sister Helene, you child of this people that knows not what it does.

The inmates of the camps were recruited from the entire population. Women were no longer viewed as human. (SS-men also had mothers....)

Rattling and scraping, the footsteps of the execution-er, the doctor, the personal servant—"Well, are you ready?"—with the entourage coming along behind. The greeting, with his paw raised, the predator, the hero (popular in slippers and with a napkin after the war, later in field gray again). "Are you ready, nurse?" An impatient snapping of the fingers—"And the cross gets thrown out today?"

"Yes, Sir!" And the personal servant is already tipping it, and the servant woman, a representative of that miserable sex, is already hurrying.

Elise Panse, courier of the resistance group of the murdered communist Hubert Knes, often hidden in the bushes until three o'clock in the morning, waiting for a promised message from the partisans (or carrying one). The sick courier on the cot, the bed, in his situation, the man with the nation that is to be destroyed (Austria), with the name that is to be destroyed. (Stands for Josef Heinrich Kornfeld, monarchist, officer in World War I. Gave help, shelter to those who were persecuted, took them across the border in his own automobile.)

Stands for Josefine Brunner, courier of the organiza-tion that was led by her and her husband in Wörgl, Tyrol. *(Andreas-Hofer-Straße, Speckbacherstraße, Jose-fine-Brunner-Straße.)* How could I have been a female partisan, Your Honor? I was simply a courier....

"No, Doctor!" The voice of the nun, the voice of the sister, the strong voice of the woman (who does [not] desecrate the operating room). Silence. A silent encoun-ter. The glance. The headband, beneath it the gaze again—*"Either the crosses remain, or we will go, too!"* The chief physician lowers his eyes (impatient snapping of the fingers). The tray with the rubber gloves is already approaching, the powder box is already approaching (rice flour?), an impatient beckoning, powder, of course. The coat is handed to him, the bandage is tied, the muslin cloth placed, the swab picked up, the patch of skin cleansed, the suction mask applied, the head pulled back, the body tipped quickly onto the grating, onto the cloth remnant.

The heads are removed from the phenolated water and placed before us on a stone table. In October of 1945, the heads are placed before us on a stone table in the Institute of Anatomy. After long interference we are initially confronted with ten heads that stand before us on the stone table. *This eternal searching for corpses. Afterward they lie around here again. Seventy percent of those brought to justice are criminals anyway.* In October of 1945, Institute of Anatomy.

He offered resistance, he lifted his hand, he rebelled against unjust force (the godless king). Doctor Jakob Franz Kastelic rebelled; Leopoldine Kowarik, postal employee, rebelled; Karl Lauterbach, soldier, rebelled. *Dr. Kastelic's head has been nicely sewn onto his body.* So Annie sees her brother now, and unfortunately she must also testify that it really is Jakob. As stated, October of 1945, Institute of Anatomy.

Didn't they rob the cloisters, plunder the churches, drive away the monks, the nuns (give them special treatment) at night and at dawn? When the fathers ran barefoot up *Hahnenkammstraße* to us in the hotel, one was even in uniform, at home on leave, with his tonsure grown back in again, his beard shaven off. ("Don't say a word to anyone, understand?") When they stood barefoot in the night (at dawn) at the door (when she stood naked and half frozen before the barrack door), when we didn't let her in, when we didn't let the half-frozen Jewish woman come in, when she ran back out and tore loose a naked women from the pile of frozen corpses, lay down across the body, and thus concealed herself as she trembled. When the SS did not search carefully, when they crept into their barracks to their wives, when we sat in the barracks and knew nothing, when we sat and knew nothing about anything, when the yellow, greasy, evil-smelling smoke drifted over from the platform and we knew nothing, nothing at all, when they stood barefoot in the doorway and....

The women could not be effective. The women could not be an effective compensating factor. The women could not be an effective compensating factor in the amelioration of aggressiveness, because of their exclusion from public life.

Motherhood was used as a means of bringing pressure to bear. There were no laws for the protection of pregnant women, no paid vacations before and after giving birth. Medical counseling centers were closed, women's organizations were liquidated.

The lonely nun in the operating room understood. The lonely nun in the operating room understood that it meant being disobedient. That was the beginning of her struggle, that was the beginning of her resistance, that was the start, that was the beginning.

In the workplace, women who were opposed to the regime found more opportunities to join the resistance.

In her workplace, Sister Restituta recognizes that it is her duty to work on the earth for the welfare of the soul and the body and for honor. Restituta restored honor *(restituo l'onore)* to the Order of Christian Love. *(O Signore fa' di me un istrumento della tua pace.)*

Systematic resistance by women. It didn't exist. Sister Restituta kneeling in her room and pondering. Sister Restituta kneeling in her room and plotting (in the

Lord)...rise up according to the vow, people and country! Sister Restituta at her workplace. Sister Restituta dressed in the habit of her order and without the habit of her order (starved down to a skeleton). Putting aside the stiff band of the order and running her worn-out fingers through her hair (close-up, pan shot). Sister Restituta with paper and pencil: "Lift your heart and hands to heaven." The prerequisites for overturning the regime from within were missing. The lonely nun Restituta (a real child of Vienna) sitting in her room, writes (in reality she dictated): "If the army could have been won for a coup d'état..." Slowly she writes down her words. The nun's handwriting is slanted and uniform. The nun's organ playing is cheerful and spontaneous. For this nun, the activity of composing slogans is unusual, yes, extraordinary. "Or if an overwhelming majority of the people could have been won for the resistance...." And she writes a rhyme and writes a line and tears up the paper. (Soon there is only one sheet of paper left, with narrow lines, the address at the top and to the left, pre-printed, prison regulations, school notebook format, state court.) "...and had been able to draw a large portion of the army to the side of the opposition..." And she writes a rhyme and writes a line and goes to the window and examines the blackout curtains and listens for the footsteps (not yet, have no fear) and walks up and down. And in reality she had no time at all for such things.

The surgical nurse washes the flayed body. The Red Cross nurse's aid Pauline Wittwer from Feldkirch cares for the suffering prisoner of war, and she covers the bareness of the naked man. (She covers his nakedness.) She covers him with a piece of linen. Restituta returns to the stretcher and occupies herself with the gang member and behaves in a conspicuous manner for the longest time. (While I knew everything about Dachau from my relatives.) In the newly constructed wing of the Mödling Hospital (near Vienna), Restituta didn't want to listen at all, in her ridiculous get-up, naïve as the people. *(And thus the emperor's property is demonstratively spared by the peasants at great sacrifice.)* And so, naïve, poor, and peaceable (and blessed, of course), she wipes his wounds and wipes his forehead and wipes her forehead (headband, starched, white) and bends down and receives a piece of news (after all!), a slogan (treacherous, conspiratorial), and goes to the washroom and tears off her headband, her veil, without a prayer on her lips, without the memorized prayer text *(for they know not what they do)*, goes and sticks the clandestine message of the communists into her stockings. Restituta goes back to her cell and writes what she has just heard with a tiny pencil lead in the hand-sewn, lovingly decorated little book (for Anni Haider, companion in sorrow), and when she comes out (cut), nothing but a skeleton (cut), the hood is (cut), the habit is (cut), the veil of choice, the collar are (cut): what the fathers once promised, what the soldiers once promised. (Soldiers, remember your first oath: Austria!) The slogan is (cut). She writes. She distributes the sheets of paper, the appeals. She carries out resistance. She invites resistance. (In reality she went into the x-ray room and dictated.) She is unambiguously guilty. Yes, I am guilty, Reverend Mother, Reverend Sister, Reverend Priest, I am guilty (not as they wished, not as they thought, not as they chose). I am guilty of breathing in the poisonous clouds of smoke of the cremation ovens. I am guilty of watching the humiliation of my fellow citizens who are without rights. I am guilty of being the vassal of a fiendish system, of the final consequence of godless

71

Mammon, the idol Baal, called capital. (Forgive us. We really didn't know that. We were always so obedient.) Listen, Sister, a poem, somebody ought to copy that down!

"Resistance had to begin where the state's methods failed in spite of its every effort: with the individual." (Inge Brauneis)

The individual man on the stretcher, on the cart, the individual man. Was he a communist? A socialist? An atheist? A Bolshevik? A radical? A sympathizer? An artist? A demonstrator? A rebel? A human being? (Interesting!) The brother, the father of the nun.... (The accused justified himself by saying that at most sick prisoners were brought into the camp on wheelbarrows, never dead ones.) A child of his people gave the battle cry. *(People of Austria! Defend yourselves....)* She passed it on. (We want to be a united nation of brothers, or something like that.)

So-and-so-many little notes written and sent to so-and-so-many field post office addresses. So-and-so-many times were the letters cut from the newspaper by gloved hands that put them together and glued them down. So-and-so-often were the glued-together notices attached to walls, thrown over fences, carried into houses, handed on. So-and-so-often was the material brought in from Czechoslovakia, which was still free at the time, secretly printed, carried from one district in Vienna to another, and distributed in the factories. A package was shoved under a tavern table during a meeting; the roles of a couple in love were played. ("You know nothing about the package, if somebody asks.") And so-and-so-many times everything went well. But once she was caught, and then she went to Ravensbrück, Comrade (Amen).

The nun Restituta in her cell, in the nun's room, in

the nun's habit, does none of that. She writes in her simple, narrow, slanted handwriting and carries a song on her lips. (Nearer, my Lord, to thee. Rise according to the oath, people and country.)

And she writes and uses her saliva to glue the badly gummed envelopes shut, field post office address such-and-such: *Not dumb is Brother Laced-up Shoe, / Watch out, he'll turn the guns on you! / The day of retribution is not far away, / Remember, soldiers, your first oath today: / Austria!*

Helene sitting on the last bench and remembering....

I ask you: Should a person write that way? Can and should a nun, a woman, should a weak woman, can a person write that way these days?

The surgical nurse quietly moves her lips, counts the seconds, counts her heartbeats and watches and prays and waits and thinks.

We are telling the story of the nun Restituta, former-ly Helene Kafka, nun of the Women's Order of St. Fran-cis, called Seraphicus (Francis! Francis! I'm calling you!) of Christian Love, surgical nurse in the newly constructed wing of the Mödling Hospital near Vienna, arrested and accused (cut) of having composed and duplicated tracts (cut) that urge the people to fight for liberation (careful, not another word), on the basis of information given by the doctor, her superior (member of the armored SS, wearer of a uniform, no criminal record, in general an upright man) (close up, fade slowly). We are telling the story of a simple woman of the people (Austria), who alone, left to her own devices, called people to the struggle (even if the Church doesn't want to admit that it is true). We are telling it because when we heard it, oblivion was starting to spread, oblivion as heavy and dense as the odor of corpses, over our cities, over our villages, over our roofs (no wonder, with that conscience). Oblivion and slander were starting to spread.

We are telling it as it could have occurred, and as it might have been. At a time when in Ravensbrück in the Uckermark region (called a youth camp) certain doctors carried out their notorious and unknown experiments on women, when our sons dissected the anatomy of their brothers, the delinquents, when the skilled students broke the women's bones (that comes from obeying, that comes from listening, that comes from discipline), when they infected them with virulent tumors and pathogenic agents—very scientifically, of course—with Latin names, in the name of the occupation force, when they amputated bones from one leg and implanted them in another (yes, in research, we have always been a world power), when they reduced human beings to skeletons (nothing for whiners, whining patients are extremely undesirable), when the ungodly representatives of a respected station in life (at the top of the people's popularity list) helped eliminate those with swollen legs. (When we, of course, knew absolutely nothing about it.) (Secret! Maintain the strictest silence about it!) For orders give no indication at all, printed sentences say nothing at all, entire *combat* books say nothing at all, ethnic regulations mean nothing at all, the nightly convoys, raids, arrests, deportations, documents and facts, living witnesses simply say nothing at all. ("So, Madame Witness, decide: Was it a Jewish child or an Arabian? The accused is an honorable man—*and yet, he is an honorable man.*) Everything has occurred before, has been here again and again. It was constantly with us, was still with us. Who will be so petty...? (Really, who is against human rights?!) When all this happened, and while all this was permitted to be

74

(for the real danger is always somewhere else entirely!), Sister Restituta walked through the operating room (but not for much longer, I'll promise you that) with a prayer on her lips. She counts the seconds, she counts her heartbeats, she watches and prays and waits and acts.

At a time when so-and-so-many priests, members of religious orders, Catholics (Protestants, International Bible Students, Jehovah's Witnesses) were annihilated, destroyed, tortured (abandoned by their church, abandoned by their bishop, expelled from their order, expelled from the congregation, expelled from the convent), Helene Kafka, a real child of Vienna, picked up a pencil and wrote with slanted, uniform strokes, with Latin, Gothic letters. (Were the letters Latin or Gothic, Madame Witness?!) She wrote her letter "To the Catholic Youth." (The appeal is not badly written. It has a psychological effect. Gestapo.)

She walked through the operating room. She entered the hospital chapel. She paused in front of the picture of Mary, in front of the picture of St. Francis (frescoes, Italian school, twelfth century). She knelt in front of the tabernacle. She poured fresh water on the flowers. She cared for the crosses with her own money (unnoticed for half a year above the entrance, then a hospital worker took them down). She straightened the altar cloth. (She picked up the dust cloth.) She obtained new candles. (She baked consecrated wafers. Of course nobody said that, but she baked them.) Again she obtained new candles. She saw to it (perhaps) that fathers from the nearby St. Gabriel Church read the sacred mass at least every two weeks, when the priests were all in the field, the pastors too old. She comforted the sick. She gave the workers an extra portion. (She fasted.) She gave an extra portion to her cell mate. Annie Haider gave the prisoner

Restituta an extra portion.

Eleana, the daughter of the partisan, Eleana and *mio Papà, il partigiano.* I'm so proud of him! (Gold medal, Order of Merit, 1948, in the name of the Republic, signed—De Gasperi.)

In the evening, I was ready to go out. They were playing *Lohengrin.* (What else?) So I was standing in the vestibule. The wall was here, the bath was not tiled, but nevertheless there was the Venetian mirror and a carpet. In those days I was a frequent visitor at the *Dorotheum* (as a buyer). So I stood in front of the mirror. I tried on the little gold pin to see how it went with the green dress, and then I rejected the idea of the pin. In spite of its simplicity, it would have been conspicuous. So I was just putting the pin back with the glass beads, shells from (cut), when my hand froze. Then my heart seemed to freeze, I stared into emptiness (cut). Those are not fanfares, those are not hussars, not centurions who spare us. That's the steps creaking, that's boots scraping, those are footsteps on the scoured stairs, they are shouting (and still haven't learned any discipline from us Germans, Tyrolean accent, women's camp, French barracks, two weeks after the liberation, the gossip of the female guards, period). Be calm. Maintain your composure. Whatever happens, maintain your composure. (It was such a trauma that for some of our female citizens it was 1970 before they could bring themselves to wear boots, even in the depths of winter.) My hand begins moving again (with perfect composure, of course), retracts the movement (close-up), terminates the movement. My hand takes the gold pin from the box. My hand finishes the movement. My hand puts the pin in my hair (Nazi-porno, a fabulous business, Comrade), an expensive clip in my flowing hair. There is a knock at

76

the door. My voice is calm and cool. There's a song on my lips. My stride is lively. "What can I do for you?" (The witness will not remember that clearly.) The door opens and there stands a personal servant, a girl in a dress, with a gold clip in her hair. "What can I do for you?" The voice is fastidious, slightly irritated, the clip a good imitation. (The girl is German to the core.) In those days it still worked: All I say is, "Czernowitz."

I saved for the ticket, made the journey, arrived in Vienna, went to the opera. (Think how hungry I was for German culture. In those days that excuse still worked.) So the performance is about to begin. They've gone. The trick succeeded. I picked up the receiver, dialed a number (asked to be connected), spoke to the lady, hung up quickly, went to the opera, didn't speak to anybody. I thought it over, pulled myself together, tried not to show it, greeted my acquaintances, didn't betray a single word of it, thought about tomorrow. (Middle-class, single, conservative to reactionary.)

So-and-so-many writers, artists, scholars, the cream of the German intelligentsia, went abroad, were in internment camps in France. Obtained the exit visa from the Czech consulate, remained loyal (oh, Lidice!)—*Whoever has no papers or does not have the right ones is taken from the café* (Heinrich Mann). And Switzerland uprightly and calculatingly closed its borders.

One look into my room and the men were well informed. No picture (cut), no book (cut). Only the upright piano, with the cover pushed back, the song book open, the Köchel catalog (cut). The desk and the other things were added after 1945. Briefly stated, I went to the opera, probably didn't listen attentively to *Lohengrin*, thought about the lady. "Tell your papa (general in the First World War), if I am missing tomorrow, look for me (click), please, look for me." At seven in the morning I went to the *Metropol Hotel*. Headquarters of the gestapo, front entrance. (If she had entered in back, she would no longer be sitting among us today.) I walk with my head erect, I carry my head high, I step up to the door, I knock, I try to knock. The door opens, it springs open, the room, the personal servant, an ugly room, the ashtrays (not) screwed on. He's wearing a uniform. The gentleman from yesterday is wearing a uniform today. The gentleman is a high-ranking officer who doesn't remember the oath. I stand before him. I look at the chair. I am permitted to sit down. ("Sit down!" or: "Sit!" or: gesture toward the chair, or: a raise of his eyebrows in the direction of the chair, or....) Footsteps, with his hands clasped behind his back, his hands against the wall in front of him, beaten-up, robbed of clothing, beaten unbelievably hard, beaten to a pulp, beaten on the way, rendered unrecognizable, two children shot with one bullet. (It helps save ammunition.) Or....

"Why did you call me?"

"Out of envy. That doesn't surprise you?" (That doesn't scare you?) "My cousin. (My female cousin.) There are people who envy you, unfortunately."

I just say, "Czernowitz," and "Remember how hungry I am for German culture" (turn the page). After that, Ferri sent for the confirmation of his baptism. After that, I was less afraid. After that, our marriage failed. After that, the war was soon over. After that, my ex-husband committed suicide. After that, the simple woman from the village cared for the grave.

Sister Restituta in the May devotions in honor of the Virgin Mary. Sister Restituta in contact with the Catholic youth. Sister Restituta a promoter of choral singing.

Sister Restituta hurrying along the corridor. Her veil flutters like a flag in the wind. The cross clatters softly against her chest (against her side). The nun's flat soles slide softly and quickly over steps and corridors, up into the choir loft (nearer to Thee). She sang in the choir, of course.

This was not the Nun of Monza. This was not the Abbess of Gurk, not Frau Ava, not the Nun of Gandersheim. This was a woman from the regular clergy (who counted the days, folded her arms in her sleeves). The cross dangles at her side; the veil flutters in the draft (as in the hospital).

Is it true that she once went disguised as St. Nicholas? Is it true that she liked to walk across the cemetery? Is it true that she did not obey until she was in the dungeon? Is it true that it was only by grace that she...? (Of course, only by grace, how else?!) Is it true that she was alone? Is it true that she was satisfied with the food? (Water soup, potato peels, anything is all right with me, Reverend Mother.) Is it true that she only became obedient in prison? Is it true that she—only through prayer, of course—was able to lay aside her domineering nature?

Do you remember the scandal in the Kitzbühel sanatorium? Not only was he divorced, not only had he remarried (after that, the convent immediately withdrew all the nuns) right after the war.... (The convent didn't withdraw anybody because of Restituta.)

Alone and on her own. It is a long time from June to February. February 18, 1942. Ash Wednesday. Did she count the days? (By then her days were numbered.) See the lilies of the field, they do not count, they...(cut).

Did lilies grow in Mödling? In the field? In the hospital garden? (They don't count, they....) No, lilies don't count now.

A white page in front of her on the table. A white sheet of paper in front of her on the table. An empty, white sheet of paper (with narrow lines) in front of her on the table. Her hair is short. A nun's hair is short. (The Holy Father wants it that way. He likes to have everything uniform.) The hair of a nun without a habit is short. The worn-out fingers brush briefly through the hair of the nun without a habit. Her veil is not fluttering in the wind. We are not standing on hills in the sunset. This is not the wind of the prophets, it is the storm of the quaestors. It is the draft on the stairs and in the corridors in the People's Court (a people on trial). A white, empty sheet of writing paper (with an imprint, narrow-lined, prison paper, wartime product, with wood content, coarsely fibered, absorbent, like blotting paper, gray and dismal). In the lonely room (solitary confinement) the lonely woman who chose the right part— Helene chose the right part—sits in the nuns' room, in her nun's habit, while confined to quarters (at night?), and writes to distant soldiers, and writes "To the Catholic Youth," and writes to the Reverend Mother. *(Because we can't say that we fall into the feathers, we say that we fall into the rags.)* Franciscan mirth, Comrade.

Stubbornly and cumbersomely the text flows into her pen. The text flows onto the paper (this text flows onto the paper):

"..., don't let yourselves be blinded, wasted, don't flee. Arise to your oath, people and country!...Put aside the old ideas, get rid of the old hierarchies, do away with the old obedience. The distribution of property (Francis), no above, no below.... Above all, make the military democratic.... Above all, make the schools democratic.... Above all make the hospitals democratic,

80

and the officials, make the executives democratic. Above all, make the land democratic. Don't speculate, according to ability and desire, according to what is permissible and necessary, not to each his own (nefarious statement). Let man be good! But above all, rational! Let man be merciful! But above all, full of dignity! Reason says: Justice! Reason says: Let goodness reign. (Goodness commands that reason reign.) *Lay your ear / on the people's heart.* Anni said that—while the storm of war raged around her.... Think of the substance that taught you. Think of the history that you push aside. Who erected the bridge? Who felled the poles? Who bled? Who baked the bread? (Whoever baked bread / tomorrow will be *dead*). Who wrote history? Who made history? (Yes, who did it?) What did the priest say? Who cooked the soup? Who cared for the children? Who washed the sick? Who made the dead?"

Who committed murder at the Perschmann farm? Who drove the farm's inhabitants, thirteen people, together? Who? The farmer, the sister, the grandmother, a teenage maid, the farmer's children and those of his sister and some of the neighbor's children (the youngest nine months old). Who drove them together before the front door? Who gave the people the signal? Who fired the shots? How many fell immediately? How many were horrified and tried to flee into the house? How many of those who had already been shot at reached the protection of the entryway (narrow and long, a wooden railing, the faded planks, the smell of curd soap, the knotholes, the inherited rooms and decorations of the houses)? Who followed and killed the people in the vestibule and in the kitchen (my flesh and blood)? Who heard the terrified whimpering of little Gottfried? Who fired a salvo behind the stove, so that it became as silent as death? As silent

81

as death, I say. (Whose heart does not break when writing this, when screaming this?) Who set the Perschmann farm on fire? In Unterpetzen, in southern Carinthia. (Slovenians? Not worth mentioning. They claim there were so many of them. In reality there were hardly five thousand any more: Injustice has a name, an address, a date, a time, a place, all known and gladly provided. Klagenfurt. Provincial capital. 1977).

Ribitsch, Brunner, and Ranacher formed a gang with foreign workers in the fifth and sixth years of the war and terrorized the area / Klementin and Jelic / brought weapons, delivered ammunition / Maria Peskoller, Grete Jessernig, Rosa Eberhard led foreign workers, deserted soldiers to them, bandaged the wounded, and helped in other ways in German-speaking Upper Carinthia. (Dishonorable, of course, to punish them with death.)

Who made the wine? Who harvested? Who staggered? Who pressed the wine? Who created the dead?

Who came into the village of My Lai in two trucks? Who came into the village on March 16, 1968? Who threw hand grenades into the bomb shelter? Who drove the villagers together? Who shot women, old people, and children? Who stabbed the babies with the bayonet? Who fired six shots into the children? *The older boy fell forward to protect the younger one.* Who gave the command? Who carried it out? Who covered up the massacre? Who acquitted the main culprits? Who never even indicted the people who were really guilty?

Who threw the dead into the trench? Who placed the living in front of the trench? Who made the cannons? Who ordered them? Who paid for them? Who should pay for them? We, the nation, the people, will pay for it. We will pay bitterly. (I would urgently advise her not to continue writing that way. That sort of thing doesn't sell at all.)

Who put fish and meat together? Who mixed wine and vinegar? Who mixed flour with sand? Who strewed ashes? Who reduced a people to rubble and ashes? Who dispersed a people to the four winds, burned to ashes? Who did it? Who did it?

Godless mammon, the idol Baal, called capital. Don't let yourselves be bound, nor blinded, nor wasted. Bad oaths should be broken, bad regimes should be broken, bad deeds are a crime....

Lonely and upright in her room, the nun. The night overtakes her. She tears up the sheet (with the narrow lines covered with writing). The ink has run out, blood has flowed, time has run out. She writes in her cell:

A handwritten newspaper, in secret-message form. Commentaries on articles from the *Völkischer Beobachter*. Articles by Franzl. Speeches from the English, the French, the Soviet radio stations. The Stalin speech of 1942 about the Don River Resolution and the provisions of the Atlantic Charter. These papers were written in several editions by Restituta, Wilma Tessarik, Haas Franzi, and in part by me. (Document office. Archive material.)

The reading of Stalin's speech in the confessional— the priest illuminated it with his flashlight. Finally he gave me the cross to kiss and said, "Remain seated so that it looks like you offered the prayer of penance." Hard work began for me after that confession. The newsletter had to be written, my tasks as supervisor and nurse lay before me, and I did not want to give up that work, in order to be able to help my comrades. And at night they dragged me out of bed, under the pretext of "a dying person." They dragged me into the nurses' station, where supervisors and nurses sat and requested a discussion night. (What will happen after the war? What is a people's democracy?) Anni Haider. Solitary confinement. *Schiffamtstraße*. Restroom telephone. Inquisition Hospital. Escaped from it.

Confinement! The nun and surgical nurse from..., born on..., in (Bohemia, a real child of Vienna), single, supposedly no previous criminal record, on February 18, 1942, arrested temporarily, as yet without a defense attorney. I accuse her: of having undertaken (cut) and the military forces of (cut) of high treason a) and b) an area belonging to the Reich (cut), by the authority of the (cut). In the criminal case against..., on the basis of the hearing on October 29, 1942, the participants of which were Senate President (cut), Supreme Court Judge (cut), the SS-Chief of Staff, who (growing more and more dashing, cut), W-Standard Bearer and Chief of Police (cut), State's Attorney (bellowing), Court Secretary (devoted servant, cut): sentenced to death and to the loss of civil rights for the rest of her life *(restituito l'onore alla chiesa)*...also has to bear the court costs (cut), by rights. Reasons. (Pan shot).

The accused claims to have had the original of...read during a visit to the hospital...lost it and for that reason to the soldiers...who demanded that it be returned shortly thereafter...in the flyer German Catholic youth... in an abject manner...follows from the contents of this concoction...clear and unambiguous (cut).

Above all, I greet you warmly. Has Mother Superior already performed her devotions? Mine take quite a while now, but I have learned many things from them (not the way they thought...). About fourteen days ago I received a letter from Sister..., written very unctuously as always, but no greeting from the Reverend Mother, nor from anyone else. I really had to take courage in order to give my order in this...as well.

Restituta! Take the secret messages. Who knows what they plan to do with me. *(And Restl put everything in her stockings and went to her cell.)* This friendship with the communist women must really have been compromising, don't you think?

I had to maintain silence about everything, of course, otherwise the later death candidates would possibly not have received a priest who could speak their native language (watch silently).

Starved down to a skeleton, with her hands tied behind her back. (When I asked, "What have you eaten today?" she answered, "Potato peelings and they were black, but anything is all right with me." Yes, confinement was a blessing, a real mercy.) Emaciated and still envied, a former nun, the accused, sits in her cell knitting. (That was before the verdict.) Believe me, that is because I was permitted to see you again after your acquittal!

She knocks, she shakes the door of the cell, she demands: "Open, open up! Off to the battle prayer! Pray for Anni." The door flies open. The cell door flies open. The entire Inquisition Hospital is in an uproar. The battle prayer is being said, the needle is being prepared. (The needle?) You would not have remained in the death cell, Anni! That's all we can do, that's all we do. And she wrote the secret messages and gave instruction (at night on the restroom telephone), and reported to those below us in the death cell, and raised them up, and reported to the priest. And the priest handed out the secret messages: "If you can keep quiet, the gestapo will never find out about us!"

Cut up pieces of cloth. Gut them into strips. Sew the strips to each other. Wind them onto balls. Keep back a tiny scrap, braided into pigtails, two tiny shoes sewn. *(For Anni!)* Made by the barefoot, penitent nun, slippers for Anni. (Her hair was very short.)

The door opens. It opens and there is a bodyguard, a personal servant, a body. The door opens and the nun in white.... (Think of it, without her habit, without her veil, but she did it for Christ. Didn't he die naked?) The door opens. I was the garrison priest in my subsidiary appointment. At three o'clock sharp, I was in the state court. As I walked through the door, I could see already. I accompanied my soldiers (cut) and then waited as always in the corridor to bless the others as well. The door opened and Restituta walked out accompanied by two people (cut).

Comrade Restituta, dressed in white.... (Objection, objection! Might we not expect a more favorable decision?)

Don't believe that I weep because I must die. I weep for joy, because you are alive and I can see you once more. When the war is over and Austria is free, continue to fight so that *something like this never happens again!*

Lonely and starved down to skin and bones, the formerly stout, supposedly domineering nun with the Czech name, who perhaps suffered from gall-bladder disease, now a delinquent with her hands tied behind her back, Restituta, left to rely on herself, thrown into the hands of the enemy. (She walked solemnly and calmly; she cast a glance at me.)

She often climbed up on the table. When we called her to the window of her cell, she climbed up on the table and spoke, so kindly, Viennese. And then the word of God. She was a missionary. Now and then weeping was heard. She cast a glance at me, she looked at me.

She walked on. We stood around her. *Three priests and an English minister.* Then I heard her say (cut).

After receiving the holy sacraments, in a loud voice she renewed the sacred vows (cut), asked in a loud voice for forgiveness for those who bore responsibility for her fate (cut). Sister Restituta recited her vows in a loud voice and afterward said a few words in favor of the conversion of enemies (cut). And with joy she encountered a father from Maria Stiegen. (In her youth she liked to come to our church.)

6:30 p.m.: *I am going to the feast, I am going to heaven!* (The door opens and a body....) *I die for Christ! I lived for Christ!*

Afterward, we gave those who had been executed the last rites while the executioner cleaned the blood from the guillotine next to us.

THE GYPSY WOMAN

NAME: NOT GIVEN
Born: Unknown
Deported: Between 1938 and 1945
Exterminated: Between 1938 and 1945

Why don't you want to write about the Gypsy woman? Why don't you seek out the Gypsy woman, write down her name, birth date, arrest date, internment date, deportation date, sterilization date, renewed deportation date, and finally the date of her extermination? Why didn't you give the name of the Gypsy girl, search it out, write it down, question the survivors, do research, collect data, read, make notes? Why didn't you find a suitable name? Why didn't you select a suitable name? Why did you discriminate against the Gypsy woman? Why did you treat her as a special case? You say you know no Gypsies. You say you have never seen any Gypsies. In your youth there were no Gypsies anymore, only the itinerant tinkers from Italy and the basket weavers, the broom makers, called cart people, who lived in the vicinity. You say there were tinsmith families. People assumed they had immigrated years earlier from the South, perhaps from the Dolomites, and perhaps it was all just a rumor. One descendant became an athlete and world famous. His sister directed the boarding house. She had the darkest skin of all of them.

You say you saw your first Gypsy woman in Florence, about 1956. She was carrying a child in her arms. She was begging. The child was bundled up so tightly it required effort to recognize it as a child and not as a doll. You say the woman was young and pretty. She was wearing a long, yellow, flowered dress. At the time that was extremely unusual. By rights, everyone should have turned around to look, but nobody turned around, and nobody paid any attention to the woman. Moreover, you were completely alone in your amazement. It frightened you all the more, when you suddenly thought that you were the victim of your imagination, of a strange vision. Instead, the woman held out a firm, demanding hand to you from beneath the child. Her hand was brown and black, namely black under her short fingernails—they had been trimmed with a knife—and around the brown creases of her knuckles. Her hand was young and broad. She quickly and firmly took coins or banknotes away from you. The crumpled bills disappeared beneath an apron or a stomacher, a cloth that held the suckling child—or the doll, you were not sure—tied around her neck. Her naked feet shuffled across the curb stones in sandals. Unconcerned about the traffic, the yellow figure glided safely into the nearby park and disappeared, with the scarf that covered her thick braids askew. The woman seemed unsympathetic to you. But you felt a trace of sympathy rise within you, sympathy for yourself and for the bundle that you could just as easily have carried from curb to curb, the bundle or the doll. Your figure would not have been firm and demanding. Your gait would not have been shuffling and unconcerned.

Aghast, you followed this apparition with your eyes, and in so doing you met the mocking gaze of a Florentine housewife, you say. Hiding your tears, covering them up, holding them back, again and again you cried, *"Ma cosa c'è, ma chi è!"* And when you said that, the housewife overcame her suspicion about your complicity and laughingly answered, *"Non lavora mai, questa gente."* To which you sanctimoniously responded, *"Non ci credo."* And then you said, *"Ma cosa sono."* The housewives' answer—in the meantime others had stopped, supposedly in the vicinity of a market—was full of vague intimations. They said that the people in question were lazy rabble, that there were more of them running around, and that a person should not give them anything or indulge them under any circumstances. You claim to have said, "It's not the child's fault." To which they responded, "Child?! These people simply have children in order to beg with them."

So you knew instinctively, or claim to have known she was a Gypsy, and accordingly you had the choice of concerning yourself more intimately with the Gypsy problem or, while feigning indifference, pushing it aside. You decided in favor of the second alternative, you say.

You were poor, you were perplexed—the demanding hand and the trussed-up child (or doll), the long dress, the braids, the displaced scarf, the begging, the coin, the banknote. You followed her with your eyes. You could not comprehend that it was not you instead of her disappearing unconcernedly among the bushes of the park. To be sure, you had a job, but not a good one. You were poorly paid. You were living in a foreign country. It was a rich city where being poor was humiliating. You were young. You hardly had more than the clothes on your body. You were afraid, had the fear of a foreign, short-sighted woman. Everything happened very quickly. Barefoot, wearing flat sandals, she had made her demand firmly and curtly and probably also wordlessly, before you could think and ask anything. The local housewife had stopped. She had watched scornfully and had seen your perplexity. And you, you had recognized very clearly the disparaging, comparing gaze. You had the feeling that you would soon go begging the same way, with a tightly wrapped child (or doll) in your arms, with hysterical, short-sighted fears. As if rooted to the ground, if there is such a thing, you stopped and gazed in the direction the woman had gone, as if looking at a vision.

Why didn't she dance? Why didn't you dance? Why didn't she carry a knife between her teeth? Why did she carry a tormented child around with her (which was asleep, by the way)? Why didn't you carry a tormented child around with you?

Why do you claim you knew for certain there were no longer any Gypsies? Who claimed that all the Gypsies had been exterminated? Why didn't you ever ask for more details? Exterminated *how*? Why did you run away, or at least make a wide detour, each time a woman in a long dress approached you in Florence, walking like the barefoot woman? Why were you afraid? Why do you use the Suez crisis as an excuse? Why do you pretend the crisis in Hungary eclipsed both the Suez crisis and the crisis in southern Tyrol, and that everything together covered up the matter of the Gypsies?

Why do you remain silent about the Gypsies after the war? Why don't you report that you really did see Gypsies after the war? Why do you remain silent about the Gypsy pilgrimage?

You say they were not Austrian Gypsies. You claim they were Hungarian or other Gypsies! You allege that they came in automobiles, entire caravans of them. At the time, people supposedly talked about the earlier covered wagons, drawn by emaciated horses. You say they were American cars. You say they said they were on their way back from southern France. They were returning from a pilgrimage, they said. They were permitted to camp on the village green.

You say you went there once, too. You say the men and women on the green seemed like innkeepers or merchants, like fat merchants, and there was nothing romantic to see in them, at most something to fear. But that came from your short-sightedness at the time, you say. Loud music from phonographs resounded above the tops of cars that were equipped with long cables, and you also connect the memory of carpets with that episode.

You say the people were fat and dark-haired. You say that at the time they did not seem young to you at all. They seemed to you to be at least thirty years old. You say as much as you looked around, you didn't see any children. You claim you saw no children on the village green, which was now a Gypsy camp. You declare that you did not picture Gypsies to be like that. You claim to have doubted that those Gypsies were real Gypsies. You say that long after their departure people were still describing the possessions of the Gypsies down to the smallest detail, from the portable radios to the trailer houses. You say that perhaps it occurred in 1945, or in 1946, or later. You say that in your opinion the woman was too old to wear her hair down. You say that as a child a person has certain ideas about adults. You say the woman was just as fat as her companion. He wore a mustache and a hat that he never removed. You say people called him the ringleader. The others stood further back, in the hop field. You say you don't know whether the place was actually a way station at the time. His hat was pushed back into his neck, and the man sat on the hood of his American car.

You say you did not see traveling Gypsies until 1965. You say the children were unbelievably beautiful and pathetic. You say they begged. Your assert something to the effect that the Gypsy children ran after you along the little provincial street of the town and flatteringly asked for your bracelets. You state that they almost overcame you with tenderness when you stopped. You say it was difficult for you to take off the bracelets, distribute them to the children, and still retain at least one of them. You assert that a native then became angry. He bellowed at the children that they should not bother

97

foreigners. You state that the native tried to force the children away like rabble. You also state that it was only two bracelets anyway. They were not made of silver, and you just wanted to share with the children. You tried to make it clear to the children that you wanted to share. You say the children were content, even before the angry native tried to drive them away from you. Moreover, you say you had the feeling the native wanted to take the children away from you. You had the feeling he wanted to tear the children (although it can be proven that you had none of your own at the time) from your arms, from your breast, and load them onto trucks. You admit that this feeling was exaggerated. You claim that the sight of the children, little, barefoot boys with brown curls and brown eyes, tugged at your heart, that you had to weep in that provincial town. You say you wanted to take them with you. You admit that you weep too easily.

You say you admired the older girl. You say you asked the girl if you could take her picture. You say you photographed the girl the way a tourist photographs peasants where you come from. You say the little girl was nine years old at most, and she had dark blond braids tinged with red, and thin, brown arms. You say the girl wore gold coins on her ear lobes, around her neck, around her waist, and on her nose. The photograph shows clearly that it was not a coin on her nose, but a liver spot. You say the girl was adorned like a bride. You say the girl wore the treasure of her clan as a dowry around her neck and around her waist. But the photograph awakens the impression that it was a matter of bait or showpieces or both. You admit that in the final analysis you didn't want to know anything. You confess that you had reservations about the shady customs of the migrating Gypsies.

You say that later they showed you the courthouse in the country's capital city. On Thursdays the Gypsies had their court day, or rather the court reserved Thursdays for the Gypsies, you claim. On Thursdays the women crouched in long, colorful garments on the steps of the courthouse in that country's capital city. The steps are both numerous and low. On Thursdays the feuding clans sat, according to you, on the large outside stairway, with the women smoking and the men gesticulating while they waited for the verdict. Sometimes natives approached the outside stairway of the courthouse and looked at the Gypsies, laughed at the Gypsies, and praised the patience of the authorities with the migrating people (who, by the way, always walked there). The felt hats of the Gypsies reminded you of the alpine regions. They had bushy mustaches, thin, sun-creased faces, you say. The flower sellers, on the other hand, reminded you of the nineteenth century. Or rather of certain motifs from the paintings of that era.

Later, you saw the Gypsy women in the parks of the country's capital city. They were nursing their babies. Springing from the bushes, they caught up with the overcrowded, slowly moving streetcars and then huddled there on the floor and continued to nurse their babies. The fertility of those people had a provocative effect, because it constantly exposed the vulnerability of the human being, the susceptibility of human flesh. You saw young girls of unbelievable beauty, who were still children themselves, sitting in the sun with their tiny sucklings. The children were wrapped in dirty rags. You wondered how they survived. Once you approached curiously to look at a child.

You say you suspected it was not advisable to look too curiously at the children of the Gypsy women. You

99

claim to have read something once about the evil eye. Nevertheless, you approached. Of course you try to justify it by saying you wanted to find out about the living conditions of the young mothers.

You admit that much of what you know about the Gypsies discredits them. You say, you admit besides, that much of what people say about the Gypsies discredits the people who say it. You admit that the story you could have written about the Gypsy woman does no credit to you.

The young Gypsy in the courtyard of the restaurant next to the road (by the lake) stood before you and brazenly sang to you. He nonchalantly sang his sentimental ditty from the 1920s directly to you and didn't even wait for a tip. Your local woman friend, who had owned Gypsies or at least their campgrounds before the war, smiled derisively. That sly dog of a Gypsy saw that you were a foreigner. That Gypsy rascal turned your head on a whim, with a tear jerker that was, by the way, sung improperly (as only a Gypsy can adulterate a song). Smiling and good-naturedly your friend admitted that his accordion playing had not been bad and that the idea of that particular tear jerker had been astoundingly appropriate. Finally, you admit that you stood up and were angry. Why are you ashamed of Gypsies?

Why don't you describe what you saw in the arms of the young Gypsy woman? Why don't you describe the naked little skeleton in the girl's arms? Why don't you admit at last, what you saw on the sidewalk of that particular capital city? Why don't you describe the dirty rag the young woman used to wipe away the honey-yellow excrement of the newborn child, the excrement that continued to erupt from the little body? Why don't you admit that the mother, the child-mother, the mother of the child, didn't even deign to look at you, but simply continued to catch the honey-yellow excrement in the dirty rag, and that you don't know what she did with it then? That she didn't even look up when you shoved the bank-note under the head of the suckling child and departed as if somebody were after you? Why do you believe you have to disassociate yourself? Why do you always claim that it serves you right, that it really serves you right?

But why do you bother with the drinking-water episode? It is well known that in these large cities there are drinking fountains for the populace every few hundred meters. So it is superfluous to report extensively about provisions for drinking water in large cities. Thus the story about the Gypsy women at the fountains is also superfluous. The Gypsy woman with the transparent, ready-made blouse and the brassiere in her hand. All of the male occupants of the passing streetcar (with you) stared and laughed and shouted at the Gypsy girls with the transparent blouses and at the brassiere in the one girl's hand. The girls wiped the backs of their hands across their lips and walked barefoot into the bushes wearing their floor-length skirts and what were almost brothel blouses, as if they were on an island and not in that country's capital city, even if they were on its outskirts. The two Gypsy girls scorned the men with their cheers, their shoes, and their distorted faces. What concern was that of yours? Admit that the girls walked vulgarly and scornfully away from the fountain and straight into the bushes.

The fortune teller. She was at least forty years old, and she was accompanied by a ten-year-old girl and a two-year-old boy. As one might expect, the children went barefoot, you say. The Gypsy woman was wearing

101

a short work dress, a bandanna, and shoes. She called to you, you say, with a domineering gesture, of the kind one sees in Romance countries. You obeyed, feeling guilty and frightened because you had been staring at the child again. You followed all of the witch's directions, participated in the mumbo-jumbo, and clearly saw that she was brazenly robbing you. Horrified, you watched her spray milk from her breasts on the ground and saw the child stand at her breasts and suck. Intently you watched everything, as if in a dream, and only when she dismissed you with the same gesture, only then did you run away, stumble away, flee. What point are you trying to make with this story? What is the purpose of this report?

You gradually became accustomed to the Gypsies. The children knocked on your window almost daily. You heard them knocking early in the morning, opened the window, and handed the old bottles, glasses, and clothes out the window. You asked the children why they didn't go to school, why they didn't learn to read and write. They claimed they had no money for the uniform. Angrily you went to your friends. Your local friends answered with a smile, "We know the tune." They imitated the Gypsy dialect and in a distorted voice they said, "We don't have no money for rags."

After that your friends said—at least that is what you allege—they had tried everything. They had directed these people, obtained housing for them, given them jobs (even ones for which they were not qualified, which had been a mistake). Of course, they had left their jobs one day, torn out the parquet floors, made fires in their apartments, raised chickens and pigs in the bathrooms. (You can't drive it out of them.) You thought of the southern Tyroleans, the so-called refugees, who kept their chickens behind the stove, but you kept the thought to yourself. You stood there silently and decided not to tell your friends anything else. You claim that back then you quit talking about the Gypsies.

Then you heard about informers, about block wardens, about authenticated infringements, all by Gypsies. Then you left the country and forgot about the Gypsies.

Suddenly, in Vienna, you constantly encountered Gypsies. In the street around the corner there were Yugoslavian foreign workers, officially called *guest workers*. They were Gypsies. The children said so one day. You invited the children to visit you. They played with your little boy. Your little boy screamed. He wasn't used to so many children. You practiced German, reading, and writing with the children, all of whom attended special schools. You let the children draw. Then the little boy demolished the rocking horse, the bigger girl scribbled on the bathroom wall, and the older girl painted a holy family: Joseph in jeans, Mary with breasts, Jesus in a little red dress. You kept the pictures but told the children not to come again for a while, after they had hit each other on the head with the wooden shoes, after the bread lay in crumbs on the floor under the table. You were amazed at how precisely they obeyed. They never came back.

Before that, the little girl asked you, "How many languages do you speak?" Before that, the little girl laughed slyly and asked you, "Do you speak the Gypsy language, too?" Before that, they told you they were all attending the special school. Before that, they stared silently into space when you talked about professions, about technical schools, about school. It got on your nerves when the little girls always wanted to carry your

103

little boy around. Your little boy immediately began to scream if a girl touched him, but on the other hand he demanded more often that you carry him.

Once the girl talked about her father. "He spits in my eyes," the girl said. "He doesn't hit us if he comes home and we haven't cooked dinner yet. He just spits in our eyes."

Several times you were pestered out on the street in broad daylight when you were expecting your child. Once even by a local citizen, but the child had already arrived then. So what do you want? Why are you telling this story?

You say the foreigners can be recognized by the way they walk. Their clothing is less conspicuous than that of the traveling Gypsies. Thus the men walk in front with long strides, followed by the women, with the length of a stride between them. Each woman has a cigarette clamped between her teeth, and the heels of their shoes are too high for their feet. They seem to walk on crooked legs, thin, crooked legs, you claim. Of course, you are not sure whether or not they are Gypsies. What do you care if they are Gypsies?

They are always addressed with the informal *du*, and people only yell at them, you say. That comes from the instinctive assumption that you only have to yell at foreigners, and they will understand you better. This misunderstanding is based on the substitution of linguistic functions, you say. In such a communication, what is lacking is not contact but the right code. But the local citizens insist on yelling and using the informal form of address.

You say the girls on the street around the corner are always looking out the window. You claim they are still of school age, but they long for nothing but to have their own children. You say they seem to long for nothing more earnestly than to escape from the authority of their fathers in order to come under the power of a strange man. Why do you say that? Why do you discuss that?

You report that a family moved into the building where you live. The family moved in, although the apartment had previously been purchased by two young men. On the first cold day, smoke billowed from all the stoves in the house. Clouds of smoke moved through the house, and the new family couldn't cook anymore. Some said they were Hungarians, others said they were from Burgenland.

Suddenly the caretaker locked the bicycle shed, an old laundry, and distributed expensive keys. The price of the keys was astonishingly high. You asked the people if they needed help. The mother, a pretty woman of indeterminable age, silently continued to stir the pot on the stove. Her husband sat at the table and remained silent. Finally the woman said the caretaker had to know what was happening. The bad chimneys were the caretaker's responsibility. Not a trace of Hungarian. They spoke an Austrian dialect. Didn't they get a report on the condition of the chimney? What for, with the high redemption fee? So, cheated after all. The apartment was decorated with colorful wallpaper; it made an oriental impression and was painstakingly clean. Then the chimney sweeps came and new fireplace doors were installed. The defiant attitude of these people from Burgenland seemed strange, but at the same time you had to admit they were right, you say.

Then the children of the family said they were Gypsies. You claim you had no idea they were Gypsies. They behaved quite differently from all the other representatives of their people you had seen before. The children said, "We're Gypsies." Then you noticed the dark skin and the dark hair of the girls. You say you thought they were possibly Burgenland Croats. You are not actually familiar with representatives of the Austrian minorities, you say. Then you learned that the mother raised nine children from a total of fourteen pregnancies, of which, as they said, three of the children lived in the house. But on a daily basis you saw many more people in the kitchen. Each time the door opened, there was a surging throng of young, brightly clothed girls and some young men, who were playing music. The two youngest girls said they attended the special school. "Because we weren't able to speak German very well yet," they said in flawless, accent-free German. "In the special school we learn just as well, only slower," the girls said. You wanted to find out if a transfer from the special school to the main school was possible. You say you didn't do it. You became afraid of the responsibility connected with such a question.

Your little boy now only wanted to live amid the bustle of their kitchen. Suddenly, however, he was afraid of Krampus,* of ghosts, phantoms, and dogs that were not there. Angrily you forbade him to visit the B. family. From then on, the much older children of the B. family had to come to your apartment. Your husband did not agree with that. He reminded you how much the people liked children and about the instruments your little boy was permitted to touch, even though each of them was worth a large amount of money.

Then the youngest child in the B. family told how his father ran for his life. The youngest son of the family from the house where you live told about his father and

*Legendary companion of St. Nicholas

his flight through the bushes. He was fourteen years old. He carried his youngest brother, a fourteen-month-old child, in his arms. While they were fleeing, a twig snapped into the child's face and injured his eye. The child screamed. In spite of his father's best efforts, the child, his uncle, screamed loudly, said the boy—you say. Then the pursuers, who were armed with long knives and had surrounded the small patch of trees and bushes, knew exactly where they were hidden, said the youngest B.—you say. Then the boy—the father—dropped his little brother in mortal fear and ran on, said the youngest B.—you say. The mother's family survived. The people in another village hid her. Then they stabbed the little brother—the uncle—with knives, said the boy—you say. "My father still weeps even now, when he tells about it," said the boy—you say. "My father walked to Hungary," said the boy—you say. Very incautiously and quite superfluously you asked who the murderers were, you say. The boy was frightened at the question. "I don't know," said the youngest B. "I think it was the Russians or somebody."

You screamed at him. That was a mistake, but for a moment you couldn't think clearly either, and you almost believed it, you say. "Just think about it!" you screamed. "It can't have been the Russians. The Russians fought against the murderers."

"Oh, yes, the Nazis," said the boy meekly. After that he didn't want to talk about it anymore, you say. When you later showed him a book about the extermination of the Gypsies, he didn't react at all, you say. He doesn't want to know anything about his own history, you say. Just who of us knows all about his own history? Just who of us knows all about our own history?

The janitor was an alcoholic, you say. He was emaciated. His face, hair, and clothing were gray. He often appeared suddenly out of the darkness, you say. He lived in complete degeneration, almost decay, you say. In his complete degeneration he once opened the door, and stench like that of animals streamed out of his apartment, you say. You were disgusted, but you greeted him nevertheless, you say. First he raised guinea pigs in his apartment, then white mice. He took these animals for walks on the patio and made admiring comments like other people do when they point out their pet dogs. Sometimes you heard him crying and/or kicking up a row, you say. It usually happened when you were at home alone with your little boy. Often the drunken caretaker or janitor rang the doorbell looking for some key or other. You never got rid of the feeling that he should be washed, should be given the opportunity to wash himself. An almost pathological feeling of responsibility for the house warden or janitor oppressed you and simultaneously aroused great revulsion in you, you claim. You didn't even tell your husband about this feeling. Yes, you didn't even formulate it properly in your mind. The feeling just arose, you say.

Then there was the matter of the dead pigeons. The attic in the old house, full of rubbish and junk, was suddenly occupied by numerous fluttering pigeons. A broken attic window or a damaged dormer window appeared to be the cause of it. The attic smelled like pigeon dung, and the smell, or better: stench, mingled with that of the guinea pigs from the ground floor. You could hardly open your doors anymore. Then every time you went to the attic to dry the laundry, the pigeons were a little quieter and more disheveled. That was perhaps weeks or even only days later. You forgot the pigeons when you left the attic, and when you entered it again, you were all the more forcibly reminded of them. You entered the attic with the laundry. You were the only resident of the house who dried laundry in the attic, and you had the feeling that you were not alone. Then behind the beam on the floor you saw the dying pigeons, at least twenty of them.

You were petrified with fear and revulsion, but keeping your neck stiff and turning your back on the pigeons, you hung up the laundry anyway. You moved slowly, as in a film by Bergmann, you say. Next to the dying and already decaying pigeons, you calmly—at least you were not screaming, even if you were choked with fear and felt cold shivers down your back—hung up the stupid laundry.

You informed the other residents, especially the woman with the first-class bathroom fixtures and the inappropriate tiles. The woman who owned the nice fixtures agreed to go to the attic with you. At the sight of the pigeons, the well-dressed and flawlessly groomed woman let out a short scream of anger. An hour later the caretaker cleaned the attic, unquestioningly. He carried out the lady's orders (and they were orders) quite submissively. Shortly thereafter the attic was free of pigeons. After completing his work the caretaker stood in the attic sprinkled with lime and with his eyes open wide from the exertion, and then he walked slowly down the steep, rickety attic stairs. You wondered for a long time, why he didn't really protest against those requirements. Later your little boy's bicycle was damaged in the shed, you say.

The caretaker had a friend, you say. He had a flat boxer's nose and long, dull, ashen hair. He wore high-heeled shoes and had a mustache beneath his flat nose. He often stood in front of the caretaker's locked door and could hardly be distinguished from the dark door panel. He did not turn around, or he lowered his head if he happened to be looking in their direction when somebody went by.

Sometimes the friend placed a bag or a net containing packages in front of his friend's door. Then you saw the caretaker wobbling out of the surrounding taverns again. He screamed into the night on the patio and smashed pieces of his own furniture.

Then came the business with the renovation. The roof was supposed to be repaired again, and the chimneys were scraped out. On the roof there were heaps of junk and tiles that nobody took away, neither the roofers nor the chimney sweeps. The chimney doors were all open. The caretaker was not informed about it until the chimney sweep's apprentice stumbled over the piles of rubbish. That is, you informed him. The caretaker slammed down the telephone receiver. Only after the master chimney sweep complained did you meet the caretaker on the attic stairs. He came down the steep stairs like a figure out of Balzac. He was covered with mortar from head to toe. You fled into your apartment and turned the key twice. You asked yourself why nobody let the caretaker take a shower. Everyone knew he had no water in his apartment. He said he didn't need any. Everyone knew he hadn't had gas or electricity for years. He secretly tapped into the house's electricity. Did people know that? Did they tolerate it? Didn't it matter to anyone? You did not remember that there were public baths, you say. You had this unpleasant guilt feeling because he stuffed the garbage into sacks with his bare hands when he was threatened. He knuckled under and simultaneously brought the building into an undescribable condition. You imagine that the caretaker was the image of the building's inhabitants for those outside. You had the fixed idea that the caretaker was the image of the house.

Later the neighbor woman from the third floor came with the note. They wanted to get rid of the caretaker and have the Burgenland Gypsies, the B. family on the first floor, as caretakers. Everyone had already signed the petition. Then the B. family, with its many children, could use the caretaker's neighboring rooms for their own children. Suddenly you refused to sign. But when they told you the story involving the Gypsy girls, you had had enough, you say. The caretaker and his friend had badgered the Gypsy girls and their mother, as soon as the father was out of the house. They actually besieged the apartment of the B. family. More than once, the police had to step in, the neighbor woman told you —you say.

The two youngest girls in the B. family—who were still of school age—took care of the household almost by themselves. You met them shopping, carrying water, and washing the car. At night, or really at four in the morning, they were also seen carrying the instruments belonging to their father, their older brother, and their cousin from the car into the house. If you asked the girls if they also played an instrument, they laughed as if you had told a good joke. Once the youngest girl asked her father to let her play an instrument. Proudly she said that her father would soon buy a piano. Then it was never mentioned again. The youngest son practiced his violin diligently. He even took violin lessons and was the only one who learned to read notes. The sisters were employed as waitresses or as unskilled workers. The girls who attended the special school, the two youngest ones, monitored the homework of their little brother, who attended elementary school and later the middle school. Your son was again the daily guest of the B. family. He defended himself against the girls and admired the male members of the family. The girls anticipated his every wish. You didn't like that, you say.

You tried to encourage the girls to attend a school, undertake an apprenticeship, or attend a trade school. The nearer they came to graduating from the mandatory school, the prettier the girls became, the less they talked about school, and the more they talked about earning money. The third youngest married a mechanic and gave birth to a son. Very often she visited her parents' home with her child, and sometimes her husband took his youngest brother-in-law to the Prater amusement park. The oldest daughter became engaged to an Israeli, a former Polish national. The little kitchen was crowded more than ever. But the oldest son's wife never came with her little girl anymore. She didn't like it when Mrs. B. touched her granddaughter.

The caretaker was finally evicted. Before he left, he smashed all of his own windowpanes. He put his furniture and all his possessions in the shed or the cellar. He threw all the keys away. A petition was handed around, saying that the residents wanted the B. family as caretakers. They were in agreement that cold water would be piped into the caretakers' apartment at the expense of the building's residents. It was said that the caretaker had moved in with his brother, a farmer. Later he was said to be in jail.

The fourth daughter, the two youngest ones, and the youngest son kept the building and the sidewalk clean. They were cheerful. Sometimes they were heard laughing loudly on the patio. Many of the building's residents were away. On the second floor the renters whitewashed the walls and decorated them with flower pots. In so doing they mocked the caretaker, you say. The building management distributed the payment slips for the plumbing. The installation of the plumbing took its course. Water was piped into the kitchen and on through the wall into the apartment of the B. family. A shower was planned for the caretakers' apartment, and the oldest brother was supposed to hang wallpaper after all the rooms had been fumigated. The fumigation promised by the building management still had not been carried out. The plumbers pried and hammered in that air, in that stench, you say. The hallway was full of dust and garbage. The children of the B. family did more work than ever. Fortunately it was vacation time. The filth-caked building was supposed to be cleaned after the plumbing was finished. The children wanted to paint the building doors. "Perhaps red," they said—you say. "Preferably brown or black," laughed the older sister, who had taken over the position of caretaker. Then the discrimination began.

Women who had previously done nothing more than greet each other in passing, visited each other's apartments and exchanged liquor and jam. In the process they railed against the Gypsies. (They said *Gypsies*, not *Hungarians* or *the B. family*.) As somebody who happened to know about that, you protested against their prejudices. You reminded them about the persecution of the Gypsies. "They are much too young. They haven't been persecuted yet," was the answer.

Again the possessions of the Gypsies were described down to the smallest detail, you say. People constantly mentioned the many children of the B. family, you say. Women with heavy shopping bags put down their burdens on the dirt-covered stairs and talked about the payment slips and the Gypsies.

You reminded them that they should have gotten the building management to finance the water pipe. "We would have paid for it anyway," was the answer.

"So why all the excitement?"

"They've ordered a laundry table. They'll have a shower stall. At our expense. The Gypsies."

You saw the bills for the appliances. You saw the bundle of banknotes in Mrs. B.'s hand. Apparently all her working children had contributed money to her for the washbasin and plumbing. "We don't want any credit. We don't want any debts," the fourth daughter said.

The renters talked about the Gypsies' possessions. "They have enough money anyway," they said. "We're not going to pay."

You reminded them about the signatures. "They aren't valid," the women said.

"The Gypsies are sticking it to us. The Gypsies are lining their pockets at our expense. They ordered a large washbasin. Not with my money," said Mrs. Sch.

Meanwhile the contract finally came from the building management. You tried to explain the official or legal language to the fourth daughter. Even you did not understand a few sentences immediately. The meaning of the sentences was that the cleaning materials were to be paid for by the management.

"They should pay for the cleaning materials with their own money, if you please," said the women. "They have enough money. Just look how they dress, the Gypsies."

"My daughter-in-law tells me how much money they spend at the textile store," said Mrs. Sch.

Finally the three girls climbed to the fifth floor with three plastic buckets full of lye, and with brooms and brushes, and amid laughter and joking they began to scrub the iron stair railing. The green color was already visible. On the second floor you could hear the women who bent over the railing and looked upward. "Now there's going to be trouble," you said and went back into your apartment. You didn't want any excitement, and you locked the door. The argument took place precisely two floors below.

The fourth daughter knocked and asked if she could sit down. She was very pale beneath her olive-yellow skin and said that she had to put everything aside. "My mother will no longer permit me to do the work," she said—you say. "I am quitting the job before it's too late," she said.

You were so angry that you became weak in the knees. You avoided the argument with the building residents and wanted to slowly build a front against them. "Nine or ten residents against two," you said. Mrs. B. would not change her mind. She said people had already been throwing rocks from the rubble pile at her door for days. They had yelled filthy comments. They had thrown burning cigarettes into the yard from the second floor, when her youngest son went out barefoot. People had been cursing the children for weeks. "This apartment is enough for us. We don't need the cleaning money. I go shopping with a thousand schillings, no more," said Mrs. B. "The business with the water is distasteful to us. Ask for your money back," said Mrs. B. "We really didn't want to do it in the first place, but the children are so disobedient," said Mrs. B. "They want to have their own way, and that's what they get from it." Then she reviled her daughters in their language.

The fifth daughter, a very skinny girl, sat in the

kitchen in silence. There was an admittance form for the hospital to fill out, for a tonsillectomy. The admission form was pre-printed in German, Turkish, and Yugoslavian. While Mrs. B. railed at her daughter in the Gypsy language, the youngest son asked you about the form, you say. "That's a form for foreigners," you said—you say. The fifth daughter smiled slightly, you say. Everyone in the room was silent, and they knew what it meant, you say. The family did not elaborate on it, but everyone knew what was meant.

"That's because they think they can do anything with a caretaker," said Mrs. B.—you say. "But they didn't say anything to the drunk," said Mrs. B.—you say. "They were afraid of him."

As you went up the stairs you noticed how clean the building had become. The garbage in the hallway had disappeared. The patio was swept. There was no garbage in the garbage cans. But in front of the windows of the B. family were the cigarette butts from the second floor. On the third floor you could see the place where the cleaning of the stair railing had been interrupted. *Nobody will ever scrub it again as long as the building stands,* you thought—you say.

A few days later you met the fourth daughter. You didn't recognize her anymore, you say. "She always wears that white make-up now," her youngest brother told you—you say. "It's very pretty," said the youngest B.—you say.

Suddenly a young blond woman was seen in the caretaker's apartment. A quiet child, pale and stunted, was only a shadowy figure against the light. A male figure sat on the only chair. The house seemed to sink back into the old filth. Then the other residents stayed out of sight.

116

The way many things began was very clearly visible in the example provided by the building where you live. Everything could be seen in a larger context. In the example of your building, society is reflected as if by a concave mirror, you say. The woman on the fifth floor commented scornfully about Mrs. B.'s many children. In addition to the precise enumeration of Mr. B.'s various possessions, the number of children they had was repeatedly the topic of conversation. The extermination of two thousand seven hundred Austrian Gypsies must have had similar initial symptoms, you say.

We have to remember the attic and the pigeons, you say. We have to remember the alcoholic who was nothing but skin and bones, his wide-open eyes on the attic stairs, and the dirty work with the pigeons, you say. The broken attic windows, the damaged dormer windows, and so forth were still responsible for the pigeons that had strayed, you say. Thus the stray pigeons were the building management's concern, the building owner's problem, you say.

Everything begins imperceptibly, you say. A person gets weak in the knees, and it is always a matter of money and profit and of avoiding this or that fact, you say. What does that have to do with the B. family? Besides, they are Jehovah's Witnesses, you say.

Your little boy continues to be the daily guest of the B. family. The B. family plans to move, you say. "Perhaps Mr. B. will get a contract at the spa in V.," said Mrs. B.—you say.

"The Burgenlanders are crude," the youngest girl suddenly observed and received a reprimand from Mrs. B. in the Burgenland dialect.

Who will tell the girl the story of the shaven, embarrassed peasants? you ask. Who will tell her the story of

117

the shaven Gypsy girls in the camp? Who will tell the story of the Gypsy girl in the reeds at Ravensbrück, giving a description of the dog, how the girl was torn apart, her death in the reeds?

A few weeks later you stepped out of the building door. To the right of the door when you go out, but to the left when you go in, is the caretaker's apartment, with its lone window next to the B. family's two windows. The window of the caretaker's apartment is next to the building entrance. The blond woman's husband looked into your face at an angle from above and then looked away, you say. He was in work clothes, a mechanic's uniform. No, he was in underwear. He was in an undershirt, without sleeves, grayish white across his belly. His belly was not visible from your position in the building doorway, at most his head, perhaps his shoulders besides, of course, in his usual stance with his elbows propped on the window sill and his shoulders drawn back, you say. Why the impression of the belly? you ask. You can't explain it. Perhaps it came from the view through the kitchen, from the first day when you went out the back door to the patio with the garbage cans and then came back. You had that view at the time, when his predecessor's dirty curtain was no longer there. Before the blond woman's clean, more brightly flowered curtain hung across the window with the ornate gratings, that typical corridor window of the kitchens in the buildings from the period before World War I. Through that window, next to the pale blond woman you saw only the man's belly. He was sitting on the only chair that had been left behind by the evicted caretaker. His dirty-white pullover was pulled tightly over his belly and tucked into his belted pants, you say. The blond woman was visible against the light. She was wearing gloves. At least later

118

she wore green rubber gloves. She was standing at the window or in the doorway, and she responded kindly to your greeting. She answered as if she had been waiting for the greeting and were relieved to be able to respond to it, you say.

That day the sun was shining. It was an autumn day and still warm. The autumn was especially beautiful that year. It was especially long, you say.

At the moment you stepped out and glanced to the right from the front entrance—because the head and shoulders bending forward cast a shadow or had the effect of a shadow—you noticed the person to whom the new caretaker was talking. He stood on the sidewalk in front of the window. You saw the brief glance to the right and the responding glance—in the one case, namely from the window, downward and to the left, in the other, namely from the sidewalk, upward and to the right, but about on the same level—as something of a change from looking up from the position on the side-walk to the window on the mezzanine. For a split second you, if not hesitated, nevertheless registered the fact, you say, that this particular building resident from the third or fourth floor had never talked to anyone before, but had now been interrupted in a lengthy conversation, you say. The fraction of a second, the mental question: Why this conversation of a man who had never before uttered a word beyond the daily greeting, and that only as a response? That all communicated itself or was somehow based on reciprocity. Perhaps your appearance, your sudden visibility in the doorway was noticed. Perhaps it made the man from the third or fourth floor aware of the unusual situation, you say. He interrupted or ended his discussion or his conversation as you took the two steps from the building entrance to the window, you say. The bloated face with the gray hair, the unshaven face, impressed itself on your memory, you say. You insist very firmly that the conversation ended at that very moment. For, on the one hand you had the feeling that both men felt disturbed by your presence, became nervous, while on the other hand you could not have turned around. And therefore the interruption of the conversation must have occurred as you were walking past, at the latest when you had taken your third step, when you were already past them, when the two parties to the conversation—or at least one of them—were still in your field of vision, you say. The steps that led you beneath the mezzanine window from the building entrance took you precisely into the line of communication, that is, through it. That was probably why the conversation was terminated so quickly, you say.

The days grew cooler, you say. The work at the construction sites along the main street progressed, you say. When you returned the same day or on one of the next days, you noticed that the window glass in the new caretaker's apartment had been replaced and cleaned, you say. The window that had been smashed out onto the street from inside by the evicted caretaker, you say. The days became cooler and the nights longer, you say. Only in retrospect does that have anything to do with the story of the Gypsies, with the story of the building where you live, you say. Why do you talk about the time of year? Why do you remember the cool season?

It was autumn, even though still early. Sometimes during the days it was as warm as summer. Once you saw the caretaker woman's pale child, or the child who was with her the first day, on the patio. A boy was with him. He looked just as pale. He wore a hat with an enormous brim. You thought about the coming winter and about the children's homework. You asked yourself where these children, if they belonged to her, would do their homework. It was September now. The days were becoming cooler. Everywhere in Austria school was now beginning.

Suddenly all the lights were on in the stairwell. The light bulbs were covered with the spherical white lamp covers that had stood in a row beneath the only window when you could still see into the caretaker's apartment. The evicted caretaker had left them standing in a row in the almost empty apartment. He had thrown away the keys but had not smashed the spherical lamp covers. Some beds and boxes were stored in the shed, some in the cellar, and some things on the patio.

Once you even entered the caretaker's apartment, you say. It seemed unreal. That is, at the time and especially later it seemed unreal to enter such a room—a room that you had walked past day after day for years, one that was only separated from the corridor by a thin wall. That was during the time of the B. family, when Monika B.—who now often wore light make-up but by nature had the darkest skin among the daughters in the B. family—occupied the position of caretaker. She showed you the rooms, you say. She pointed out the high ceilings to you. They really were unusually high ceilings. You believe that you have never seen such high ceilings elsewhere. And therefore Monika B. explained that her oldest brother could alter the dimensions of the rooms with wallpaper. You marveled at the rooms in those miserable quarters. In each case they were separated by a thin wall from the rooms of the B. family and the hallway. It was unbelievable to think that the rooms of the B. family were also that high or could be that high, that the horrendous height of the rooms belonging

121

to the B. family had only been cleverly concealed through the wallpaper artistry of the cymbal player.

Every time you entered the building, you remembered that high tube and the single light bulb on the chrome-plated rod that hung from the middle of the ceiling in that peculiar room, as from the high ceiling of a castle, a granary, a feed silo, or some other human construction, just not a human dwelling, you say. What do you know about where people live? you say. Such high rooms seem unpleasant, even to a person who is willing to put up with such a stairwell for the sake of high ceilings and bright, whitewashed walls, you say.

Once you saw the new caretaker's husband sitting astride the large painting ladder in the room with the tube, on the street side of the building. He was wearing a blue mechanic's uniform and a cap made of newspaper. He was painting the room, although the house management had agreed to have the apartment fumigated and painted. Because of the cap you think that he may have been a painter by trade. It was not aversion, you say, when you noted all the changes in the caretaker's apartment as you walked by. It was concern, almost sympathy, coupled with consternation, that caused you to note the changes in the windows that were soon curtained.

What misfortune, adversity, what conditions drove such a woman out on the street to look for an empty caretaker's apartment? What happens to make people hastily move into such an apartment overnight and ahead of time, so to speak, regardless of the barn stench and other odors, almost without furniture, as if there were a war going on? "What burden are those people carrying?" you claim to have asked the building residents. "What happened to them?"

Why didn't you talk to them? Why didn't you ask them? Why didn't you begin a conversation with her? You say, the Spaniards. For thirty years the Spaniards had lived in this city, had never learned the language, actually spoke less and less, you say, uttered only monosyllables that sounded like a parody of the Viennese dialect, an imitation, monosyllables of conformity, phonetic stopgaps to accompany gestures. "Well, yah," they said, and gestured with their hands, "Well, yah."

The man was small and slender, you say. His blue-black hair was interspersed with white strands. His furrowed brow lay in arrogant folds. "Well, yah, do everything gratis for neighbor," he said and pointed to the doors that had been painted white when you moved in, you say. He often handed a flask of *Edler Saurüssel* through the door. His wife was a cleaning woman, but never at home—"Don' matter." At five o'clock every morning they left their apartment, speaking with a soft burr. Their voices sounded like rattles and slowly died away down the winding stairs, you say. You knew that, because you were also often busy in the kitchen at five in the morning, in order to get to the office on time. You don't waste any words about it. The little man with the dark, wavy hair that was streaked with white walked straight as a stick, you say. He still walks that way. He is flawlessly dressed; he looks like a retired actor or a wine merchant. This little, very contented, linguistically inhibited neighbor was a factory worker. He is proud of his pension. He could never make it clear which factory he worked in, you say. Perhaps it was caution, you say. He claimed to be a Basque, but could not speak the Basque language, "Verra hard, well, yah." The B.s had it good in that respect. They were Gypsies and could speak the Gypsy language, you say. Why do you say:

123

were? Why do you use the past-tense form?

The Spaniard was a watchman at the factory. He has been an Austrian citizen for a long time. He was a painter, perhaps a factotum. In Spain he owns a little house in a deserted area by the sea. He doesn't understand what the pension papers say. He doesn't understand what the clerk at the employment office says. He doesn't trust banks, you say. That is why the gas man always rings his bell in vain during the summer, you say. His wife is retired now, too. Her hair is just as black, but dull. Perhaps she dyes it. She has to take care of her husband. Once she was ill. At her age she had an appendectomy. Her husband walked around as if he were lost. He collapsed: "Well, yah, verra hard, no food," you say. He began to get on your nerves with this concern for himself, his indifference with regard to his wife. He collapses because the food isn't on the table.

The two attractive, black-haired daughters are married. An entire story could be told about the Spaniard's daughters. It is startling when they speak our language, so coarse and so astonishing is the dialect they speak, you say. You don't know if you should continue to tell about the Spaniards. They have just arrived. From April to October they were in Spain. "Too much sun, phew!" says the woman. She hardly moves her mouth. When she laughs she is pretty. The pension money remains in their account here. The house in Spain is doing very well. That all emerges from their monosyllables, you say. One sits with the neighbors *drink*. His present participle has no ending. The language the reactionary mechanic K. uses with the Turkish woman is much more unpleasant, almost repulsive: "You now that clean." The Turkish woman cleans his workshop from top to bottom every day. It is as clean as a dental clinic. His language is almost unbearable, you say. The Turkish woman is about the most exploited person in the entire neighborhood. She wears a blue mechanic's uniform and a snow-white scarf, but you say that only incidentally, you say.

You try to explain the matter of the new caretaker to the Spaniard's younger daughter, you say. The daughter has a cute little child. She understands you very well. She speaks the Austrian dialect very well. She went to school in Vienna. At home she speaks only Spanish. The mother with her small eyes, her pale face—it's almost mouthless, not pinched together, no, almost mouthless, you say—doesn't move. She doesn't understand. And her daughter only translates half of it. You try to win them over for the B. family. People railed at them. People slandered them. Racism. "Well, yah." Suddenly the Spanish woman no longer understands anything at all. The daughter has never translated well. She is not capable of dealing with the employment office, you say. The pension advance through the employment office demands all your diplomacy, specifically, finding out what the Spanish woman means.

That was in April. Now it is the end of September, or October. The daughter is standing in her parents' small kitchen. Her husband has come for her. They are only waiting for the floor to dry. The Spanish woman is kneeling. She is wiping the floor. She traveled by plane for three days. There was a strike in France. "Well, yah, wanting mo' money, verra hard." Now the participle has an ending after all. Her daughter's son is almost three years old, a handsome child, you say. Like the young mother he speaks a muffled Viennese, almost without consonants, but muffled. You want to force the daughter to translate, so that she finally speaks a more beautiful,

125

and what you consider to be a less coarse language. A moderately colloquial Spanish rings out, rattling and fast. Her father responds in language that rolls and rattles. He has come out of his room. He is unshaven. Now they open up. Now they talk like living human beings, you say. The fascinating and simultaneously repellent speechlessness seems to blow away. Nevertheless, translation doesn't seem to work. They don't understand anything. They are talking about something else. They fall back into their small, mouthless facial expression, into their pale faces, at least the woman does. She doesn't move her lips. She doesn't have any. The kind, mouthless woman digs enormous wafers out of the box. The children fight over a toy. You leave without accomplishing anything. The final evening with the Spaniards in April comes to mind.

The older daughter of the Spaniards had been a widow for half a year, you say. Meanwhile it has been a year. In April she had been a widow for half a year. She has a hectic manner. The two school-age children are quiet. They speak no Spanish. When they were little, they probably had to sit next to the others who were chattering in Spanish, and listen to the shrill voice of the older daughter in Viennese. Thus the children don't understand a word when their mother and their aunt chatter with their grandparents while drinking wine and eating tortillas, you say. The children are silent, pale, and blond. Politely and shyly they press their way up the stairs. The young widow is excited. She is almost out of her mind. A visitor, a man, is in her parents' apartment, fat, pasty, and red in the face. That was in April, you say. The man talks a lot. He understands something about everything, and that is no small thing. He speaks again and again of the guarantee. He constantly offers

126

the Spaniard the guarantee. "And don't forget the value-added tax at the border." The Spaniard doesn't listen. Occasionally the visitor's female companion softly shrieks. Uneasiness prevails, as it does when you are still waiting for somebody. Then Mrs. S. from next door comes, specifically, Mrs. S.'s mother. She is the woman who will later make the comments about the many children of the B. family. For the present, the substance of her mother's discussion is that they all have relatives in *Czechia*, as she calls it. Then she doesn't mince words. The fat man's guarantee pertains to the expensive pans, the expensive cooking utensils that a person has to beg for, so to speak, for there is no advertising. They are peculiar utensils, at such prices. Well, Mrs. S. got them for two thousand schillings less, says Mrs. S. "He would have had to give the demonstration even if nobody had come, and you would have received your share regardless," says Mrs. S. to the Spanish woman. The children are in the next room. They are very quiet. They received a packet of small notebooks.

Thus you learned that the Spaniard paid his guest seven thousand schillings for the special coating. In return the man will live in the Spaniard's house on the beach during the summer. The fat man gives a terse order. His companion gathers up bags, boxes, knives, and demonstration vegetables. Meanwhile the young widow utters a short shriek. "Back home in Spain," she repeats in her broadest Viennese, which changes her face, "you aren't used to the food." And she giggles briefly. "Tell the story again."

Even her mother smiles now, "Well, yah, verra funny."

The fat man looks at the clock. *Can't do any more business here. Miserable rabble,* can be read in his face.

127

"In the work camp," he says tersely. His fleshy cheeks hardly move. If he could, he would shake his nostrils. "The long-haired people down there belong in the work camp," and he points off in some direction. His flat skull rests on the back of the armchair. Suddenly he squints his eyes. "What's that?" With the eye of a connoisseur, he rises, he acts as if he is getting up.

"Oh, that, verra cheap, hundred schillings." The women protest. They warn the father in Spanish to understate it that way. His wife and daughter attack him with their chatter.

A terribly corny figure made of wood and painted gold or silver, no, a coach, a ship in the bottle, you say. Perhaps a gold-painted Madonna after all, next to the inflatable plastic animal on the dust-free chest of drawers. "A hundred schillings," the Spaniard insists. "Well, yah." Spanish sentences roll off his tongue. It is authentic, of course, or maybe not. The fat man has lost interest. The whole thing was just a maneuver. He wanted to practice looking like a connoisseur. It must bring him many an order. Having suddenly discovered a valuable piece in the apartment, having listened patiently to the circumstances of its inexpensive acquisition, he quickly pulls out his pad and gets cracking. The effect of the look of a connoisseur has to be exploited: import, export, value-added tax. The young widow's pleas become more and more urgent. Oh, yes, the story of his friend. As a favor, the fat man tells it. You can tell by looking at him that he doesn't take such things very seriously. "So my friend went to Spain"—the widow bursts out laughing—"with his mother-in-law," the fat man continues, "with all his belongings, neighbors and friends...." Or the story went something like that, you say. "In the campground, the mother-in-law does something stupid and dies, which is a problem because of the costs involved." The fat man's companion has the boxes gathered up. The housewife slowly moves her mouthless lips. "So my friend has an idea. Who wants to pay the money for transportation? So he wraps his mother-in-law in the tent and starts out for home. On the way there is a rest stop. He is hungry. The caravan stops." The young widow shrieks. "When they come out, the car is gone, mother-in-law and all, and it was never seen again." The group laughs. You were dumb-founded, you say. Everyone gets ready to leave. The fat man gives his companion a dirty look. Everyone says good-by. "Why are you so amazed. It was in all the newspapers. I won't tell you his name, but he's my friend," said the fat man—you say. The widow con-curred with him that the transportation would have cost at least ten thousand schillings. "At home in Spain the food is so spicy." And she giggled, you say.

Now the new woman caretaker is standing on the window sill of the stairwell. She is not secured, although it is written in the contract that she can only wash the windows while wearing a safety belt. She stands there in a green apron, with bleached hair and dark roots. She is also wearing green rubber gloves, you say. You read that passage about the safety belts aloud to the fourth daughter of the B. family. Now this woman stands there, and she doesn't seem to be afraid. In fact, she seems very calm. The retired Spaniard with the appearance of an entrepreneur stands near the woman caretaker: "Why you do that?" You just happened to come out. You still wanted to ask why she was doing it without a belt, but then you let it go. You say you didn't want to get involved. Besides, somebody had already made the com-ment that the new woman caretaker drank.

Mrs. B. talked about the fact that the new woman had said she was bringing a child with her. And then her husband was there, you say. "She already smells of liquor in the morning," said Mrs. B.—you say. Now there are no longer any children there, but there are always other visitors. Once, Mrs. H., the woman in the ground-floor apartment on the right, stumbled over her husband in the dark. "The building manager has already been informed," said Mrs. B. "The garbage cans are overflowing, and we still have to sweep up the dirt. It's lying in front of our windows," said Mrs. B.—you say.

Suddenly the girls were sweeping the stairs again, you say. You asked the youngest B. girl what it meant. "Don't say anything. Everything is going to be settled now, and then our father is going to buy us a piano," the girl said—you say.

"And what about the caretaker?" you asked the girl —you say.

"She can stay here another two weeks, and then she has to leave," said the girl—you say. The B.s could have gotten it more cheaply, you say. You talked for an entire day with Mrs. B. and tried to convince her to change her mind and not give up, you say. At the time, she used her daughters and her husband as an excuse, you say. Poor people have to bear the brunt of it again. Perhaps for the B.s it was a matter of showing that nothing better would follow, you say. Then people would have to remember the spherical lamps, the piles of garbage, the plastic buckets, the garbage collectors, and the new caretaker. Somebody put the mountains of garbage in the barrels, but it wasn't the new caretaker, you say. Nobody said anything more about it. Nobody stood at a neighbor's door and discussed it. The building had fallen into its old anonymity again. Then the attractive Spaniard stood next to the blond woman and asked, "Why you do that?"

Two days later the building management decided in favor of the blond woman. The B. family finally gave up trying to reach an agreement with the residents, you say. The daughters had again received the payment slips for distribution. Again they were insulted on the second floor. Everything happened quickly and without being noticed, you say. The doors are closed. It is autumn. The days are getting cooler. People are watching television with their windows closed. They don't hear what happens in the corridor and in the stairwell, let alone in the apartments, you say.

The windows of the stairwell are scrubbed clean. In her quiet manner she washed all the windows of the stairwell while in mortal danger, which nobody noticed, of course. Perhaps she stood on the window sills with her back to the abyss above the patio. It can't be denied that in spite of its shabbiness and the scraped-off whitewash with its black stains, the stairwell already looks much better. On the two top floors, the scrollwork of the stair railing glistens. The higher you go, the brighter it is. "The building should be cleaned professionally. An intercommunication system should be installed. They should have the G. Company come sometime," said the hairdresser on the fourth floor—you say. "Then the people on the second floor would see that nobody still has a caretaker these days. Nobody will do that," she said—you say. Then she went her way. You see the residents of the building less and less frequently. The place grows quiet. But Gypsy music comes from the overcrowded apartment of the B. family on the ground floor.

Mr. B. has returned from Burgenland. The summer

131

season has ended. He must be a well-paid lead guitarist, but there is no longer any question of a contract with the spa in V. Now, of course, Mrs. B. hardly talks to any building resident more than is absolutely necessary. It is perhaps because her husband is home. Once the father even picked up the doormat himself. Usually he never picks up anything. The oldest son practices in the kitchen. He sits on a kitchen stool that he has raised to the level of a piano bench with several blankets, and he practices on the cymbals. Meanwhile, the daughters, his sisters, clean up the kitchen, you say. "Your little boy doesn't bother us. Let him stay here," says the Gypsy— you say. The other members of the family are lying around the room, probably in front of the television set. The mother is resting. She wore shoes with heels that were too high again. Sometimes she stops on the street and sends one of the children for a pair of flat-heeled shoes because she can't walk any further. The heavy woman with the yellowish skin and the long black hair remains standing on one foot and rubs the hurting toes of the other foot on her calf, you say. Nevertheless, the shoes look good on her. She actually looks incredibly good for a woman with nine children, not to mention the miscarriages. "She takes care of herself, too," says Mrs. Sch. on the second floor—you say. There is no doubt about it. Mrs. B.'s appearance makes an unusual, yes, an almost provocative impression, you say. Like their mother, the daughters have strong arms. They work hard, they clean and cook. Once the two youngest girls wore long, blue summer dresses and danced like light-ning in a circle on the patio. That was shortly after the caretaker had been evicted. "Perhaps the youngest girl will transfer from the special school to the middle school now," said the youngest boy—you say. Perhaps she will finish the compulsory schooling with a middle-school certificate, you say.

The days are cool. It is already necessary to begin heating. The small, lean Spaniard carries the oil canisters upstairs. His younger daughter married very well, a mechanic or something like that. Her little boy gets picked up. The Spaniard's son-in-law was still almost a child when they married three years ago, you say. He never said a word. He looks at the lively child. The child shouts, "*Adios!*" This particular grandchild of the Spaniard has learned to say *adios*. He was probably in his grandparents' house on that lonely beach this summer. "*Adios!*" shouts the little boy and goes away down the winding stairs. He wipes off his grandfather's kiss with the back of his hand. His grandfather smiles. He is not paying attention. He gives the impression that his thoughts are already on the next meal. The little boy disappears into the stairwell. "*Adios,* like verra much, new caretaka, well, yah." Really, the windows are unusually well polished.

It has gotten cold. The children must now be dressed warmly in the mornings. They are always bringing home some illness or other. Quickly, out into the cold, seven-thirty, eight-thirty, the kindergarten won't wait. You were in a hurry that morning. The heel of your shoe got stuck, and you almost fell down the stairs. Fortunately the corridor windows have been closed since the caretaker washed the windows, you say. On the second floor there was a small commotion. It was the two residents who slander the Gypsies, Mrs. Sch. in her nightgown and without her teeth, as always, and with her Mr. and Mrs. R. Mr. R. heats with coal. He is the only one who still burns boxes and branches at Christmas. Once you got into an argument with him about the boxes. Mrs. R.

whispers something in Mrs. Sch.'s ear. Mrs. Sch. looks at you and dramatically proclaims that we no longer have a caretaker.

It is already cold. Last Sunday, days ago, your little boy was with the B. family for a few hours. He walked down the stairs alone for the first time. You watched him go down the four flights of stairs, keeping in touch with him with brief shouts as he went. You called after him, "Be good." The caretaker's apartment had been dark for days. When you emptied the garbage on Saturday, you noticed the coat hooks. An apron hung behind the faded curtain on the hall window of the kitchen. Why did she take that apartment? Why did she move into that apartment so hastily? Where is she, when you don't see her for days? The B. family's color television set, which the blond woman had taken into the apartment that first day, was standing in the nook again, next to it an ironing board, a box of Henckel dry champagne, just the box, probably from the S. family. The box was still usable. *So she is gone. No wonder. There was no stove, no cupboard. She probably calmly hung up the apron and left,* you thought, and then you answered aloud, "We should have expected that"—you say.

Mrs. R. whispers. Mrs. Sch. asks another question. Meanwhile you have taken your child by the hand. You look at the new landing, the television cabinet, the ironing board. There is a terrible draft. The man bends forward and asks, "Do you know at all...?"

Your child tugs at your hand. "How do you know that?" A question as a stopgap, indicating a pause. Your knees buckle. You almost fell down the stairs, or maybe not. It didn't matter.

"It was a newspaper article. It was in the newspaper," says the man. "She was strangled by her male companion." The question was meaningless. The newspaper style lay in the air, subdued murmuring.

You move on. "Mrs. R., I have to go. I'm sorry." Nobody listens.

"The door was sealed by the police last night," Mr. R. said—you say.

It was cold. The ironing board stood in front of the door, on the left side, to be specific, in the niche, a deception, an imitation of the city palaces whose niches shelter twisted figures. The shabby dwelling, the stinking hole was where she met her end. The metal bar infinitely high above you held the light bulb to the shabby ceiling. Police seals are strips of brown wrapping paper. A message is turning yellow on the card. Is it possible for a card to turn yellow in just one night? you ask.

It's useless to think about what you should have, could have asked her. Looking out the front door to the right, the street window on the mezzanine is covered. The stained yellow blind has been rolled down. You have no time for conversation. It's already too cold to engage in conversation between the sidewalk and the window, you say. You go out into that fresh Monday morning. Your child asks, of course, what the man said. She had already been lying behind that window shade for days, you say.

Quickly, a newspaper! Which ones appear on Monday? Almost all of them. Your child constantly asks questions and trips along beside you. Kindergarten, elevator, quickly undress, then dress him again, a kiss. You go to the telephone, into the only telephone booth in the vicinity. You tell your husband the details. You senselessly ask, "Did you notice anything?" as if you hadn't left the apartment unsuspectingly yourself ten minutes earlier. Of course your husband hasn't heard

135

anything. The newspaper article. In a big city, it was to be expected. A fragment, with what happened before and what will happen later cut off. You take care of your errands. You go into this store and that one. You buy a book. What bothers you so much? Just what is there about it that upsets you so much?

You looked at the displays and didn't see anything, you say. Your legs, your entire body had still not recovered. You turned from *Planckengasse* into *Dorotheengasse*. A book, mattresses on the floor, but not because of extravagance. At the corner, you almost run into a woman wearing a short fur coat. She is pushing an enormous baby carriage. She is flawlessly groomed. You can see that she doesn't comb her own hair. It's a miracle that she is pushing the baby carriage herself, but she also seems disgusted about that. The dog is tied to the baby carriage. It eats more meat per day than you and your family eat all week, you say. She pushes her status symbols along in front of her. The fur coat, the carriage, you can see she is pushing an heir. What's the point of this picture? Why is it worth mentioning? She waits at the corner. Her husband keeps her waiting, or the nanny, or her mother. These mornings in the inner city—what does she know about stairwells? What does she learn by reading a newspaper article? Does she read at all? You would have liked to go back once more, you say, to meet the woman in her fur coat again, to relive the same meeting, unexpectedly, as a collision at the corner, in front of the display of one of the inner city's hundred antique stores, you say.

The long neck, the hairdo, the light-colored fur coat, the mask, an unpleasant face, a grimace, in contrast to the warm faces of Mrs. B.'s daughters. Even the Spanish woman without a mouth has a mouth when she smiles.

So why do you brood about this particular encounter? It's one of many, you say. There it is, the expression, the sunken cheeks, the more ordinary hair coloring, the earrings hanging from pierced ears, the green rubber gloves, and yet the similarity with that city woman, the same expression around the mouth.

You came home. You walked up the four flights of stairs, at least you intended to do that. From the front door to the mezzanine, a few steps. You will never count them, you say. You went past the door that was sealed with brown tape, climbed to the second floor, and rang the R. family's doorbell, you say.

The door opened. You spoke, asked questions. They let you in. You talked. Reproaches were uttered—listening, asking, answering, a game with rules, the words rattle off, the newspaper article rattles off, the preconceived images rattle off, things tick and hum along, a classical scene, a very clear case.

You talked, you pretended, you donned a flat, mouthless face. At least you tried to, you say. Formulating sentences so that they are well received, so that they are well received here—receiving formulated sentences, things that have been pawned, old second-hand junk, indignation, sadness, verdicts, suspicions, encountered texts, discarded material. It is all as dead as the dead woman. It is no more alive than her corpse, catchwords from days gone by, the legendary loyalty of the Nibelungs, Gypsies, foreigners, rascals, rabble, and other similar terms. It was like an out-of-place perforated tape from a different time, you say.

It was autumn, cold. People were freezing. They heated up their stoves, with oil, gas, electricity—on the second floor with coal. They closed the windows and doors when they came open, you say. Enter, ring the

bell, talk, remain silent, pretend, listen absently, be
indifferent, deception, imitation, apparent distance, and
a feeling of unrealness. They probably call it alienation,
you say. Mr. and Mrs. R. in the kitchen. You don't
know what they do. Nor does it matter. Perhaps early
retirement, at least Mr. R. You ask yourself how old.
You ask what they did before. You ask what someone
like that chooses. You notice, the other person has
already known it for a long time, the other person has
had an impression of you for a long time, and it's not a
good one.

Mr. and Mrs. R. on that early, now gloomy autumn
afternoon in the kitchen. They are not opponents. They
are.... What are they? It is hardly possible to understand
their story. It is only a story, a paste, a dough without
any history, indefinable wishes behind the front door,
the kitchen, the kitchen table, an altar of indefinable
wishes presented in filthy language. In front of you sat
the bailiff, the up-in-arms philistine, babbling speechlessness, the hole in the story.

You arose, you played the game with the rules, the
one called human language. You betrayed nothing. You
didn't even betray the B. family. You completely maintained your dignity, viewed superficially. You failed to
get anything done. You changed nothing. You accomplished nothing.

You got up, you say. You left the room, you left the
apartment, you left that phase, that condition of human
civilization, nothing but a stage, a step in evolution. So
you went higher, two, three floors upward. You didn't
ring any other doorbell. You didn't learn anything else.
You had to figure it out for yourself. You were able to
figure it out for yourself.

They learned about a story, a newspaper article, a

138

little front-page story, shortly after the copy deadline. It came in late over the teletype, was called in on the telephone, was written up on the monitor. The other papers will give more details, the other editors will be more or less precise. Of course, with an immediate confession a story like that doesn't yield much. You heard a story and climbed higher, up four flights of stairs, actually only three more, past the freshly polished windows of the blond woman, without emotion, without feelings about the windows, the recessed window sills, the closed outer windows. There was nothing emotional in that stairwell, you say.

When you entered your apartment on the fifth floor, you were still weak, you say. You soon had to pick up your little boy from kindergarten. The reconstruction of the newspaper article, the hour, the time of day, the day, the night, the cold autumn day, a Thursday morning—it's amazing what is contained in an article—no stove, no cupboard, the new kitchen sink torn down during her death throes. Mr. R. utters the words with relish. The Gypsies claim they didn't know or hear anything. Everything went as could have been expected, you say. Even the challenge to spit at the Gypsies was not omitted, you say.

There was once a newspaper article, a classical story of substandard housing, a typical weekend drama, like the accident rate, a meeting in the hallway. The sealed apartment, the dough, the paste without a history is responsible, you say. You neglected to talk to her. It didn't work out. You just happened to open the door and then you didn't say anything else. And the Spaniard was just asking, "Why you do that?" The blond woman did not understand him. Perhaps she didn't want to. With the help of her male companion, she carried all the gar-

139

bage from the cellar. She worked hard. She felt she was being pressed very hard, specifically by the Gypsies. If that's true, nobody can help her, you say.

The days are cooler. The culprit is lying in the psychiatric hospital. He confessed immediately. A newspaper article. He looked down at you at an angle from right to left, a doughy, not very healthy face. They say he was much younger than he looked, you say. The table on the second floor declared that he really didn't commit suicide. The table on the second floor thinks that it would be better if it didn't come up anymore, the kitchen article, the newspaper German. Why did you ask to be let in? Why did you seek the conversation and find a story? You bathed in filth, also a cliché. The realities were all present. That should be noted, you say. There was the window sill. There was the stair railing. On the third floor you can see the very scrollwork in the railing where the girls were disturbed. After that came a murder. Of course it isn't logical, but it is consistent, you say.

It was to be expected. Nevertheless, it shocked you when it happened. You don't even know why. The others must feel the same way. Nobody talks about it. Everyone hastily avoids it. Nobody stops in the stairwell. You stop on the mezzanine. Your trembling legs won't carry you past the mezzanine. Here the article is more complete. Here is where part of the article took place.

"The killer rang the bell. He held on to the door frame," said Mr. H.—you say. He wanted to speak to somebody at a telephone number. He wanted to convey a message to that number. Somebody at that number was supposed to visit him. The person at the telephone number was not available. The person on the other end of the line hung up without answering. It was repeated twice. Speechlessness is expressed here in lack of contact. Then laughter was heard in the entryway, which smoothed out the creases and flaws in the story. Those interferences are still missing in the newspaper story, in the Sunday-evening-Monday-morning story. The laughter, for example. The culprit had them call a woman. She came. They heard her laugh. "Later she went to the police and almost had an attack of hysterics," said Mr. H.—you say. Mr. H. on the ground floor. On the mezzanine the woman didn't open the door. He had to put a chair in front of his door for her. "It all happened in front of my door," said Mr. H.—you say. "I almost threw up," said Mr. H. The smell, the newspaper article, the decay. Mrs. B. sensed the newspaper article, sensed the decay through her water pipe. Originally the shower for at least seven or eight members of the family was supposed to be installed there. It wasn't possible. Nothing could be done about it. "Mrs. B. couldn't explain the stench," Mr. H. said—you say. "Of course, there was the torn-down wash basin. The walls are thin, the stench makes its way in. And besides that, if she had been lying dead under the blanket since Thursday,..." said Mr. H.—you say.

The laughter, if only the laughter could be explained. Perhaps the laughing stranger thinks that the caller is giddy from drinking sour wine, and only then does she notice the odor of decay. But what if the odor was already there? you ask. What if the odor was already there in the attic, that time with the pigeons? you say. The staggering came from Valium. How does that drug wind up in an apartment without a cabinet, without a bed? How does it wind up in a mattress nest that was not a product of extravagance? People will ask in vain about

141

the Valium, you say.

The heating problem no longer exists. She was quite calm. She stood at the window, not on the window sill. She stood on the stairs. She would have answered pleasantly. How did she see the ceiling? What did the infinitely distant metal bar on the ceiling tell her? Perhaps she was already about to leave when the rumor of the dissolution of the contract surfaced. Then she went on and washed the windows with her green rubber gloves. They say her sister was seen in front of the locked door.

The Spaniard greeted you. He called out "*Adios!*" to his grandson. He came to your apartment, you say. That day he could understand more than usual. He spoke more fluently. He claims to have seen the woman as late as Saturday. "Verra nice." A woman was with her, perhaps her sister, at the market.

He beat her, they say. It didn't attract any further attention. Actually, in the way it's mentioned you can see it attracted no attention. Perhaps that's why she waited until Thursday morning. Then he took the cord and later Valium. It didn't occur to anyone to pipe water in for the evicted caretaker, you say. People always thought about death when he appeared in the stairwell or on the attic stairs. The blond woman seemed to be ill, too, as did the child who was never seen again.

It got cold. The heating problem was solved. Weeks later you met Mrs. B. with her next-to-youngest daughter. There on the sidewalk she could talk undisturbed. Coincidentally, it was the same spot as before. Now the three of you stood beneath the covered and officially sealed window. There are innumerable people in this city who do not heat in the winter—for example, the woman who stood before the building entrance a short time ago.

142

She leaned against it. She was wearing many clothes in layers. In her hand she had a sack of sweet chestnuts. She is waiting for the path to the construction site to open up. Many no longer wait for quitting time. At six in the evening the shadows move out of the building doorways. Homeless people, even young people scurry across the street toward the construction site, to find protection from the November fog behind prefabricated walls.

Now Mrs. B. is standing on the sidewalk with her next-to-youngest daughter. Her daughter is looking off into the distance. Her gaze wanders off. It wanders into the distance. In the late afternoon you have the impression that her gaze should be disappearing, barefoot, with a bundle under its arm, into the nearby park, perhaps into the Prater. She is well-dressed. She is wearing a camel-hair coat just like her mother's, and shoes with high, pointed heels. She hasn't accepted employment since her tonsillectomy two years ago, which almost cost her her life, you say. And since then her gaze wanders in the distance. Mrs. B. says, "For us the problem has been solved. As long as we're here, nobody will move in, nobody will enter the apartment. But when we're gone...." And she paused, you say.

You ask Mrs. B. about her next-to-youngest daughter, who a few days ago..., and you describe the scene by the garbage cans. Mr. R. slammed the lid of the garbage can with all his might against the girl's wrist. Mrs. B. looks away. The girl lets her gaze wander. "We can't do anything. Really, we can't do anything. We're going to move away," says Mrs. B. *We're going to move on.* She doesn't say that. She says, "...buy a new apartment," you say.

The apartment was opened briefly under police

143

supervision. The perpetrator's personal possessions were picked up by a woman. The woman said that if he hadn't done it, somebody else would have gotten her out of the way. As a witness, Mrs. Sch. will say she saw the blond woman again on Friday. The girls are secretly sweeping the stairwell. The windows are closed. We now hear only very soft Gypsy music from the kitchen on the ground floor.

Who will tell the girl the story of the oppressed and shaven, or sheared peasants? you ask. Who will tell her the story of the shaven Gypsy girls in the camp (the story of their surreptitiously obtained or forced sterilization)? Who will tell the story of the twenty-year-old Gypsy woman—and what follows is the description of her death without succor in the reeds, torn apart by the dogs of the SS guard Erika Bergmann, née Belling—who died her special death in Ravensbrück? Who will tell her of the thirsty children in Auschwitz, about the chorus of weeping that rose and fell and filled the nights in Auschwitz? Who will tell about the sad Gypsy children in Auschwitz?

Why didn't you find a single name, any dates of birth, or any dates of deportation or extermination for two thousand seven hundred murdered Austrian Gypsies? Why do you claim that all the data are contained in your story, both the good and the bad, yes—you say—even the good?

Why, especially in the case of the Gypsies, do you speak of the living and not of the dead?

ANNI

ANNA GRÄF
Tailor's Apprentice
Born: March 28, 1925 in Vienna
Arrested: November 14, 1942
Condemned: October 12, 1943
Beheaded: January 1, 1944

With hands chained behind her back in handcuffs, led through the basement corridors to the room tiled in white, to the room trimmed in black, seized by the arms by two of the executioner's assistants, placed naked on the bench equipped with the cuff, a device to hold the neck on which the axe falls, then buried naked in the graves that are used for air-raid victims and the corpses of those who are slain at night.

The prison guard who binds the victim's hands behind her back, who leads the victim along the corridor to an anteroom trimmed in black. The table, a crucifix, and two candles—later only two candles remain. The state's attorney who very briefly reads out the verdict, turns the victim over to the executioner, and immediately departs for Berlin. The curtain that divides the room into two halves; the executioner's assistants who grasp the victim, lay her on a board, and tie her down with a belt. The members of the court who must attend the reading of the verdict but immediately return to Berlin. The clergyman who was permitted to pray in the beginning, but not after November 1, 1942, because the praying was repulsive to the gentlemen who participated. The tying down of the body and the simultaneous shoving of the victim beneath the guillotine. The whizzing fall of the blade, weighing 36 kilograms, from a height of one meter, with a striking force of 500 kilograms. The washing of the guillotine with the hose. The waiting coffin filled with wood shavings. The closing of the coffin over the head and torso. The hiding of the coffin from the next victim, in a corner. The hardly possible assimilation of the odor, and the probably impossible judgment concerning the fact that everything was washed away with water. The comprehension of the scaffold. No longer being able to comprehend the coffin.

The anteroom trimmed in black, the reading of the verdict, the curtain. The arms of the executioner's henchmen. I am naked. A board, a belt. *Wake up, damned people of this earth!*

The coffin, the corner, the hose, the next victim. The seven minutes after entering the death room. The reading of the verdict. The carrying out of the execution.

The accountantlike, flawlessly invoiced bill of the executioner who resided in Prague: 30 Marks plus accrued expenses per head.

I still have the watch. I still have the watch and the mirror. If you think they are important, I'll give them to you. I still have the watch, small, round, made of steel, with a black face, longish, oval, rectangular. Once the crystal was broken. (How many jewels?) An unknown brand, of foreign manufacture. The story of the watch and the mirror.

Was it rectangular, double, a so-called pocket mirror (polished, coated, double glued), with a design, advertisement, etched, cut, engraved with a diamond, coated with plastic, celluloid, bakelite, flammable material (suitable for the production of incendiary devices for destroying war materials)? Was it plated with zinc or silver (matching a brush and a comb)? Did it lie on the washing table (chest of drawers with a marble top), to the right of the bowl and jug? Did it belong to a set with round, with oval containers? For collar buttons, cuff links, whale-bone stays, with a cork lid decorated with the same handworked pewter.

Of course there were mirrors with Nazi slogans and symbols, the compulsory winter-aid charity, the coal claw, *Power through joy.* (To each his own?) *If you want to win, be discreet! Today Germany belongs to us, tomorrow it will be the whole world!*

The mirror that I am talking about. The mirror, the surface of a body that reflects light regularly and in so doing reproduces the image of an object. The mirror, a simple, thin plate of glass, its one side coated with a white metal, in a thin layer, to be sure, but tightly adhered to the glass. The mirror, coated with an amalgam of quicksilver and tin. (A quicksilver mirror?) The mirror, coated with silver or platinum. (A silver or platinum mirror?) The mirror, coated with an alloy that produces surfaces with especially sharp reflective qualities. (A mirror that reflects especially sharply?)

Oh, it was a flat mirror for use in everyday life, rectangular, double-sided, with a delicately faceted, polished surface, the two backs glued together, wrapped in green tissue paper and cared for like something precious. No, it was a pocket mirror, round, covered with red material (with black patent leather glued to it —the indented ends blend nicely with the beveled edge— with a flap handle), covered with felt, decorated, embroidered, the case crocheted out of scraps from the work in the prison (cutting patches, sewing them, winding the strips onto balls). Perhaps there was a funny picture on the back (Police Superintendent Schober, for example), a puzzle (plums to hang up, a clown who is losing his eyes, red carnations hanging on hooks—resulting in: Socialist Party of Austria). Perhaps the mirror once belonged to a nun, a mirror covered with black silk from an elegant little handbag, with black paper used to make the edges "nice," paper that came off as time passed. A modest mirror obtained from a relative while visiting during the holidays, which the nun accepted with heartfelt thanks without saying much. Then she passed it on to a close friend, in the state court. (That's how it reached Anni Haider.) Perhaps a female attendant obtain-

151

ed the mirror, or a mother smuggled it in, or a guard finagled it so that the women could do their hair? (There was a connection between the guards in different prisons in Vienna, honest Social Democrats.)

I still have the mirror and the watch. It is difficult for me to part with them, but perhaps, if you think they are important, I will give them to you.

How were the mirrors manufactured? Did women participate? At most in polishing the mirror surfaces, in packaging them, packing them in tissue paper, in fine shavings, in the so-called mirror boxes. (Caution! Bulk freight. Red ticket. Printed form. Exclamation point. Do not tip! Do not glue together!) And the girl apprentice played with the mirrors all morning in the draft again. (If you think they are important, I'll give them to you.)

So it is a matter of flat glass? Hand mirrors are not manufactured in the glass industry? By small business owners? They can't be returned to the manufacturer? (There follows an endless enumeration of smaller and larger businesses in Vienna, *Gars am Kamp*, and so forth. Possibly also an excursion to Brunn near the mountains, a communist town for as long as anyone can remember, or to Schneegattern, or Voitsberg.) It's just a question of what this has to do with Anni. Anni, I say, the young, athletic-looking tailor's apprentice. Even though the reader's expectation may become obsessed with the concepts of *athletic*, of *tailor*, this is a digression about mirrors. Mirrors, I say. *Mirror, mirror in my hand, whom will Mr. Policeman put against the wall today?* What does *wall* mean here? What does *mirror* mean here? The penetrating description of blown glass and cut flat glass is still missing. Briefly, it doesn't shy away from the *Glass Blowers of Bürmos*. (They were highly paid, were skilled workers, had a short life

152

expectancy, were sought-after husbands in spite of that.)
And all that because of Anni? Because an author doesn't
accept the fact that it's really a very ordinary mirror that
is obtained under conditions that bring a chain reaction
of fatal consequences along with them, be it through the
mirror's very existence in a death cell, be it through
objects and facts that are reflected in it? And under those
circumstances shouldn't its possible form, the adventure
of its genesis, be just as important as the concrete story
of its use? (In a word, the contemplation of this object
as objective observation, and what all is meant by
realism, as usual!) This one mirror, actually not a mirror
at all, no, an Early Victorian..., no, a hand mirror, a
shaving mirror that can be snapped open, a little mirror
for use in everyday life. It belongs to Anni Haider. She
saved it and gave it to a nun, and we will spare the
reader the examination of the working conditions in the
mirror industry. Although even that has something to do
with Anni, with our unique, irreplaceable, indispensable
Anni, yes, with the tailor's girl apprentice. For it is hard
to comprehend why we should present the story of a
shirt, a dress, or, to put it bluntly, the story of the outfit
that a person has to wear when (s)he is going to be
beheaded. Or does somebody here believe that these
people were beheaded naked? (Of course!) So a mirror,
with a quicksilver alloy, all for the sake of the pleasure
found in telling stories. (Even that, too! How does a
person arrive at uninterruptedly following the automatic
writing style of certain people?) The pleasure found in
doing research, just because shirts and mirrors are
manufactured by human beings like you and me, by
human beings like Anni. Understand? (Right. Now
comes the unavoidable business with the watch.)

Viventia saved both of them for me and gave them to

153

me in 1945. (That is supposed to be a quote from Anni, but not from the right one.) Viventia took everything. Viventia saved the mirror and the watch for me, preserved them, gave them back in 1945. (That she was not discovered, that she did not suffer the fate of Anni—the right Anni, that is—all that is a coincidence and clearly belongs here.) So when Anni Haider, our informant (not the only one, by the way), was pardoned to fifteen years in prison, pardoned, I say—when that happened, Viventia took the watch and the mirror. By then Anni was already dead.

And now to the watch: iron, small, with a worn-out, black rep band, purchased by a mother, saved up, set aside—the money, that is—a watch with a metal band, elastic. A person's skin becomes black from it. An unknown brand, probably not manufactured in our country, grown thin, the watch, or the band, at least the arm beneath it, grown thin, broken, eaten through, by the lead paints. (All of these are working conditions that pertain to Anni, at least to people like her, people like you, people like me.) And daily by bicycle from Schwaz to Innsbruck. Innsbruck lies south of Garmisch, but north of the Brenner Pass. Those are geographical details, and they are important. For if Innsbruck, let's say, were north of Garmisch, then we would not even have to consider the question of borders, let alone cross them. And then Anni would not have reached the point of claiming that between Innsbruck and Garmisch there is a very specific, historically established border, and it has to be respected, and it is worth dying for. (We always say, of course, that girl apprentices bring a greater occupational hazard with them.)

This watch, when it showed the time to be 5:45 p.m. (quote: "When the watch said 5:45 p.m...."), another

154

tangible clock showed the same time both in Innsbruck —on the corner of *Salurnerstraße*, on the corner of *Bahnhofstraße*, or on some other corner—and in Vienna—in the district courthouse, on the ground floor, in the death cell. That's a statement.

Now, was the watch sewn in, buried (with fingernails, digging for many nights—they say that happened), in a corner of the cell? Were there hiding places in the wall? It doesn't matter. Thus, if all these factors, and a thousand others that are named, unnamed, implied, forgotten, known, remembered and suppressed, came together.... (Do you think the allegation of torment of the reader is justified in light of the torment experienced by the person writing these lines?) *When the watch said 5:45 p.m., one of the most courageous women held the mirror out next to the barred window,* in order to see where the assigned court official was going. If he entered the upper door,... Is a digression about the court official appropriate here? Is he a human being? (Like Anni? Like you and me?) Does he have his own story? Does this, his story, have a beginning and a possible continuation? How should this story be told? What decisions do we make? (Did he make a decision?) Were the decisions pressed upon him? Are decisions forced upon us? Who decides for the author? What choice does the author have? What choice did Anni have? Anni, I say, who has waited for ninety years for the end of a life that meanwhile lasted almost nineteen years, Anni, formerly fit as a fiddle, at least athletic—she really enjoyed singing, just like you and me. She was blond, friendly, pleasant, helpful. She didn't want to eat anything. She didn't want to take away the food of other women in the prison. That happens, too, you know: people save something for someone sentenced to die.

155

They fix the condemned person's teeth. Teeth are important. That also belongs in our story: a young neck, bent back in a dentist's chair, not the most modern chair, of course, as was the custom at the time. We are certain that even a dentist's chair could tell a lot of things. (It's only a question of whether or not you can expect or demand such a thing of the reader.) And this reclining neck awakens many associations within us, but they do not belong here. They are too horrible. They can't be demanded of us, can they? But back to the court, to its officials, and we ask if the question is permitted, if we are permitted to ask:

Did he walk straight? Did he walk upright, bent, sleepily, with shuffling feet, jerkily, slowly, hesitantly, stealthily, dragging his feet, confidently, self-consciously, hesitantly, uncertainly, guiltily, deliberately, thoughtfully, resoundingly? Is it permitted to employ language to find the court official by asking questions, to resurrect him, a police official who stands for thousands, a very correct, historically relevant, little official? Not the court official *per se*, no, a person like you and me. (We know what that means, but do you and you know it?) Let's ask then, did he walk loudly, audibly, perceptibly? Did he walk silently, noiselessly, inaudibly, taciturnly, soundlessly, speechlessly, wordlessly, mutely? Did he walk quietly and softly? Was he barely audible, hardly perceptible? Did he walk breathlessly, whisperingly, hoarsely, feebly, hollowly, fadingly? (Have you already tried to add to these individual sentences, to read them aloud, to consider their amazing effect?) Did the official creep? Did he steal his way in? Did he flit through the corridors? (Do you think the women and girls in the death cells asked similar questions? Do you think the women asked questions at all? Or is it your opinion that those women were not in any position to ask each other or other people questions? Do you think that questions are generally—or here in particular—inappropriate? Do you have the impression that entirely different questions should be asked? Can you give some examples? Would you accept questions like: Why were women and girls like Anni sent to the scaffold? Who would profit by it? How much did he earn with it? Who else was involved? What kind of deals did he make afterward? What kind of business does he do now? Does he still have court officials whom he can send out? Where? In which countries? In which parts of the world? Do we know him? Is he powerful? Does he have many allies? Where should we look for them? Where can we find them? What can we do against him? What should we do against him? Do you believe there is any point in asking about the court official's motives?) Is it your opinion that certain aesthetic demands correspond to certain kinds of content? (In the case of specific authors, of course, not in the case of the author *per se*, granted, granted!)

The court official, a human being like you and me —when he walked, did he resound, thunder, threaten, roar, murmur, crackle, clank, rattle, trudge, plod, cough, hop? And what followed him? Was it screaming, yelling, bawling, howling, and wailing? Did something follow him? Could that something be heard? Was it shrill, sharp, jarring, high, squeaking, penetrating, ear-splitting, nerve-racking, nerve-rending, blood-curdling? Was the official followed by laments, distress cries, cries for help, shrieks, cries of pain, moaning? Was he followed by singing from the cells? (Suitable for a dictation, suitable for use in school, approved as educational material, by edict, not to be trusted, people, not to be trusted.)

The court official in his uniform. In clothing, official attire, livery. The court official, that messenger of death, a very ordinary human being, in a gentleman's suit, in a uniform, in a coat, a jacket, a sport coat, a smock, a frock coat, a house jacket and vest. The court official in a doublet, a jerkin, a sweater, a waistcoat, a corset. The court official in a lab coat, in a lab apron and protective clothing (the court official in the mirror).

Was he dressed, equipped, clothed, dressed up, togged, fitted out? Was he exposed, unclothed, deprived of his rights, deprived of his political power, skinned out, defoliated?

Was he naked, barefoot, shaven bald, mangy, and poor?

Was he a shadow, a threat, a phantom, a distortion, a caricature at the bottom of the mirror? Did he tremble? Where is Anni? When will Anni finally come? (She has already been walking behind him for a long time, but in the mirror I can't see Anni. In the first place, he doesn't come into the field of my mirror again with Anni, and in the second place it's not just a matter of Anni, it's a matter of you and of me, thus also of the court official.)

Was he feeble, weak, debilitated, weakened by hunger, emaciated, and ill? Was he lame? Did he limp? Did he hobble? (Was he carried on a stretcher?) Did he hang his head? Was he exhausted? Did he ask for water? Could he not continue because of exhaustion? Was he half sick from his daily rounds from 5:45 p.m. to 6:30 p.m.?

How did he view his office? How did he view his message? (Who sent him?) How did he see his work, his deeds? As a task, as an activity, his work as a job, a position, a function, a post? A service, an official duty, a settlement? Oh yes, surely as a duty. (Is he retired? Is

158

he still alive? Does he go to night school? Does he go out drinking?) Was he alone? Did he have colleagues? Did he work overtime? Did they work in shifts? Did he formerly belong to a trade union? Was he boisterous? Who gave him the names? With outbursts of anger? Was he lazy, persevering, lifeless? Was he brave? Couldn't he stop asking himself questions of conscience? Had he called in sick? Did he land behind bars?

Was he soon sent to a camp without a trial? (The drawer containing the camp's file cards. How many square meters of office space does it take for the index with the names of the German concentration camps?) Leave room for the list of the camps in Austria (in Germany, in the occupied regions). *If he entered the upper gate, a man was taken, but if he went further, they knew that one of the women would be the next victim.* (A girl is like a mirror.)

I participated in various demonstrations. Accordingly, on the 15th and 16th of July, 1927, I also participated in the demonstration against the acquittal of those who murdered the workers in Schattendorf. Sister Viventia, there was shooting at that time. Sister Viventia, back then a cardinal declared: "No leniency for the victims." Sister Viventia, they say the Church was persecuted in the Soviet Union? Who was persecuted in Schattendorf? The Church? Or did the Church persecute its believers?

A girl apprentice's reading material. The reading material of a girl apprentice before the war and the reading material of a girl apprentice after the war. A girl apprentice's reading material during the war. The reading material of a girl apprentice whose name might also happen to be Anni, who has not yet quite finished a tailor's apprenticeship and sits in a death cell (or walks

159

behind a court official on a day or an evening after 5:45, a court official about whom we have asked enough questions, to be sure, but whom we have still not found). The reading material of a girl apprentice, not a girl apprentice *per se*, but one who represents all kinds of girl apprentices. The reading material of a girl who began elementary school only a short time ago, one who began junior high school not long ago. The reading material of a grade-school girl, or the reading material of a middle-school girl. The reading material of a girl who attends a trade school. (So Anni after all!) The reading material of a girl who accepted the blessings of the dual educational system. (Or didn't they ever ask her at all?) The reading material of a girl who rides the same commuter train ten kilometers, once a week at seven o'clock in the morning, after the war. (So it's not Anni). The reading material of a girl who rides ten kilometers at seven o'clock every morning except Sundays. (Possibly Anni after all.) The reading material in rural areas in general. You would be amazed. And with that I am not saying anything at all about Burgenland. That comes later. By the way, Anni never went to school in Burgenland, not even to trade school. That must have been in Vienna. Otherwise she would perhaps have saved herself from many things.

The reading material of a rural middle-school girl and the reading material of a rural elementary-school girl. To say nothing at all of the reading material of a private-school girl from out in the country (where the travel time is omitted).

Getting up every day, commuting from six o'clock in the morning until six o'clock in the evening, for the children of the artisans and small businessmen, in Kufstein, the border city and stronghold that lies two hours

160

distant by train. (The reading material of a girl apprentice in the city.) The maintenance allowance for six days and the trip home on Saturdays for the children of small business people and perhaps those of officials as well. The private middle school for saw-mill owners, small manufacturers, doctors, and dentists—mayors, druggists and producers of raspberry syrup have no children. It stands apart, in a pleasant location, close to the newcomers who remained after the war, that is, the district leader's children, or, to put it another way, the district saw-mill owner's children. And for the grandchildren of the big landowners, whose mothers run a dry goods store or a grocery store. (And when it rains steam rises from the corner, from the woolen coats of the peasant women who only shop there for sugar, cloth, raisins, spices.) So, for the grocery store owner's children there is the girls' boarding school in Innsbruck. The same for the niece of the school principal, for the daughter of the bank director, and for the daughter of the watchmaker (and jeweler). For the children of the gardeners, the street workers, the city employees, dairy workers, soda water bottle washers, for the children of the policemen (emigrants from southern Tyrol), the seamstress, for the daughters of the innkeepers, small farmers, cottage owners, saw-mill workers (of both saw mills), workers in the ski factory, in the sporting goods store, the children of the cleaning women, laundry women, for the relatives of the messenger woman, the children of the sales clerks, the grandchildren of the private servants (what the war did not destroy, depreciation consumed), as well as for the children without families, there was the elementary school, less frequently the middle school in Kitzbühel, the district capital (very seldom the reform school, no idea where).

161

But the girl apprentices, what do the girl apprentices read?

For example, *Effi Briest*. For example, *Madame Bovary* (but secretly). Besides economics, political science, materials science, accounting. *Therese Etienne* (less). Far and wide no girl apprentice was seen reading the collective contract or the union regulations. If one were like Effi Briest. Misunderstood, sad, but just as beautiful. The mirrors are wrapped in newspaper and fine shavings. The girls from the private school walk past. They no longer say hello. Any more than the girls from Kufstein—change trains in Wörgl, railroad junction, a gray market, violent young men, ugly girls, industrial area—who know nothing of the Kufstein seamstress Adele Stürzel, that brave woman.

So where are there no ugly girls in the stories of the local people (except here at home)? In France. That was something else. And what follows is the precise description of merry, even if somewhat coarse, soldier nights in France. The girl apprentice's ears are already turning red, and she is amazed that the girls in France were not afraid. (They really weren't.) And the girl apprentice is amazed that some girls, even if they did not die immediately, but if they died afterward, for example.... But the soldier still stands there in flesh and blood, very healthy and sporty in his gabardine stretch pants. Tourism is booming in our country. Frenchmen come less often. They have no money. The soldier was actually no soldier. He was an SS man, the young farmer. As beautiful as the local girls are, no wonder those girls in France also took money for it. It must be.... Did they survive all that? Here comes the commuter train. The girl apprentice has to hurry. And the former soldier or SS man, a handsome man, wound up in British or American

162

captivity. That's very good for our tourist trade. He had the mark burned off, clever. His shoulder hair has even grown back, or almost. The story of Effi Briest may be sad, to be sure, but she didn't have to, that is, she didn't listen to the kinds of things that a girl apprentice hears. A girl apprentice doesn't succeed in looking that beautiful and sad. More is demanded of her. A girl apprentice has to endure a lot. That's not required of girls from private schools. A local boy like that has respect for the fathers of girls who attend private schools. They don't like such things to be said to their daughters. (But with the sons, on the other hand, they are not as strict.) And it doesn't matter much anyway to a girl apprentice without a father.

To have a mother like the daughter of the woman judge. Such a beautiful, strict woman. At the time of Charlemagne. The way she rides and dismounts and takes off some kind of head covering, a helmet perhaps. And dark curls (or braids) pour out. The son hurries toward his beloved mother, no, the daughter, the woman judge had a daughter. The judge's companion, called a steward, is very respectful. And not the son, but the daughter stands before the judge. She carries the gold and the jewelry in her apron and wants to pay the ransom for her brother. The judge decrees hanging and burning, says the Lombard goldsmith. He takes the jewelry and the ransom money with him.

Feet in the Fire. We don't know who wrote *Effi Briest,* who wrote *Madame Bovary,* or really who wrote *The Woman Judge. Feet in the Fire* is different. At the end in parentheses is: Dr. Conrad Ferdinand Meyer. 1825-1898. The man whose hair turns gray overnight sets the murderer of his wife free, although the children have recognized him, a Huguenot. What reminds us so much of the Huguenots? Who do the murderers of the Huguenots remind us of? Why do you read such things? War is war. Before she checked to see who wrote *Effi Briest*, she had finished reading the book and had returned it. *Feet in the Fire* was something with which we could more closely identify, and we didn't even remember the title of the next book. It was about the freedom fighters in Ireland. The older brother fights and bleeds to death, and the younger one remembers. And later he fights too, even though he didn't want to at first. But Ireland is long ago, 1912 or so. There's nothing like that here anymore, in 1809 perhaps, but then? They say people still fought in 1809, but back then everyone agreed. So we prefer the Huguenots.

All the more, since we know as good as nothing about 1703. In contrast to the Tyrolean rebellion of 1809, we know almost nothing about the Tyrolean uprising of 1703. We can assume that even Anni did not know much more than we do. There must be a reason for it. The isolated uprising of the peasants and mine workers that was so decisive for the course of the Spanish War of Succession—no wonder they die out so soon—is overshadowed by the rebellion of 1809, which was controlled from Vienna, and by the melodramatic end of an innkeeper who was unfortunately very naïve, even if he was not incompetent. The uprising of the peasants and mine workers of Schwaz, Fieberbrunn, and other mines against the rulers (but as you can see, it didn't do them any good) is overshadowed by the myth of individual men. That is acceptable and very convenient. It is easier to answer for the end of the innkeeper to school children, than for the demands of peasants and miners, to which, by the way, because of the war situation, they had to accede, as Prince Eugen predicted.

164

And so the school children do not sing, nor do the miners and the peasant bands play the song of their victory of July 1703. But they sing of the inevitable, but beautiful downfall of a loyal victim of the French. And besides that it was in Mantua.

We can assume that Anni sang a very specific song of the Austrian resistance (*You Brothers from the Cities*) to the well-known tune from Mantua. But as far as the intruder of 1703 is concerned, who was probably a Bavarian because of the French, in 1809 he was also admittedly Bavarian, but French nonetheless. And that's an enormous difference. So we prefer the Huguenots. (Nobody has to know what is going on with them.)

But as we know, a girl apprentice, who is almost a girl apprentice *per se*, understands nothing at all about literature. For that reason she confuses the Huguenots and 1809 and 1703 and the so-called recent past, or at least connects them with each other, where there is no connection at all. And Ireland? Who is interested in Ireland and in those who are still fighting religious wars these days? By the way, you can see again that there will always be antagonisms. Look at Ireland.

Ireland and Fritz, the son of the chimney sweep. He graduates from school in Kufstein, then studies in Vienna and says, "Read Rilke or *The Happy Prince* or *The Good-for-Nothing*. Don't think about things so much. Don't speak so gutturally. And your relatives, the ones who kneel in church, if you make a face like that, it's your own fault. (Fritz believes in God, of course.)

Our reading material before the war. Our reading material in the cities before the war. Our reading material, generation of 1925 (Halt! halt! There's Anni. Stop! Stand still! That really is, that really was...), shortly before the war. Our reading material in Burgenland. Our reading material on the trip to Burgenland (unavoidable, Burgenland is unavoidable, I say). Our reading material (travel schedules, bus connections), once a month, shortly after the divorce, let's say. Generation of 1900, after the fire in the supreme court building, on the trip to the village in Burgenland, to pay for child care. (No wonder it rhymes,* it's only the mother, of course.)

Our reading material on the bus, rickety, the children usually got sick. It was unbearable, the jolting, especially in the back of the bus, but the people with the rucksacks had always occupied the front seats. Our reading material before the trip to Kelchsau (a terrible, snowy hole), freezing from the cold, forced transfer, frozen fingers, alternating hot and cold baths. Aunt Fini didn't sign something and was transferred to Kelchsau. Her superior here, the school principal, is very hostile. Our reading material on the trip to Kelchsau during the war. The bus trip to Kelchsau during the war. (At that time you couldn't even read.)

Didn't the local residents, let's say the blacksmith's wife whose relatives were staying with the innkeeper (the one with the unmarried grandchildren), didn't the hatmakers, the bakers (not the one in the main square, the one in Oberdorf, two brothers, one of them a soldier who returned from Russia; his friends visited him in the bakery, later an important man in the tourist office), didn't some of the local residents, even in Außerdorf, where later the Innsbruck-Salzburg expressway passed by, hide Sepp in May of 1945? Everyone knew about it, even which alpine pasture. He had the mark burned off. Did he kill the paratrooper, whatever else he did? Or did

*The rhyme appears only in the German original.

somebody else do it? Or were there two paratroopers? And remember the Poles. (They were so angry after the war.) Everyone claimed not to know where Sepp was hiding, even the American occupation forces. The officer squinted his eyes angrily. He was interested in the cables, not in those allusions. (Were there really any allusions like that?) The entire village, at least the part on the west side, talks openly about Sepp's hiding place. The quiet ones in the corner mourn for their sons. They smell like manure. Their farms are generally rundown and poor. (Didn't the blacksmith's wife, the village blacksmith's wife, the wife of the plumber, throw herself out the window? After all, they had champagne and even meat. Or was it for some other reason?)

That didn't interest the Americans. But they beat the cattle dealer so badly that he never recovered from it. (There was also a Pole with them.) But by then the cattle dealer, as you know, was already a financially ruined man. He no longer mattered.

Our ride on the streetcar in Berlin during the war. Our ride to the People's Court in Berlin during the war. Our ride on the metropolitan railway, the subway in Berlin after the war. Our ride on the subway during the Cold War after the war. Our ride through Berlin after fleeing from Berlin (purely economical reasons). The advertising, the media, the lure of the displays (in Berlin after the war). Our flight by metropolitan railway from Berlin to Berlin after the war.

A girl from Cologne during the war. The girl with the pale skin coloring and the black hair during the war. The child that had to be protected, should have been protected during the war. Why are you so poor? Because of the bombs? Tell us. Why do you flinch when the teacher asks you something? Why do you have a sister

167

who is much older than you? Why is your mother so old? Why do you live in a hotel during the war? Why doesn't the teacher like you? Why don't you get called on? Why doesn't she make you take your turn? Why do I only go to visit you once? Why do I feel so strange when your sister is so nice? Why do you talk through your nose? Why have I forgotten your name? Why does the teacher scream at you? After all, you do come from the Reich. Why do they say you died before the end of the war? Why do I feel so badly about it now? Why didn't I feel badly about it then? Why do I ask why you flinch during the war? Why do you twitch that way? (Was your name Mathilde?)

Our reading material during the war. Our reading material before the war. Our reading material after the seizure of power in Germany. Our reading material in the Vienna Woods, before the war again and again. Our reading material while hiking in our beloved mountains, in our beloved forests, *Red Youth, Advice to Soldiers, Pathway and Goal.* "I am very happy up here. With fondest wishes. Yours, Anni."

History books or what we heard in school. What did we hear in school, about battles, about glorious military campaigns and the unexplainable disappearance of peoples? Where can they have possibly gone? They must have simply packed their bags and begun to wander. (In 1254 the Aragonians replaced the entire population of Alghero [Sardinia] with Iberian immigrants.) Departure from Aspang Station, 8:25 p.m.: Celts, Basques, Rhaeto-Romans, Gypsies, Dacians, Illyrians, Indians, and others.

The unambiguous matter of the First World War and the subsequent unambiguous matter of the Second World War. (This year we didn't even get to 1918. First of all

168

there was the material, and secondly the nonproductive hours, Colleague.) And yet: *You can only be right in one thing: either when you overthrew the empire, or now when you deny its crimes.* Designated number one, designated number one on the list of undesirable intellectuals in Germany, seventeen lines, in small print, no comparison with his brother. Not considered to be noteworthy, not designated as reading material, it did not penetrate our consciousness at all.

"And why did he live so alone in the castle? The Belvedere Garden, the view of Vienna. It's not what it used to be either. The skyline. There are gaps, not only in our memory. I'm talking about building gaps. But the tower back there, red-white-red, Mama. A little patriot like his father," says the father. The parents walk down the gravel path. They go down the steep carriage ramps. Not Anni's parents. In connection with her, we can't talk about parents, only about her mother. They go down the carriage ramps and ask themselves: Did they wrap the horses' hooves in cloth? Did they wrap Anni's body with cloth? Did they lay carpets? How did the coaches get up the steep paths? (After all, we live primarily from the tourist trade. Or does somebody have a different opinion here: mine workers, pitmen, farmers, artisans, girl apprentices?) The garden ends in small paths that radiate out among geometrically pruned tree and hedge structures and lead onto an oval lawn (all that is missing is a comparison with a cemetery, but it is missing), lead to a pool, to the suggestion of a pond, the reminder of an artificial bomb crater. (This eternal searching with the flares, this constantly repeated searching, this infinite number of negotiable paths, all this just because of a girl apprentice, or, if you prefer, for the sake of a girl apprentice.) The garden, almost vacant as always, the

169

fountain with five bowls. Women tourists balance their way from one statue to the next. (We already said it, tourist trade.) Young ducks seek refuge among the decorative stones. (Now they really have nothing to do with Anni.) Trenches provide a view of gigantic foundation walls. In front of us is the entrance to a secret nuclear air-raid shelter, to a corridor through which food is taken to the prince, to a freight elevator between the two museums. We reach *Prinz-Eugen-Straße*, walk out of the stillness of the garden onto the busy street. We walk along the outer wall in the direction of *Schwarzenbergplatz*. We look through the gate into the private park —after all, it is also a book about Vienna. We look through the bars. We see only a gravel path and trees, nothing else, deserted, in the middle of Vienna. We turn toward the square. We want to go to the Russian Memorial. We say *Russian Memorial*, not *Memorial of the Red Army Soldier*. We walk in the direction of *Schwarzenbergplatz*, in spite of everything an accumulation of historical names and deeds. It should be worth an excursion.

"The Russians are angry," says the patriot.

"Who says so?"

"Because they had money to buy weapons, more weapons."

The fountain rushes. The spume sprays as far as the benches. It is as cold as in a cold-storage building in the middle of Vienna.

"But the Russians didn't start the fighting."

That was quick-witted. We are quite shocked. Who tells a four-year-old that nations are bad? Thus we learn personally, at least through the flesh of our flesh, that there are several factors in the development of a child, in the development of a story, an interlacing series of

170

excursions, so to speak. The child quit listening long ago. He is concerning himself with the policeman. The child represents his generation and nothing else. (Or is there supposed to be something more behind it after all?) The evening sun shines on the hero's memorial, we think *hero's memorial*. Two policemen, not an honor guard, only what is contained in the agreement. A little chat or chatter, and the dog is permitted to lie in the grass without a muzzle, then back to the guard post. The evening sun shimmers in the golden crest of the monument (that was never reflected in Anni's eyes, that much is certain), in the Soviet crest, we assume. But who knows right off the bat the nature of the Soviet crest, unless he is involved because of hate or love? (Hand on your heart, Anni! Do you hear?) Light falls on the golden letters in the red marble and in the rounded structure behind it, Cyrillic, gold-sealed message, about the names of those who fell in the liberation of Vienna. The powerful discourse about those fallen soldiers. It was written, it is still being written, so that we can enjoy the coolness of the fountain today—which can't be said about Anni, which can't be said about those like her. Our important and personal experience today, during this walk through Vienna, the statue of the soldier who looks out across the fountain, proud and alone, a soldier, to be sure, not a soldier *per se*, but one who represents a very specific category of soldiers. Here the excursion becomes almost dangerous, not only for us. No fountain can cover up the tall statue. What does he see? Does he look into a better future? Who can think of the statue of the happy prince now? I think of Anni. She died with a song on her lips, Anni, who would be so happy to walk past here today. I look at the monument now with other eyes. I try to see it with Anni's eyes.

Our reading material on the streetcar during the war, *Schwarzenbergplatz*. Streetcar line seventy-one. Destination Central Cemetery. Our garden work at the Central Cemetery, our waiting for the arrival of the bodies from the Institute of Anatomy, our search in the trench grave, the secret notations in the group book.

Our search for gardening work, our search for work. The idea of looking for work. The idea of looking for gardening work at the Central Cemetery.

Garden, an enclosed piece of land in which useful and decorative plants are raised. Kitchen gardens, decorative gardens, flower gardens, gardens for educational purposes. Botanical gardens, school gardens. Careful working of the ground produces greater yields than farming. Decorative gardening. The natural style versus the geometrically regular style according to the French model. The Vienna City Park in contrast to the Schönbrunn Palace Park. The Vienna City Park compared to the Schönbrunn Park (or to the Belvedere Garden).

Cemetery, place, enclosure, place of burial, churchyard (cemetery gardener), cemetery peace, administration, graveyard, enclosed field of God, fenced place, burial place, cemetery essence, enclosure, enclosed, fenced space, seclusion, cloister, yard, churchyard, yard of honor, garden. A cemetery is like a garden. Real estate, piece of ground, earth, piece of earth, field (garden), place, market, market place, church plaza, churchyard, cemetery, cemetery peace. *How much earth does a human being need?*

I buy the ticket. I have a ticket. I pay (perhaps) thirty pfennigs. I have friends in the Simmering Station. Friends in Simmering advised me to go this way.

I have a ticket punched. I hold the ticket firmly in

my hand. The conductor is a woman. (More women are being hired now. The men have gone into the army, been drafted, gone off, been arrested, condemned, beheaded, Franz Mager, 48, streetcar worker, Vienna, district court, cell 120, February 26, 1943.) She takes my ticket. She punches it with the little, red, hooked hole-punch. Her fingers are in gloves with half fingers. The fingers are only knitted half length, so that her sense of touch is not impaired while she tears off, sells, and checks the tickets, while she takes care of the equipment. A pad of tickets, the back of the punch quickly lifts the ticket from the pad. The fingers that are blue from the cold take the ticket, tear it off. Date, line, and time of day. Meanwhile watch the passengers. It is cold. The door is half open. There is a draft. The sliding door can only be opened with two hands, a metallic blow with the punch against the door glass to warn the passengers who lean against the sliding door, to warn the soldiers on leave from the front who lean against the sliding door, to warn the Austrians who lean against the sliding door. The passengers are crowded together by the running board. It is hard to ring the bell. The women conductors stand on tiptoe. Their tight skirts hinder them in their work. The caps on the peroxide-blond hair are attached with hair pins. Today many people in uniform are traveling. The poor soldiers on furlough. They sit and gaze silently into space. An officer climbs in and demands the seat of the soldiers on furlough. The conductor has rung the bell. She is agitated. "I ask you not to use that kind of tone." The conductor Elisabeth Castek protests against the barrack tone of voice. She raises the hand with the punch and pulls the leather strap that extends forward and rings a bell by the driver. One ring means depart, two rings means stop. A soldier wounded in the war blocks her view. She has already become accustomed to the sight.

The matter of the First World War and the unambiguous matter of the Second World War. But why did the Americans ally themselves with the Russians? (The French have nothing. Any child can see that.) Well, you wonder about that. Perhaps they couldn't have done it without the Russians. Aunt Marie says there aren't even enough mushroom places for the residents anymore. The Germans simply robbed us. They did not want to learn that you must not simply pull the mushrooms up, but you must twist them or cut them. Otherwise you destroy the mycelium. (And the never-ending cries of "Yoohoo!" in the woods, that stupid "Hoohoo!" But suddenly every man had a wife from abroad. Do you remember?)

The blacksmith's wife really did jump out the window because of him. Then she was in a plaster cast. She liked to read novels so much. No, they fled separately, incidentally on the same night. Each fled in a different direction, and then the scene at the border. She took poison. He came back alone (not Sepp, her husband). Each of them fled in a different direction, and then Sepp went to the alpine pasture and hid.

When and where do rural people read? Do they read in the railway station, en route, in the trains, out in the country? What does the railroad station look like? Which stretch was it? Was it damaged by bombs? Who built it? What connections are there, and is it fortuitously located on the main route to the West? (This important railroad connection, with two tracks, and the heroes who prevented them from blowing it up, 1945.)

Walks along the railroad tracks out in the country. Walks during air-raid alarms. Nothing happens to us, but in Wörgl it's different. (A part of the populace flees toward Kaisersgebirge, always with the most important documents in a small suitcase.)

Our reading material during the war. Our reading material before the war. Our reading material after the seizure of power in Germany. Our reading material in the Vienna Woods belt, again and again before the war. Our reading material while hiking. A sunny winter day in the Lower Alps. *Two dozen male and female students, we had climbed with our skis from the fog-shrouded valley to the heights of the forested mountains.* The letter to a dead friend, written by his friend who is now dead, Hugo Kaudelka to Kurt Horeischy (the chemist who gave his life to save the electron microscope). He experienced the battle, but not the victory. With him fell a German named Hans Vollmar. Two assistants who risked their lives for the freedom of research in Austria, an Austrian and a German, on April 5, 1945, on *Währingerstraße* in Vienna.

Our excursions before the war. Our hikes in the Lobau region during the war. Karl Brzica with his friends who amused themselves there in tents and boats. Our friendship with Karl. We felt drawn to Karl. We felt recruited by Karl. We paid the membership dues, ten pfennigs a week, just to see Karl, just to be with him, we stated credibly and unrefuted. It was Karl, Poldi's fiancé, and although that love seemed hopeless, we laid aside all our reservations. We followed our instinctive feelings for Karl. We became psychologically dependent on Karl and had only one goal before us, to be in the vicinity of the man we loved. (That saved Valerie Anna Marie.) Our meetings in the *Schönbrunnerallee* during the war. Our assignment with the pamphlets, our excursion into the sixth district. Our reading material in prison, our reading material in the cell. (On January 6,

1943, Karl Brzica was condemned to death in Berlin.)

Our reading material once a month, shortly after the divorce, the Great Depression, unemployment. You had to stand in line for days to get work. If you had relatives in Burgenland, you could consider yourself fortunate. Perhaps that would insure the survival of your children. An unmarried woman during the Depression. A woman, a day laborer who places her little daughter Anni in foster care. A woman among many, who works her way through as a cleaning woman, a messenger, a window washer, a laundry worker. (Even today, in contracts for apartment building managers, the use of the laundry room for washing laundry from the outside is strictly prohibited. Similarly, begging and soliciting are prohibited in apartment houses in Vienna, as well as on the Danube canal and in Leopoldstadt. Later loitering was especially prohibited.) Flora Schön, you paid a high price for loitering. Chaim Heinrich Treppler, you paid a high price for picking up cigarette butts.

The reading material of a girl in high school is different from the reading material of a girl in middle school. (The comments of the lecturer about Thomas Mann in the German class. The rumors about the school principal's past. The woman is entitled to a license. During the last days of the war, the license for a private school was worth about as much as a free ticket to South America. The high-school girl understands that, but the middle-school girl doesn't.) So the school principal drinks because of a guilty conscience, according to the high-school students, those former boy and girl apprentices. The German teacher and his obscene laughter at the mention of Thomas Mann's name, in Vienna in 1961. "You should read his brother," somebody says later in a café. "He's much better."

Our reading material shortly after the end of the war. The secret reading of a long poem—that was all during the May devotions to the Virgin Mary. The great storms of prayer must have helped. You would be amazed, Reverend Sir, how crowded the churches are here. A thin booklet, black, white, and a lot of red, a man like a tree, struck by lightning on the cover. The long poem about an old man with a white beard. An SS man taunts him, "You're crying because your whore is dying." And *Feet in the Fire*, the persecution of the Huguenots, the old married couple who took so many sleeping pills and didn't wake up. Why didn't they wake up? Because the authorities insisted that they get a divorce. What does getting a divorce mean? That's when you are married and then aren't married anymore. Where were they? In the building where Aunt Hedwig lives. The proletarian poet's widow couldn't save the old couple. Our feet in the fire. We never compared *Feet in the Fire* with the concentration-camp poem. We read that poem like a folk song, author unknown, secretly, with our feet in the fire. We were ice cold in our shirts, in our prisoner's clothes on the parade ground. We stood at roll call and saw the old man before us. We knew nothing about Lessing's seventeenth letter on literature and suspected a great deal about the dignity of the old man whose tears dripped into his beard. His raised countenance, his sublime countenance. The booklet fell out of our hands. We really waited to see if the old man would ever be remembered in school, the old man, and the Huguenots, and the Africans, and the Indians, and all the slaves of modern times. But the closer we get to recent history, the more dangerous it is, because we do not report about it objectively, because we do not give a scientific and well-balanced account of historical truth.

"A foolish girl," said the history teacher. "The Russians and the Serbs have always been the warmongers." We have to point with one finger now. We have to stretch out one finger, not the entire hand anymore. From now on, everything else will be forgotten, including certain songs. Some melodies are still permitted, but with different words. But that was shortly after the war. Later the old words were also permitted again. For that reason a change to Romance philology was recommended. There you could at least be spared certain texts. They still rang in our ears, you see. Shudders still ran, a cold sweat still ran down our backs. For those of us children with Romanic blood in our veins, the Romanic blood froze in our veins at every step.

The blacksmith's wife poisoned herself in Reit im Winkl, and the girl who was later an apprentice thinks that she once saw Sepp, with a furrowed face and smooth gray hair combed back. Can you tell by looking at him, can you tell by looking at a man, if he is perhaps a murderer, if he perhaps killed somebody? Nobody remembers a mark below his shoulder. Maybe that was all talk. Who ever branded people like cattle? The blacksmith soon married again, this time a local girl.

Did you know there were girl apprentices who bought themselves expensive art books after the war? Did you know there were girl apprentices who clamped those expensive art books under their arms after the war? Did you know that the girl apprentices with the expensive art books would also have liked to read the books after the war, but could not understand those books? ("We really did have such gaps," says Barbara.) And that they therefore simply carried them around in order to be regarded as something better? (Barbara says.) And that we knew nothing at all about the war

178

after the war? The parents who said that they didn't know anything were very careful to see to it that their children didn't know anything. And that's why those girl apprentices felt deceived by their expensive art books, by their reading material, for a long time after the war.

When we see this stage play, we're happy that we live in the present. When we see this production of *Woyzeck*, we're happy that we don't live in Woyzeck's time. Woyzeck, the good man without morals, has to gather wood along the brook. In our national army such things really don't happen anymore. When we see the dramatization of *Leutnant Gustl*, we are happy to live in the present.

The adapted novella by Schnitzler also sees the positive things of the monarchy. Scenes really occur there (close-up, outside/day, semi-close) when the director pauses. I mean, there are compliances as if it were still a hundred years ago, and yet scenes occur that are unthinkable today. That's why we are very happy to live in the present.

Our reading material on the streetcar, January 1944, heading for the Central Cemetery. Our thoughts about the meetings, about the excursions, about the hikes. Our thoughts about the letters-from-the-front campaign, about the production and distribution of *Advice to Soldiers*, about the plans for acts of sabotage. Our thoughts about the reading material in prison. Our thoughts about the reading material in the death cell.

What I want to say with that after the war. What I want to say with that, with the reading material, with the girl apprentice, with the excursions, with the art book, with the deception after the war. What I want to say with it, with the death cell. That we were so hungry in the cell. That we were so thirsty in the cell. That we were so hungry and thirsty for knowledge and for justice. That we were not sated. That in our short lives we were not sated. That we hungered, that we surely hungered during our childhood, generation of 1925, with our mother separated from her husband very early and the child and her siblings soon given into foster care (you guessed it, in Burgenland). That our lives were so short. That our lives were a venture (possible associations: front or roulette, decide for yourself). A hope, a deep inner fulfillment. Whether *deep* and *inner* refer to *hope* or *fulfillment*, there was a song on our lips, about our homeland, for the people. That such a thing seems peculiar to those who did not participate must be calculated in. Don't worry, it is calculated in. *Onward, and don't forget.* Even if we forget, there will always be people who remember it. (The perplexity, that unbelievable perplexity at every step. If somebody could only explain it.) Under the Christmas tree in the death cell, the girls sang the *Internationale*. Who would have believed it?

Burgenland. That region that descends, that sinks slowly from the Rosalia and the Leitha Mountains to the plain, the region around Neusiedler Lake, the southern hilly region. The Parndorf Heath, that scarcely fertile moor, the countryside east of the lake, with ponds and tarns. Burgenland. Meadow land. Land lying west of the lake. (Those all seem to be vocatives.) Hilly land covered with elm trees and rich vineyards. Land of fruit, land of sugar beets. Southern region with tracts of forest. Tracts of forest alternating with fields. Burgenland. Forest land. (Did you know that the vocative has almost died out in German, yes, that it actually doesn't exist at all?)

Burgenland, a region that lies under the influence of

the Hungarian climate. Burgenland, a brown-coal region of apparently little importance. Burgenland, a land with a few sugar factories. Burgenland, also inhabited by forty thousand Croats and nine thousand Magyars after the war. Burgenland, after 1647 a Hungarian province—following a plebiscite in 1920, an Austrian province. (Did you know that vocatives, imperatives, and other one-word sentences, taken out of context, often can't be distinguished from each other? Yes, that's how difficult and how simple it is.)

Burgenland, with your single-street villages, with your small, black-clad women. Burgenland, with your storks and your endangered bird paradise, with your lake region and your increasing tourist trade. Burgenland, your gates bear the symbol of the sun. Burgenland, your real estate is cheap abroad. Burgenland, your people radiate something that is completely unknown anymore and therefore also unmentioned. They construct roads in Vienna. They are building the subway in Vienna. They live in barracks in Vienna, and on Saturdays they go home from Vienna. (There is possibly a connection to Anni in those things, but only possibly. We aren't certain.) Burgenland, what happened to your Jews? What happened to your Gypsies? One really doesn't ask those questions, at least not in our literature. Burgenland, your owners, your fields and forests, your view across the Leitha Mountains, your bus connections, your culture experts, your bishop, your governor, your capital city, your ghetto, your immigrants, your strange guests from abroad, from the Federal Republic of Germany. Burgenland, your castles that have been bought up. You land of Anni's childhood, I think of you often.

Externally, everyone was calm. Externally, all the inmates of the death cell were calm. Externally, the

181

tailor's apprentice Anni, Trude Müller, Leopoldine Sicka, and a strikingly beautiful girl were all calm.

And Anni sang the songs again. Songs of the Alps, folk songs, children's and hiking songs. When you come home, sing them to your children, Erna.

Death cell. A barred window up high with a rounded arch. A table (with a table cloth), two benches, a flower vase, a booklet on a nail. (Inventory? Rules of behavior?) A snapshot probably taken from the bed, or from the door.

Trembling, weeping, they sat and lay on the floor, almost insane when the keys rattled. And again Anni sang the songs, from her childhood, from her time in Burgenland, from the time when she hiked, the songs of home that she so dearly loved. Anni, tall, blond, and athletic. (It was in the early summer of 1942. No, it was a year later. As you can see, we can no longer depend on the witnesses.) She candidly kept me company as I scrubbed the corridor. She never complained about her fate. After I was arrested, after I was arrested on that autumn day in 1941, in the early summer of 1943 Anni kept me company as I swept the steps and corridors in the building on *Schiffamtsgasse.* Anni, just turned seventeen. (*The second and the fourth girls were juveniles at the time of the deed!*) Arrested three weeks before her journeyman's examination, just when she would have begun to earn a little more money. Her last earnings were fifteen marks a week, of which she gave seven or eight marks to her mother and saved five. *She must pay the court costs.* Anni, arrested in November, born in March, born in Vienna, single, widowed, for her fiancé, Karl Golda, died of typhoid fever on October 17, 1942, in Kharkov. Anni sings in the cell.

They were not the young men in the fiery furnace.

It wasn't Daniel in the lion's den. They were the girls of the Communist Youth, Anni, Trude Müller, Poldi Sicka, and two others, one of them a strikingly beautiful girl. I don't know who.

Flight into art. Flight from truth in art. Flight from truth in reality and art. (Art as a mirror of reality.) Flight from the truth into the phony truth of art. Flight into commercial art. Flight from progressive art into avant-garde art. The flight of the avant-garde into experimentation. The flight of the experiment into the new-realism movement. The flight of new realism into photo-realism. The flight of photo-realism into documentary art. The flight of documentary art through the natural exit (if possible without a stomach ache). The flight of phony art into so-called art. Free trips, free tickets, free visits, documentation, documentary art, live broadcast, audience survey, supercooled voice, cooled tone of voice, chilled critic. You're just jealous, of course. The flight of the media from reality. The flight of the audience into the media (the audience's fault). The flight from reality into the phony world of the film (pure garbage). The flight from the film into the video (embarrassing). The flight from the video into a fabricated, phony reality (exorcism, extremism, terrorism, money). The distribution net of bourgeois art policy, and in the middle of it a few German-German fish flop around. (The city of Vienna, for example, has only positive advertising. You don't get anywhere with negative advertising there.)

Anni and her siblings were placed with strangers in foster care. For years Anni lived with foster parents in Burgenland, and then later she came to Vienna and began the tailor's apprenticeship. It is certain that from her earliest youth she was acquainted with hunger and privations, but there was also her cheerfulness, but there was also her capacity for friendship. Anni's trips into the mountains. Her enthusiasm for sports. Everyone gave a little extra for the tours, a few pfennigs for Anni. An apprentice doesn't have that much money.

We suffered the severest hunger. The confined women suffered the severest hunger and rapidly lost weight. Anni didn't want to accept anything. Many of them were now only skin and bones, and Anni, the youngest, didn't want to take anything or wanted to share immediately. *(At Christmas a police official brought baked yeast dumplings and a Christmas tree, beneath which they sang the* Internationale.*)*

Hunger during the war. Hunger as a means to destroy the enemy. Hunger as a means for mass destruction. Hunger used to weaken resistance. Hunger used to reduce the necessity for guards.

The first phase of food fantasies, of theft, of roots, of buds, acorns, rats, cats, waste, brown coal. The phase of licking the empty kettle from the turnip stew. The phase of clever tricks and of attacking the food carriers. The phase of unrestrained greed and the barbaric struggle for survival.

The second phase of the changed facial expression, the veiled eyes, the mindless gaze, the pale gray skin color, the clearly protruding cheekbones, the plainly visible eye sockets. The appearance of the elongated head and the appearance of the shrunken head (the water beneath the skin). The softer speech, the slower breathing, the great effort with every movement. The edemas, especially on the feet, on the lower and upper ankles. The diarrhea, the long periods spent in the toilet compartments (in mortal danger), the back-and-forth between the outpatient clinic and the block toilet. The excrement, the stench, the anticipated end.

The making of charcoal from bread, from wood. The preparation of filler from paper, leaves, pieces of wood, sand, earth, and sawdust for the walk to work. The loitering around the crematorium. The obvious symptoms of mental illness.

The third phase of the standing groups making swimming motions as if praying, like the Mohammedans do (thus the camp expressions: *Moslems...swimmers...*).

We offered no resistance. We didn't commit suicide. We meekly allowed ourselves to be murdered in groups by individuals. We waited patiently. We stood. We sat. We lay, until it was our turn, often without supervision. Nobody tried to flee. We waited for an injection in the heart or for the shower. We dragged ourselves onto the trucks without hesitation, although we knew that on the trip from Mauthausen to Gusen we would be murdered with the hydrogen cyanide compound Zyklon B.

Artificial coffee, black, unsweetened, the cheapest kind. Turnip soup, half a liter at noon, another in the evening. The turnips rot in the SS cellars. Eating turnips in the punishment block is prohibited. A slice of bread, only one, for twenty-four hours. No salt in the soup, no fat. Those who work in the weapons industry. (Beginning in 1942, Siemens-Halske also recognized the signs of the times and built a production plant near Ravensbrück.) To be sure, no objections were raised on the part of the factory when the prisoners supplemented their completely inadequate outer clothing with material belonging to the factory (cleaning rags, insulation paper). But in the first place, three thousand women took factory-owned insulation paper, and in the second place it always rustled so loudly beneath the women's clothing. So the supervisor, a civilian, a normal employee of the firm, who was walking along the rows as usual, heard it rustling so unpleasantly. The Russian women had sewn undershirts for themselves from newspaper that belonged to the government. Then it had to be reported. After all, it was his duty to walk through the rows. And then we drove her, the Russian woman, into the furnace room and beat her to death with a piece of wood. That was common then where we were. (Witness: Berta—escaped, came home, testified, recorded.) So, a person who works outside receives three potatoes a day (whether or not he is entitled to a pension, I can't say), sweet, frozen, spoiled, but potatoes, twenty grams of wartime margarine, and a spoonful of wartime jam on the weekend. That is the menu at Ravensbrück in the winter of 1944. By then Anni Gräf was already dead. Poldi Sicka, Franz Sikuta, and Karl Mann were dead, as was Karl Brzica, handsome Karl, Poldi's fiancé.

When we drank malt coffee, when we drank fig coffee, when we drank barley coffee from Aunt Tina's store, there was a famine in the prisons, a famine in the camps. ("I can't eat anything else," a woman in Tyrol said. "There's a famine." She seemed bewildered. She rejected the food. She incurred Aunt Tina's displeasure.)

Twenty thousand slices of bread and twenty thousand slices of sausage. The prisoners for whom they were intended are being punished and work their shifts at the Siemens factory without any food. If that isn't business, I don't know what is. The idea of the elite, the natural law, the racial law, the law of those people, the law of those creatures is: you get fat from eating yourself. There's a war going on. Under the circumstances everyone takes what he gets. Everyone eats what he gets. Everyone steals what he can get—heroic, racially pure, and bull-necked—from living corpses, from

186

exhausted vermin, and from the dead (for example the packages from relatives who had gone without for those who had traveled through the chimneys long ago...).

A still-life painting in the forests of Mecklenburg, photo-realism, April 1945. Pot-bellied and wheezing, a specimen of the master race hastily gets out of a car, stolen, of course, north of Fürstenberg an der Havel, between the lakes of a moraine landscape. Wheezing and fat, this magnificent specimen, this jewel in boots hurries into the thicket. Behind him the escape car is full of sacks of noodles, semolina, milk cans full of butterfat, pails full of jam (wartime jam), rolls of cloth, authentic Smyrna carpets, the finest curtains, chocolate, and many other things. He moves hastily and clumsily, leaving the stolen goods behind, to save his fat belly from the Red Army. In the forests of Mecklenburg the women found automobiles, left behind and stuffed full. The dead had starved for that. The survivors had saved it. The armament slaves had sweated it from their skin and bones. Paint me a picture of the sacks and pails in Mecklenburg's forests, just beyond Ravensbrück.

Then came the columns of prisoners. From Hungary they were driven over the Austrian border in front of the SS, driven with blows from rifle butts to dig trenches and build redoubts. And after finishing their work, they were slaughtered. Others were driven further west. At Riederberg beyond Vienna, at Präbichl in Styria, and in many other places they were shot, stabbed, slain. Then came the treks. Cows with projecting horns, water buffaloes from Hungary, wagons with linens and corn. Along the country roads of Austria moved innumerable wagons. Many people went on foot. Now and then a woman crept into a house, asked for a piece of bread, a spoonful of soup, some fat. What drove them? Why did

187

they come? What were they doing before? And the Ukrainian women prisoners of war danced round dances on the meadow behind Leni Gratt's restaurant.

Flags were sewn. Not white ones, no, they had to be red-white-red. Nothing else would be credible. The flags that were hidden in attics, rolled up—where did the cloth suddenly come from? They took off the swastikas, but many had hidden the old flags. Many brought out the old flags and could only be right once—*when you toppled the empire, or now when you deny its crimes.*

The route from *Hofherrgasse* to the Central Cemetery. The route from *Hofherrgasse,* Vienna 10, the *Favoriten,* into the main street of Simmering, to the Central Cemetery. (It leads across the Lobau, it leads across the hills, it goes along the *Schönbrunner Allee,* it leads through the fifth district, it leads, I confess, through various telephone booths in the tenth district. Autumn 1941, it leads through many post offices during the shipment of highly treasonous printed materials. Spring 1941, it leads above all to Leopoldine Sicka, cover name Ida, daughter of a bakery worker, unskilled worker, later a trained mechanic with a weekly wage of twenty-two marks, arrested on a streetcar. She was strikingly pretty. Was she the strikingly beautiful girl? It leads to Karl Brzica, serious Karl with the winning nature. It leads through weekly training discussions, for eight months beginning in early 1940. It leads to the front, written fifty or sixty times by hand: *Help end the murdering.* It leads through the collection of toothbrushes, fountain pens, combs, films, aluminum powder, celluloid dolls, and timers for the incendiary bombs. The route to the Central Cemetery leads through treason.)

I walk the route along *Hofherrgasse,* to the corner of *Erlachgasse,* around the block, along *Absbergergasse.*

188

(Valerie lived here. She got off with eight months.) The number six streetcar comes from *Gellertplatz* and goes along *Quellenstraße*. It turns into *Absbergergasse*, then into *Gudrunstraße*, in the direction of the East Station. It passes through the underpass. The gray buildings, the merciless rumbling of the trucks. Stretches of *Arsenalstraße* have no sidewalk. Then the pedestrians in the tunnel press their way quickly along the wall and across the street. There's number six. The conductor has already rung the bell. She stretches. She leans out of the streetcar. Her hand clasps the leather strap. She twists her upper body forward and has one leg stretched out behind her, like a figure skater. She waits until the pedestrians pass through the dangerous underpass and reach the tram stop on *Geißelbergstraße*. (Careful! You don't know if you are being watched.) The number six meanders onward, no, it rushes, it rumbles down the long stretch. It pounds, it rattles, it roars and grinds. *Nemelkagasse, Kremenetzkygasse, Puschkingasse,* to the left, therefore on the north side, the Aspang Station, to the right, therefore on the south side, the East Station. Further down are the railroad's main workshops, no trespassing. The task forces of the Austrian railroad, Josef Steurer, for example. *(It is now one-thirty. At six o'clock I will no longer be alive, but my last thought will be of you.) Leberstraße*, underpass, *Am Kanal*, we are in Simmering, at home in Simmering. The people press toward the exits. Gravel has to be spread at the *Lorystraße* crossing, an injured war veteran. Fortunately the braking maneuver was successful. Now the *Sedletzkygasse-Grillgasse* loop. I go to the exit. The wind, the sharp January wind from the Simmering Heath, the trade wind from the Hungarian plains. I hurry across *Grillgasse*. No, I have ridden past it. I have ridden through the entire loop. I have ridden line six back to *Gottschalk-straße*. I get off and walk to the main street of Simmering. I reach the streetcar stop for line seventy-one. Is it early in the morning? Is it late at night? It is getting earlier and earlier. It is night. It is afternoon. It is January 11, 1944. Was there an air-raid alarm yesterday? Will there be an air-raid alarm tomorrow? What is the news from the eastern front? What's the news from the western front? They can already hear the guns in Poland. There is already the sound of battle around Birkenau. This time it's an old conductor. Yes, there is a shortage of men. *Domesgasse, Braunhubergasse,* then comes the east railroad tunnel, then the *Laurenz Pharmacy.* Over there you turn off to Kaiserebersdorf. There are the row houses for the Chilean refugees. In the winter it is so cold there that you can't sit without a head covering. On the right is the freight station, the shed, to the left are *Dürnbacherstraße* and *Nierenbergergasse.* You recognize the towers and walls of the Central Cemetery now. On the left there are gardens and the crematorium. On the right is the Israelite section, in short, the Jewish cemetery, *Weichseltalweg*, First Gate. I remain seated. My knees are so weak, my knees are trembling. Is it early in the morning? Is it late at night? I get off at Second Gate. I cross the street. (That's not easy in heavy traffic.) I ask for work as a gardener. It is January 11, 1944. I do garden work because I am waiting for my child.

When we look at a work of art, we are not interested in the life of its creator. We are not interested in whether a poet describes a true or a fictitious love, or a symbol (Beatrice). A girl apprentice doesn't understand that. A girl apprentice would like to know: Which side was the poet on? So the girl apprentice asks about the poet's life. She must ask about it. The girl who will finish her tailor's apprenticeship in three weeks asks: "Is the poet on my side?" (At least he was on Beatrice's side. He wrote in Beatrice's language, the language of her people. He wrote other works in Latin. The women could no more read Latin than the rest of the people could. So the poet made an effort to write as clearly and as beautifully as possible. That saved him.)

The jam bucket on the cellar stairs. Aunt Tina's delicatessen and the wartime jam. (After the war somebody broke in. Too bad about the many jelly glasses and the preserving jars containing veal and the canned foods from the Swiss care packages, especially the Nestlé.) We don't mean the jam from the local woods. (The berry comb, an instrument used by the professional berry pickers. It worked well for one or two summers, and then the patch was destroyed, and there were no more berries to be found. The berry combers wandered on and left the destroyed berry patches behind. The same with the mushroom hunters. They trampled what they did not recognize. They were often more involved with destroying the good mushrooms with which they were not familiar than with gathering the kinds they knew.) The image of the honey pot pushes its way in front of the image of the jam bucket. The honey was solid. Back then we were permitted to bore into it, crook our forefingers, lift the lumps of honey from beneath the darker liquid layer, and put them in our mouths, secretly, on the cellar steps, next to the pantry. Then came the kettles with dried fruit, the sacks of dried mushrooms. A short time later the boarding house had to be sold. Shortly thereafter we moved. Shortly after that the jam kettle stood on the cellar stairs at Aunt Tina's place, with the pig feed for the potato farmers. Sailer, known

191

at home as Rainer, and the cows of *Zur schönen Aussicht*, two thin cows covered with dark green scabs spanned in front of the cart that was used for transporting the boxes of soda water for the vacationers from Germany. The image of the jam kettle, that greenishly shimmering tin, crusted with dirt, set up in the sealed train cars, slopping over or kicked over by a dying prisoner, spreading a pestilential stench.

People starved in Vienna, starved in the district court, starved on *Schiffamtsgasse*, starved on *Morzinplatz*. (The designation *Hotel Metropol* must be discontinued immediately. That building no longer has anything to do with a hotel.) The women in the district court rapidly lost weight.

She starved and loitered on *Porzellangasse*, at night in front of the windows of number fourteen. The Jewish woman Flora Schön, imposed name Sarah, Jewish, single, born in 1868, lived unregistered in an empty store to which she had secretly obtained the keys. In order to avoid evacuation, in order to avoid starving to death, dying of exhaustion, dying by gas, dying of asphyxiation, Miss Flora, 74 years old, sat starving in a store. (Miss Schön had seen her best days.) Flora wandered around the streets at night starving, or perhaps only in the evening, perhaps even on *Porzellangasse*, her former home. She was caught and taken to the collection camp on November 12, 1942, on the anniversary of the Republic of Austria, for the purpose of evacuation, of course. (Two days later it was Anni's turn. Two days later it was Anni's and Valerie's turn because of their participation in the Communist Youth. Anna Gräf confesses. Valerie S. denies it.)

On October 9, 1942, at 8:25 p.m., the 45th Jewish convoy (the 13th daily convoy to Terezin) departed from

192

Vienna's Aspang Station with 1322 people aboard.

The dentist's chair in the Vienna district court. We
see Anni. Her beautiful young throat is bent back. I
smile at her. Pain convulses through me. Anni's young
throat and our glances. Anni's gesture, her deprecatory
hand movement. (In the late summer of 1943 Erna Hed-
rich saw Anni for the last time.)

It was at the dentist's office in the district court. Our
hope was the dentist in the district court. To meet one's
husband, to meet one's lover, to meet a relative, to see
a comrade. The office hours in the Vienna district court.
The trip to the district court, the excursion. The mothers
waiting in front of the gates of the building on *Schiffamtsgasse*. The mothers who went to *Schiffamtsgasse*
every day in order to have a chance of catching glimpses
of their children. Mothers who put on pretty dresses,
applied a little make-up, and radiated hope that after
months they would receive news about their children,
letters, messages. (Mother, when they send you my
clothing, tear out the lining, open the cloth-covered
buttons, examine the shoulder pads. Mother, that's
where my last letter will be, that's where my last
greeting will be. There you will find my last greetings to
you. I will die erect, Mother. Don't be sad, Mother. It
is better to die erect than to live on your knees. *I am
only a soldier of the just cause who has been called
away*. Head high, Mother. Your child greets you.)

We waited until it was our turn to be called. We
waited in the prison corridor. The door to the dentist's
office was open. I saw Anni, who was sitting in the
dentist's chair with her head bent back.

I see the picture before me: Anni, with her head
leaning back. Anni reflected in the mirror. Anni as if in
a mirror. Anni, at an angle from the side. She looks into

193

our faces, but as if in a mirror, as if from above, as if from behind, as if from a mirror's perspective, as if from a different perspective. We look spellbound at Anni's neck, slender, young, athletic. The neck of a blond woman. The neck of a would-be journeyman tailor. The neck, bent backward and somewhat thin. The throat with the pleasant voice, with the slight Burgenland accent. The neck on the dentist's chair. Anni, loved by her colleagues, favored by the female guards, given privileges by the personnel. The dentist's clinic as an opportunity to see comrades, to give messages to relatives, to give hope, to give news about the course of the war: When will my liberator come?

I see the picture before me, the morgue behind the precincts of Ravensbrück, the work of the dentists Harms and Hellinger. According to the established procedure, the dentist, slender and tall, with his hands in rubber gloves, approaches his victims with an electric lamp and a pliers. You can hear the clanking of the pliers, the dull sound of the body being thrown back. Then the booty—crowns, false teeth, and gold teeth—is wrapped in paper and brought to the garrison headquarters. Now the corpses lie like fish with open toothless mouths. On their shoulders they bear the receipt stamp verifying the dental examination. Otherwise they will not be accepted at the crematorium at all.

I rode my bicycle through the gardens, past the brick ponds, toward Laaer Berg. I rode through *Bitterlichstraße*, through *Bleichensteinerstraße*, through *Grenzstraße*, toward the freight station. Above *Hasenleiten*, I turned off to *Gadnergasse* and could still hear the whistles from the freightyard until I reached *Schemmerlstraße*. I was familiar with a small gate on the East-Station side. It was used by the garden personnel and by the grave diggers, and was perhaps hidden by the bushes. It is often advisable to take that route when the special streetcars stop, when the whistles resound and the boots crunch across the gravel, when the special details carry out their special assignments.

The court official in the mirror. He has started his rounds. The court official does not go through the gate, he goes further. One of the women will be the next victim, one of us, several of us, trembling and crying, almost insane with fear. Can seconds be so long? Next door a door opens. There is a soft order: "Take off your shoes." We rise, we begin singing the songs. Our fettered hands, these hands that are weakened by hunger and fettered. We are ice-cold and half insane with fear. The court official stands before us. We must take off our shoes. We walk barefoot with our hands bound behind our backs. We sing, *Brothers, to the Sun* and *Our Thoughts Are Free*. Above us our comrades hold the mirror out. Careful. He's coming. He's here. A few letters: *Help end the murdering!*, to a soldier. A Viennese girl. Beginning November 1, 1942, the clergyman was prohibited from praying during the execution because the recitation of the prayers was offensive to the gentlemen who participated.

I notice the rotten fragrance of the cemetery flowers. I walk along the wall. I have something to do here. I have important garden work to perform. I must straighten up wreaths and bouquets, gather and arrange them in piles at specially designated places. I must arrange the pieces of corpses in piles. With coal forks I must continually arrange pieces of corpses. I must gather candles from the lanterns; I have to remove old candle wax and turn it in. I have to straighten the bows on wreaths, arrange the branches in vases, decorate the hall,

195

trim the plaques of honor, decorate those who lie in state.

I see the graves. I see the open trench graves, the trench graves in rows—for the bombing victims, they say. I came through the secret gate on the East-Station side. I know where the trench graves are, the graves of those for whom there is usually no money. They are open. They are waiting for their contents. I weed the gravel path, the worn dirt path in front of the trench graves. I rake the ground. I pull out the weeds in clumps. I pile up the weeds. I wait.

The anteroom trimmed in black, the reading of the verdict, the curtain. Two executioner's assistants, a board, a strap, a guillotine. The coffin with sawdust, the corner, the hose. Gräf, Anna, tailor's apprentice. Müller, Gertrude, sales clerk. Buresch, Franz, soldier. Homolka, Emil, clerk. Rubas, Waldemar, lithographer. Schmidt, Leopold, waiter. Lachnit, Friedrich, ship-builder's apprentice. Böhm, Johann, metal lathe worker's apprentice. Fuhry, Wilhelm, lathe worker's assistant. Sikuta, Franz, lathe worker's assistant. Bernhardt, Michael, mason's assistant. Reitbock, Josef, mechanic's assistant. Name, date of birth, address, date of death. The seven minutes after entering the death room, from the reading of the verdict to the completion of the execution. The beginning of the executions usually at 5:30 p.m., the completion at 8:00 p.m.

The delivery of the bodies to the Institute of Anatomy for processing and preparation. The stacking of the delivered corpses on top of each other like blocks of wood. We are overloaded. We are filled to bursting with corpses and parts of corpses. We have prepared proposals. One submitted proposal was also rejected elsewhere because of overloading. Butchers wearing rubber aprons remove larger pieces of flesh with knives, then they boil out the heads and bleach the skulls. Corpses and body parts beyond what is needed are transported by streetcar to the Central Cemetery at night and buried there in mass graves. *A human being needs six feet of earth.* That estimation is greatly exaggerated. *But stored human heads float like turnips in cement tanks.*

I have accepted work as a gardener. It is January. I wait. I have things to do. I am busy. I carry out garden work. The processing plant has mountains of body parts three meters high. For that reason additional executed people are delivered to the plant only when called for. I am waiting. I will identify the trench grave. Night is falling. I will use the remains of the candles to see Anni, my daughter, one last time.

STEFFI

STEFANIE KUNKE
Née Jelinek
Teacher
Born: December 24, 1908 in Vienna
Arrested: January 9, 1936 and (about) April 1938
Died: December 26, 1942 of typhoid in Auschwitz

One...two.... When did you learn to count? Who taught you? Beginning when, where, with whom, why did you learn to count? Did you grasp it quickly? Were you gifted in counting? (When does a human being count? Not glass balls, caramels, snail shells. Not primroses, crocuses, water rings. Not...one..., and that eternity between one and two.... One.... That's me.... One life and...one more.... That's you....)

One...two.... Who taught you to count so competently in the Viennese dialect? Use your fingers, Steffi, and count.... Who taught you to count even more competently in everyday language? That's right, one and.... Just who was it that taught you to count correctly in German? All right. And who is holding on to your wrists? And on the Saturday before Pentecost, who pulled you onto the whipping bench in the cell block or the detention building—called the bunker for short—and held your wrists clamped tight like a vice? (Who jerked your feet back in a kind of box so that your body stood slanted and tense and therefore especially defenseless?) Who has such skilled and ghastly knowledge of leaning, stretched-out, emaciated anatomy (and no escape from the single rod of the leather whip)? Personally ordered by Himmler, witnesses and supervision, camp commander, protective custody camp leader and signature of the camp doctor. (Very well beaten. The flesh, to the extent that it is still present, has holes in it as thick as an arm, my *Führer* of the Reich.)

You won't use your fingers for counting again very soon. Go ahead and try to pull your hands even a millimeter from that vice of other hands. You see, we told you so. The leather whip with the single rod is also available in bundles, in *fasci*. (The Home Defense Force has it good, they learned Italian and studied fascism in the original language.) The symbol of the new masters, the rod, whistles mercilessly against your back. It spares nobody, not even revolutionary socialists. You probably did not expect that. The rod, you see, spares nobody. All are equal before the rod: communists, socialists, social democrats, the revolutionary socialist, as previously mentioned, but middle-class people as well, yes, even people from the Home Defense Force. That should make a person think. There is something equalizing about it, something wise, so to speak, almost like a natural catastrophe against which, as every child knows, you can't defend yourself. (Some prison guards, Home Defense people, incorrigible as they are, are fooling around. In Mauthausen they can fraternize with the former politicians from the Schuschnigg period, the lousy bastards. What do you think of that?)

Who is beating you now, Steffi? Who is using the whip, an established means of German discipline? Is the woman you protect beating you, the woman who lay before you on her knees? (Don't betray us, through all eternity, amen.) Come out for roll call. There are the rabble now. They stand shorn and gray. Hunger and cold and work for you and nothing else. (That wasn't a bad idea, to use the prisoners' stamp money to buy bread for your own belly and get rid of the letters in sacks by the ton. It's a sign of the drive for self-preservation, almost a sign of breeding.) There must be order. (There follows a flood of sarcastic comments of the kind that every school child knows from personal experience. Now it is a matter of finding a place to begin.) Letters, for example, hundreds of letters, composed and delivered very properly, with the painstaking omission of any details about the camp, then found in straw sacks, for our daily bread. That was in 1938 or 1939. (Now was it

1938 or 1939? Which was it?) Now, beneath the whip of a real criminal, of a petty thief, nothing more, we learn to count, and the year is 1940.

Question: Would you have betrayed the woman to the SS? We couldn't do it. While standing at attention, between work shifts, with empty stomachs and in mortal danger, we couldn't do it. We had learned to talk without moving our lips, and from row to row the answer was: No.

Just once to be able to move between two...and three ..., but not a millimeter is permitted. The body is taut and bent forward on a slant. The whip is still hitting the institutional clothing. Unfortunately the prisoners are still smearing the good institutional clothing with blood...and three...and four. The distinct beginning, the mandolin orchestra, three, four, now the guitar. Today the guitar maintained the tempo very steadfastly again. Count along aloud, guitar. The streetcar is coming. The guitar on the streetcar—a conversation—maintained the tempo. The most important conversation of my life took place on the streetcar. That's where it all began. Steffi, guitar, very gifted. Steffi hears that she is very gifted and intelligent. Beethoven, guitar, mandolin orchestra. Hans encouraged Steffi to learn to play the violin better as well, but not until much later. Hans recognized Steffi's talent immediately, fostered her inclination. Aunt Flora also encouraged Steffi's talent and inclination. Steffi, who grew up in a household of women, was only interested in humanistic education at first. Now it is different. Steffi has a boy friend. The conversation on the streetcar: your talent, your life, for the working class.

Back then in Mauer, the house on *Langegasse*. The one-room apartment with a kitchen on *Langegasse*. The garden through which she reached the apartment, her

205

aunt's apartment, her grandmother's apartment, in short a household of women. Aunt Flora, unmarried, handicraft teacher, single, a typical woman's occupation and a civil servant—what you might call independent. (Learn to stand on your own two / feet.) The apartment in Mauer, back then still Lower Austria, today Vienna 23. A person who lives there is already out in the country. During the first months of Austrian fascism the police administration was not very strict there. That is how it happened that Käthe found a house where we were in Mauer. Käthe, whom we then meet in Ravensbrück. Käthe Leichter, née Pick, briefly a resident in Mauer (until we meet again in the Jewish block). Käthe, the unyielding one, meets Steffi by the punishment block. (Do you still remember? Mauer? The house music? The garden? The green landscape?) Käthe's blue eyes ask: *Will you endure to the end?* The apartment in Mauer, still Lower Austria. People there live as if in the country, far from the capital city, and yet nearby, in the middle of the green countryside.

A quiet child, Stefanie. She has lived with Aunt Flora in Mauer since her earliest childhood. Three generations of women. A dreamy garden and three generations of women.

Back then in Mauer, a small, one-story house, a simple apartment that was accessible through the garden. In the fragrant garden of Mauer near Vienna. Three generations live out their lives there (born in 1850, 1879, 1908). Aunt Flora, handicraft teacher, a typical woman's occupation, independent, jumps in when she is needed, remains with her mother, takes in her brother's child. (Ignaz, brewery worker, corresponds with Rosegger who publishes his poems in *Heimgarten*.) Perhaps because she has no dowry, perhaps because of her mother and niece (we're talking about Steffi), perhaps Aunt Flora read *The Woman* (Anniversary edition, Stuttgart, 1909). Maybe Bebel's epochal writings were also in Aunt Flora's bookcase, next to the writings of the forest schoolmaster and the *Heimgarten* (her brother's poems)?

Wrong, she counted wrong. Another blow. Continue. In the women's household in Mauer, in the garden house in Mauer there were never any blows. Ignaz, the brother, was sickly. An employee of the city brewery, a dreamer and a poet, he corresponded with Peter Rosegger (as previously stated, *Heimgarten*). He had become ill right after the child's birth. Of the mother we know only that her name was Marie, née Ourednik, and that she was a seamstress. She probably took care of her husband and maintained the family, and Flora, the sister, took the child. The grandmother is happy to raise the child. The liberation of women can only be achieved by improving their economic situation. Thus Aunt Flora was very careful to see to it that Steffi learned to count early, that she learned to read and write. In addition there was the money for the child's food. And it remained that way under a silent agreement. The child was with Flora. So Steffi grew up in a household of women and was soon a diligent, successful schoolgirl.

One...two..., and many years in between, three...four.... The bench, the table, a box. A person lies down across it, rather she is thrown across it and pulled back. Perhaps she has bared her upper body. She is accustomed to nakedness, of course. As soon as you enter the camp (Ravensbrück is not Steffi's first camp, Ravensbrück is no novelty in that regard), you become accustomed to nakedness all too soon. The sharper order came later. *Blows on the unclothed bottom.* That's how delicately they expressed things back then. Anyway, the building was already standing, a building with two hundred cells, a hundred on the ground floor and a hundred on the second floor (incidentally, that's not an insinuation), and a purposely planned room with a flogging bench, so providently did they build in those days. Mental arithmetic is in great demand here, at least counting, at least to twenty-five, clearly, flawlessly, loudly, with a firm and yet not all-too-loud voice. Go on, count! After all, you were a teacher's assistant, Steffi. Clench your teeth, but not too tightly, otherwise you can't count. Stronger people than you have died because of it. So if at all possible avoid even the slightest hesitation and moaning. Think of the mandolin orchestra, or of anything at all, it doesn't matter what. *You must not forget that here you are no longer a shop steward.* Käthe passed that golden rule on to Rosa Jochmann. For here, on the bench, everything looks different, but behind it, if you survive here, there are hundreds of emaciated, worn-out hands. They are ready to help you. Thus Rosa welcomed Steffi in the spring of 1941 and made her the block secretary in the political block. That's an important position, and that was also Steffi's best time.

Now note, it's not all over and done with here. It's never all over and done with. As long as we breathe, it's never over and done with. (Remember Socrates, and if you don't know what happened to Socrates, you will perhaps learn about it here with us.) So, act as if you agree with everything. Try to protect the prisoners and act as if the SS were magnificent in everything. (For you must know that you are dealing with primitive human beings, whether it suits posterity or not.) So deceive and sabotage and protect the prisoners. Don't forget that.

For the time being you must break stones, unload ships, /and usually endure punishment without food. For the time being you must be cautious and hide your face. (You know they are more primitive than primitive.) Your face will easily become a provocation. Your face is still too beautiful, a stumbling-block face. It could easily serve as an excuse for a flogging (which you will endure alone without a sound). It will end with the possibly dangerous faint.

So blows rain down on Steffi. Strokes of the whip fall like hail. (It can be seen that we are dealing with a natural event.) When did it begin? How did it begin? How can it be recounted? It can only be indicated piecemeal in individual images. The counting of the blows was not the worst thing. (The worst thing was the separation. The worst thing was the homesickness for Vienna. The worst thing was—I admit it—the despondency, the resignation.)

"After all, you're talented." Hans's self-confident, slightly sarcastic voice, a baritone. (To hear his voice once more, to meet his gaze once more, at the beginning of the *Spring Sonata*.) What are two years compared to an entire life? Give me just five more, please, please, and I will endure everything. Two years of bliss. Was that our happiness? The apartment where we conspired. The wedding was in September of the famous year 1934. We lived in a central location. We lived in Neubau. That's a district in Vienna. But since this is a time-lapse presentation, first of all we are waiting for the streetcar. There must be order. Line 60. Departure from the Hietzing Bridge. You can see the walls of *Schönbrunn Castle*. The *Church on the Plaza*, the *Park Hotel*, the beautiful red streetcar, our people, as the reader knows, of course. Beyond them eagles crouch on the bridge.

They are unavoidable. I simply must describe the eagles. They remind me of the lions at the Nußdorf Locks, and together they are magnificently laden with symbolism, for decay and calmingly distant past. Nevertheless, the crouching eagles still wear a crown. Every tourist guide knows that the cupola of the Neuburg Cloister monastery bears the same crown, the House of Austria, or some such thing. Part of the resistance movement even cites this crown as its authority, or could have cited it, Catholics for a democratic but Austrian empire. Karl Roman Scholz (attention, statement of a name, a momentous ritardando), a canon of the monastery, may unconsciously remember the crown on the cupola, he and eight other Catholics, to the death. Whether it was dishonorable is not known. That was probably in 1940. We are patient. The red streetcar will come soon. We are still waiting. The view from the Hietzing Bridge, with the Vienna valley before us. We are waiting for number 60. We are waiting for a better future. We hope that we will soon have weathered these twenty-five blows from the rod. Beneath the blows we remember, try to remember. Were we happy? A garden? Dreaming and writing poetry? Humanistic education? Knowledge is power? What we once learned? What we once....

The teachers' college on *Hegelgasse.* (Philosophically, Steffi is a disciple of Kant). Aunt Flora was a wonderful example in everything. While some are for Nietzsche, others accept Kant. In that, Steffi is in the best of company. There is a German poet who was exiled to the country that was his homeland. France was his homeland. He is just now writing his *Henri Quatre,* he is fighting for the United Front, he writes *La haine* and does not mean his own but the hatred of the others, the hatred that found him (that found you, Steffi, that

210

found us all, brothers and sisters, *I in Ravensbrück, you in Sachsenhausen, in Dachau, or in Buchenwald*). By way of Rousseau and Zola he found his way to Kant, and by way of Kant he found his way to the nationalization of coal. It was only a figure of speech, but it hit the nail on the head, the *Kopf*, which none of us wanted to read. He sat there and wrote his fingers raw against the coal monopoly. *Whoever has the coal controls the war*, or something like that. And it could mean that whoever has the energy controls the war. "Whoever has the banks impedes the war." Käthe said that. She also read the French authors, Flaubert, Maupassant (but they send the eight-year-old out of the room when discussing certain topics), Zola's world of the *Rougon-Macquart*. But not until the early war years did she read *Germinal* and *L'Argent*, and then again the books of her childhood, *Les misérables, Die Weber*, and finally Heinrich Mann's *Der Untertan*. Käthe, prisoner E-196, bears witness of these, her reading materials in the Vienna district court, cell E-125. Perhaps she also read the *Kopf*, written in painstaking detail during the eight-year struggle against the warmongers. During this time Käthe works to improve working conditions for women. "For the fight against women working is a diversionary tactic that serves fascism in the final analysis," Käthe wrote. So the arc is drawn from *Rudolfsplatz* 1. (Behind the park, across the street, the Brochs lived on *Gölsdorferstraße*.) We are in the textile quarter, on the corner of *Franz-Josefs-Kai*. Every child knows that or should know it. Hermann is nine years older than Käthe, who doesn't live far from here, at *Rudolfsplatz* 1. She mentions the rising second generation of capitalists who finance the one-year voluntary enlistment in the cavalry for their sons. One could think she meant Hermann Broch's father with that.

The author, like Käthe, was arrested in 1938. He got away. His file probably did not yield much. Strange and—as the whole world knows—degenerate, but unintelligible—and sometimes that's good—it's called the *Schlafwandlertrilogie*. Well, we know that these so-called artists make a rather sleepy impression anyway. Let him go. Watch him. Watch him carefully.

That is why Hermann is safe in England when Käthe is writing her memoirs in her cell. (During the preliminary investigation that was still possible.) The stairwell, where Käthe's mother threw herself down, what a flight, what a solution, Käthe's mother and Egon Friedell. (Excuse me, that was a different part of the city.) Now an elevator has been added there, reconstruction money, long, long after the deaths of Käthe Pick and her mother. Hermann Broch's mother died in Terezin.

We said an arc is drawn, symbolically of course, from *Rudolfsplatz* 1 through Lübeck to France and on to us at Ravensbrück. (Question: Should that be explained solemnly or objectively now? The claim will remain incomprehensible anyway.) For, as we know of course, the author must never show that he knows that he knows something. That's the great strength of literature, of course, that it can convince a person that he already knew all that before. (It is well known that we remember familiar things much more easily, but nobody is supposed to notice it.) In short, repeat slowly and clearly: Against the background of the social novels of the nineteenth century the children of the patricians found their way to socialism by way of literature and experiences at home. (Listen! Listen!) Steffi, as a member of the third generation (offered association: patrician, bourgeois, petit bourgeois, further: first-generation capitalism, second-generation capitalism, social democracy), the child of commoners, Steffi, residing in Mauer, finds no library in her home, but finds Rosegger nevertheless. She attends the public school, not the lyceum for the daughters of officials, which was in itself progressive for Käthe's parents. Steffi composed. She is about to take possession of her musical legacy. (No wonder. Vienna is a world city in the area of music.) She almost has the legacy in her pocket. She was just on her way to Eisler and Brecht. Her friend sincerely tried. His baritone really sounded good. He always accompanied her himself on the piano. The autumn landscape in Mauer, the many shades of green simply cannot be reproduced. In France the resistance is in the offing. In Austria the struggle continues. That is a figure of speech, but it is in print on thousands of pamphlets. Since the night of March 12th, the slogan has been: *The struggle continues,* signed CPA (Communist Party of Austria). The A is very important. At that time, who of us believed in Austria? Yes, the self-hatred of the rump state, or something like that. But the slogan about the struggle is already making an impression in the prisons. It is—that was the salvation of many—also making an impression in the camps.

So looking toward the center of the city, with the matchless green behind us—the landscape painters have always feared that matchless green of the Vienna Woods —we stand and have that green and the Mauer hill or the Kalksburg cupola behind us, the community woods, the rifle range, the defensive alliance—bury the weapons. The blackberry patch, night shadows, ruins, training ground, Nazi territory, later national army territory, much later location of the Wotruba Church. Into the city, a vigorous morning walk, a morning bicycle ride down *Lange Gasse* in Mauer (and it is long), in the

213

direction of the city or into the city. We like the rhythm. We are precisely in rhythm. (The reader noticed that long ago, of course, much sooner than the author.) *Kroißberggasse* leads off to the left, as we already stated, in the direction of the city. There stood the Kunkes' villa. Director Norbert and his wife Cilla came from far away, supposedly from Poland. Back in the time of the monarchy they came from the formerly Austrian area in what would become Poland. Director Kunke, perhaps a friendly, perhaps an educated, perhaps a puritanical, perhaps a free-thinking man (has nothing to do with textiles). A son, two daughters, an obedient descendant, takes up a bourgeois occupation, insurance agent. The word gives security. Viennese Municipal, Tuchlauben, Inner City. A person can make music on the side, of course.

Did marriage offer better possibilities for Party work? After the reversal in February, which will still be exploited, Hans and Steffi will have been dead for a long time. But first of all the painful matter of the letter of June 17th, of that confounded year 1934, and the speaking style of Comrade Felleis, Roman Felleis with his evidently unrefined pronunciation. (Of course the reader knows immediately that it is now a matter of decisive questions: Should the fact that he is a proletarian be a burden to the socialist? And should his origins keep him from talking?) Comrade Felleis's proletarian intelligence (in spite of his pronunciation, mind you). This is a memory honoring a not-very-well-known revolutionary socialist, a memory of his honest efforts to gather forces and build a new organization (February shock and June rage). But unfortunately, unfortunately our best forces crossed over to the communists. You guessed it. But Hans, the enlightened middle-school student, the successful business-school student, the promising member of the Socialist Worker Youth.... Enough, no dates. Here it's a matter of deeds, political reviews (with Hans Kunke signing as the writer), Brecht and Eisler songs. (You know he had a beautiful baritone voice.) Beginning in 1934, he was a member of his party's central committee. His wit could be biting, but it was never malicious.

Five...six.... That's not right. We were happy much longer. Intelligent and talented, sarcastically talented, a generous, sensitive intellectual, Hans. We attended concerts. In the time that remained to us, we made music at home. Käthe Leichter also made music at home. The reader didn't expect anything else, in a music city like Vienna. He expected Hans to sing Brecht and Eisler with his beautiful baritone voice, and that he would set Morgenstern and Wenzel Sladek to music with his piano fingers. Surprising, to be sure, but it was only to be expected. (Who is really speaking here, the victim, a fellow-sufferer, or a female author? It's strenuous, almost like searching for an apartment in Vienna.)

They finally settle down, seventh district, not far from *Seidengasse*. They are already being watched. They lull themselves into thinking they are secure. They are no *tabula rasa* in the security office. They just can't believe it. They can't believe that the *Political Review*, that all of their work was in vain.

We were too secure. We were too sarcastic. We were too careless. We were too obstinate. (We were not conspiring enough in establishing the apartment.) We hoped for an Austrian version of the Nazis, although we did not believe in Austria. In defining the limits on the left, we overlooked the enemy on the right. We were too proud to flee the country (but perhaps we only lacked the right connections). Which factors made Hans Kunke into the great opponent of the United Front? (Was it right that he had to pay so bitterly for it?)

The trouble with the lower echelons. They really wanted the United Front. Meanwhile, a camp is being set up for us at Lichtenburg. That's supposed to be a play on words, tactically joining the United Front and turning the lower echelons around. The enemy won't be that furious.

Six...seven.... Seven women eat turnips. Seven women eat dirt. Before you turn around to look, they are gone.

Once there were seven women at the Lichtenburg Fortress. (The author seems to have taken on too much. She can't maintain the language level.) Seven Austrian women among 860 German women. Put names on the table, addresses, occupations, not so many deeds, more dates please. Susanne Benesch. Here! Herta Breuer. Here! Steffi Kunke. Here! Irene Laner. Here! Grete Stabei. Here! Hanna Sturm. Here! Marianne Schlaringer. Here! Once upon a time there were seven women from Austria. They came to a fortress that had already existed for a long time. It had been built for women, but not for those seven. The fortress was far away from home, somewhere in central Germany. The women could be proud. They were the first ones from Austria at the fortress, an advance guard, a real vanguard. When the Ravensbrück camp was ready for use, they were again the first. Suse Benesch was slain soon afterward.

Seven women at Lichtenburg. (It really sounds good. It was also a place for widows, but more about that later.) *And once I saw Suse again.* That sounds good, too. That sentence must definitely be included. *And once I saw Suse again.* That wasn't near Sesenheim, it was at

216

Ravensbrück. Suse staggered across the camp road. Before that, she had to pound stones, drag barrels, carry bricks, dig in the earth with her bare hands. She built a villa for the SS. She dragged herself onward to work outside the camp. And a fellow-sufferer remembers: *And once I saw Suse again*, before she died. The fellow-sufferer's ability to speak gave out. That can happen. In the emotion of remembering, the fellow-sufferer uses Goethe's language to talk about an enemy of the German people, Suse Benesch, slain at Ravensbrück.

The long way from *Lange Gasse* to the long street in the camp. In between: interrogation, arrest, and release. Shortly before the annexation, the Austrian fascists released prisoners. (The card index was already in Nazi hands.) Back to *Zieglergasse*, Vienna, the Neubau area. She made music with Hans and composed a song. Hans made a copy of it. Hans Kunke wrote the date and her name at the bottom. *Song to the Unborn Child, April 8, 1938, by Steffi Kunke.* It was like a farewell.

The long way to the Lichtenberg Fortress (near Prettin on the Elbe River) goes past the Rossau Barracks (red brick building, the Elisabeth Promenade) to *Morzinplatz*, the former *Hotel Metropol*. There she meets old acquaintances. Some of them know the building from happier days. (Käthe Leichter, for example. Her Romanian grandparents lodged there.) And the time-lapse camera goes on again: Arrest on the *Brillantengrund*, arrest on January 9th, in the evening. The year 1936 is getting off to a good start: everything, everything in vain. Defense alliance, paramilitary training, even General Körner's battle strategy. He did not keep it to himself, but he could keep it. They kept their weapons ready and became hardened in defense tactics. They soon awakened in an interrogation cell.

217

But before that, military exercises, burying weapons. Yes, even in Mauer Steffi's younger friend, Anni H., buried weapons. She wasn't twenty years old. The eternal, grinding waiting in their positions for attacks by the regime and the national guard, until they are weak, until they are crippled. Seven women at the Lichtenberg Fortress. That sounds nice but definitely isn't. Suse Benesch in solitary confinement. The fortress walls are cold.

We're talking about Steffi. We're speaking for Steffi. Steffi is occupied with counting. Right now Steffi is striving to escape with her life once more. Steffi has all she can do not to miscount. The rod whistles relentlessly. Steffi is also unrelenting. She counts as long as she can, clearly and plainly but not too loudly. It could sound like moaning, and that irritates the masters. We, too, were unrelenting, with ourselves. Relentlessly and at all costs, we carried out the Party's change in course, against the lower echelons. We were against a mass organization and for a cadre organization. We changed from the short to the long perspective, from the United Front to the demarcation against the communists.

Eight...nine.... The concept of the Austrian nation. We rejected it. Steffi and many leaders of her party rejected it. Austria was nonsense promoted by communists and democrats in all camps. Hans and Steffi are addicted to the ideas of a greater Germany. Only bitter experiences brought the socialists to revise their thinking. The idea of a greater Germany, a mistake, paid for too dearly.

Police interrogation at *Morzinplatz*. We missed the opportunity to leave the country. We remained behind. We were left over. Others came back illegally from safety in exile into the so-called Eastern Province. Hedi Urach, for example, then the girls from France. Many

218

of them wind up in Ravensbrück. Many are saved by the resistance in the camp. The side entrance at *Morzinplatz*. We missed the opportunity to leave the country. We also disdained accepting the instructions from abroad. The organization craze that came from abroad was for us at most a stimulus for jokes. The side entrance was on *Salztorgasse*. How many there were who did not come out again! You didn't enter by the side door of your own free will and under your own power.

The large entrance door and a hallway to the barred door. Behind it a room for admissions officers. On the left, the prisoners' waiting room, then the confinement room with, as far as I know, eleven cells, five cells on one side and six cells on the other, each two meters by five meters. They were divided by barred gratings that produced spaces of two meters by two meters and two meters by three meters respectively. Light burned night and day. To the right of the grating was the cot, and high up in the outside wall there were totally blacked-out windows. Two doors to the stairway, one next to the outside wall of the admissions room, one leading from the confinement room. From there you were led to the upper floors, to the fingerprinting room, to the special prisoners. The screams usually came from the cellar.

The history of the Lichtenburg Fortress, the history of the stronghold. In 1812, Napoleon's Russian campaign makes a fortified city out of nearby Torgau. What is to be done with the convicts and those who fall into the category of prisoners? Take them up into the fortress. So the windows are barred, walls are moved, and cells are erected. An architect can always be found for something like that. (Who knows, otherwise they may yet demand and receive from the conqueror the freedom and equality that his campaign embodies for the poorest of people in spite of everything.) By the way, the rulers promise reforms of their own accord. Napoleon does not force them. *(When he had gotten rid of the gentleman, the king of Prussia broke his promise. It would have been amazing if he had kept it.)*

And thus, in addition to the dissolution of the guilds and the (formal) granting of equality to the Jews, the Russian campaign remained at least as an example to be copied at the appropriate time. We won't give it up for anything less.

The landed gentry did not really recover from Napoleon until the end of 1848. Even Torgau and Prettin have revolutionary democrats among their citizens. Where to send them? Of course, the fortress. We don't travel in the other direction until November 1918. At that time the soldiers' council freed 76 military prisoners. Don't worry, that doesn't last long, and three years later the wind of the old masters blows again. (They are also generals, big landowners, and industrial magnates of the empire in the Weimar Republic.) There is still room at Lichtenburg Fortress for two thousand of the seven thousand who fight in March of the year 1921. (A good beginning. The average of 800 prisoners is exceeded for the first time.) Vienna's hunger riots come on the first of December (and yet the workers of Vienna were still collecting money for the endangered Soviet Union).

On June 12, 1933 it happens. Lichtenburg Fortress becomes one of the first concentration camps in Germany. (Generals, big landowners, and industrial magnates are satisfied.) In September Mr. Dollfuss follows with Wöllersdorf. (Many members of the defense alliance received political indoctrination there for the first time. So everything, as we know, has two sides.) The two thousand men from the Lichtenburg Fortress march to

Buchenwald on July 31, 1937. In the middle of December the women are there. Steffi came in the early summer of 1938.

On the evening of January 9th, the wife of the aforementioned Hans Kunke, the teacher's assistant Stefanie (departs from the corner of *Zieglergasse/Burggasse*, rides streetcar 48 to the beltway, changes to the emperor's city train, the Hütteldorf line, rides to the Ober St. Veit stop, and walks along *Hügelgasse* to the girls' elementary and middle school on *Feldmühlgasse,* Vienna 13, eats the croissants of Baker Bauer on *Burggasse* for breakfast and corrects the notebooks in the teachers' room).

Stefanie Kunke, convicted of assisting her husband, on the basis of handwriting—demonstrably hers—found on the pamphlets. She denies it, of course, but after all there is the confidential message, then the former insurance agent, nondenominational (just between us: Jew), about whom it can certainly be assumed that he.... (Then there is the enumeration of his functions in the central committee of the Revolutionary Socialist Party, and his report to the leaders in Brunn is attached.)

On the evening of January 9th. It is 1936. The year is still young. The school vacation has just ended. The information-service material has just been freshly duplicated the day before, ready to be distributed. The pamphlets entitled *Capitalism is War, Socialism is Peace* have been brought across the beltway from the depot at *Pfeifergasse* 3 in the fifteenth district. (Josef Neubrunner has been arrested. Heinrich Widmayer and Anna Lechner from *Loquaiplatz* have been arrested. Julius Uhlir and especially the brothers Alfred and Franz Hummer have been arrested. It's not far to *Myrthengasse*, just twice around the corner, Colleague.)

On the ninth of January the waiting is over. On the ninth of January the trap snaps shut, and in her apartment Steffi—as her husband's assistant she has not only a typewriter but also more than two hundred kinds of printed matter stored in containers (so the version about storing things for unknown people does not hold up)—Steffi comes in close contact with the enemy from the right. He has been waiting there. Käthe had already warned about him in 1919.

But before that Steffi had become engaged. Before that Steffi was in love. Before that Steffi was a student, *Hegelgasse* (always for Kant). Before that it was clear to Steffi that you had to start with the children, especially with the workers' children who suffered because of the educational privileges of the others. (Their own semi-education was less obvious to the middle-school students.) So Steffi became an elementary and middle-school teacher, all the more because she believed in Otto Glöckel, in his school reform, in practical teaching methods, in his idea of community education. (That's what was taught at the teacher's college.) And just as Steffi began to teach, there was the set-back with the middle-school law, the crazy notion of the two class tracks. That is how you pursue the politics of possibilities while losing utopia. (Käthe warned about that.) And with that Steffi soon helped to sift out ten-year-old girls for the second class track (perhaps), and took courses in law and political science at the University of Vienna on the side, and in addition was (perhaps) a member of the Communist Students, and in addition (probably) already had a personal file (see confidential information).

When did it begin? It began on the streetcar—back then many more people rode the streetcar—after a session, after a meeting of the district organization, perhaps in 1929, perhaps as early as 1930, an intervention, a brief comment, a good beginning in the mandolin orchestra. Steffi's lectures are suitable for printing. What does Steffi lecture about after Hans Kunke's question on the streetcar? (Your intelligence, your talent for the working class.) There are ten lectures for the training of the local group, with discussion: *What is Fascism? What is Imperialism? Basic Economic Questions*, and *The Ethical Co-existence of the Two Sexes*. Besides that, Hans's exciting musical revues, as we already know, political texts to familiar melodies. Anni H. is the producer, and the local group can't keep up with the performances. It goes on like that until 1934. Käthe has already been warning against wait-and-see tactics for a long time. She has long since been demanding offensive action. Long ago Käthe formulated the slogan: *They say Bolshevism and mean the Republic.*

And so they strive not to be swallowed up. After 1934 Steffi and Hans strive very hard not to be swallowed up by the communists. And by 1927 at the latest, they had already been roasted.

While we are writing our gestapo reports—it is August 10, 1935: Ernst Blaukopf, the son of Leibisch and Berta, née Horn—Leibisch born in Poland, Jewish, authorized to live in Vienna, merchant, unemployed, living in poverty. Leibisch's unemployed son Ernst, furrier's assistant, registered as a lodger in his parents' apartment, is said to undertake a trip to the Comoro Archipelago, a trip that he actually cannot afford. According to his own assertions, he plans to remain there for eighteen days with two like-minded friends. The names of the friends: Stiller and Meiselmann.

Ernst, who claims to be affiliated with the social democrats, stood watch while the communist Isidor

Meiselmann painted billboards. The painted slogans were communist. For standing watch he got four weeks, for the communist pamphlets, six weeks. At the end of April he was arrested with thirteen other radical leftists in the central cellar at *Taborstraße* 8. His return is noticed. The dependable informant is notified.

Informants. Contrary to the general assumption, they were present among both the socialists and the communists. Didn't Käthe have her own personal Judas? He pats the children, acts concerned, and asks about her valuables. Passport, code name, travel route, border crossing—everything divulged, even the clandestine communications connection with the prison, which was the pretext for the trial and concentration camp. Everything was buried there, by the tree, and the first place the gestapo went in Mauer was to the tree. But Käthe, with her hat pulled far down over her face, wearing a long overcoat, hurries from *Belvederegasse*, through the city hall park, to the Votive Church. It is Käthe's third-to-the-last known walk through Vienna, on May 30, 1938. The lilacs were surely already in bloom, and that is not a figure of speech. The Votive Church was surrounded by a sea of lilacs. On the way she made a telephone call at *Rudolfsplatz* 1—the news that the gestapo had been in Mauer (and had dug), the assignment to her fourteen-year-old son: "Go to your friends' place. I'll follow you there immediately." At 6:00 p.m. Käthe appears on *Belvederegasse* (Käthe's next-to-last walk in freedom in Vienna). "You must be very brave now. They're going to arrest me" (and on to *Rudolfsplatz*, Käthe's last walk through Vienna). Her son obeys and regrets it to this day.

They forced us to say: "Be brave." Later they said, "Be brave, be quiet." And they laughed and exchanged glances. We said, "Be brave," and hated the fear and the foreboding within us. They were brave and would have liked to weep. But your courage, Käthe, lifted the others up. Your courage preserved the Jewish block. (*Tipsy, Tipsy,* Sunday afternoons, the story, history lessons, poems, songs, everything, everything.) Your courage was the courage of your son. He also helped Steffi. Käthe, awarded your degree a second time through being deprived of your doctor's title for us, your strict, tall Pick grandparents can be proud of you.

For the time being, Hans Kunke, the highly gifted musician and obedient son with the bourgeois occupation, is a functionary who molds the Liesing group (Socialist Worker Youth). For the time being, Hans sings the songs of Bert Brecht and Hanns Eisler in his beautiful baritone (against the stupidity in music, hoping for its legitimate impact on politics). For the time being Steffi eagerly follows Hans's correspondence with Bruno Walter. For the time being Steffi and Hans usually spend their vacation in the mountains. *(They carry enormous rucksacks and hike from cabin to cabin.)*

The hiking from cabin to cabin, the silent agreement in walking through Austria's mountain world, conversations, perhaps purely theoretical, plans, evaluation of the situation, the Great Depression, the struggle against unemployment, the confidence in constitutional law, the jokes about the bourgeois reaction, the *Manifesto*, the *Origin of the Family*, Franz Mehring, Max Adler. Then *Moscow 1937*. The heads roll there. We want to shed less blood (and do not suspect that it will be our own). How could the weak be challenged? What are our goals? Does the Party also have weapons? Käthe asks that anyway. And in the evening the view from cabin to cabin and that faith in legalities. Hans likes to sing and sings well. His musical arrangements of the gallows songs have melody and rhythm. In addition, when there was time, amateur music. Hans accompanied himself. He challenged Steffi to practice the violin more. Steffi especially liked the *Spring Sonata* and Eisler's workers' choruses. Eisler called it the *return of material to its practical function*, that is, after he left the twelve-tone system and found a new tonality. But Hans and Steffi only experience Eisler's greatest popularity indirectly, in the Spanish Civil War. And later, in France, Hans and Steffi are already dead.

France, here we encounter François Albert Fabre, in civilian life Kurt Blaukopf. We remember Ernst and his trip to the Comoro Archipelago (right, the brother), with my friend Meiselmann and my friend Stiller and Stiller's sister. The week in Comoro (perhaps in tents next to the water), the meadow landscape, Isidor Meiselmann and Ernst, both born in 1914. (Isidor works at *Herbst and Caon*, at *Morzinplatz* 3, in the textile quarter. The stay was exclusively for recreation. During the second week of his lawful vacation, Isidor was at his father's home in Prague.)

The quiet days in Comoro. One of the men brought his sister along. It would perhaps be our last vacation, if it was a vacation. We'll never forget those quiet days in Comoro. Ernst Blaukopf, born in Buczacz, Poland, now residing in Vienna, *Leopoldgasse*, unemployed, at present a fugitive (with friends in Comoro, etc.).

Beethoven, especially the *Spring Sonata*. It will still take a lot of time to lay claim to the great legacy of music, before it becomes the possession of the workers. Hans encourages Steffi to practice her violin playing again. Hans has recognized Steffi's talent. She will be a teachable pupil. Steffi, raised in a household of women, has a boy friend who encourages her inclinations, who recognizes her talent. Steffi's companion, an enlightened student, a good head, with round, horn-rimmed glasses and attentive eyes, with his hair combed back. He wasn't big. The SS did horrible things to him. But that was later. Nevertheless, not much time remains for Steffi and Hans. Get ready. Did you look closely at your friends? Did you look into people's faces? (Will you stand by us? Will you maintain your composure? Harder times are coming.) Hans wears a leather coat. He looked very good in that clothing. A digression about wearing leather clothing, to say nothing of boots, is needed here. Who wore what kind of leather coat? When and where? Hans loves the mountains. By his own admission he is no more capable of parting with them than with women. (His wife is now Steffi), the one with the ready laugh, with the regular teeth—just the things that happened to our teeth in the camp—who is perhaps not otherwise proud, but decidedly too proud to let Hans notice her liking for him all too soon. That's how it is. Theory is one thing and practice is another. Besides, there was no time for an infamous, for a tawdry love story. Not until long after the discussion, long after the lecture (if it was a lecture). Not until the beginning of the *Spring Sonata* does Hans's beloved face lose that trace of sarcasm. And perhaps high in the mountains, after hiking for days from cabin to cabin, we were young, we were happy, and the tension, the duty fell away from us. Time was not good to us. Who knows, were we really good to ourselves?

While the first wave of arrests cripples the Party leadership of the social democrats, in the second district and in the Prater area resistance begins to develop. The barber with the funny name Peisach Berl Bindel is a little knot in the distribution network of the illegal newspaper *Rote Fahne*. The thread stretches from *Schreigasse* 12, that is, *Adambergergasse* 2, which is the same thing, for that is Bindel's store. The thread very plainly stretches over to *Leopoldstraße* 16, to this unemployed furrier's assistant Ernst Blaukopf (I mention only Comoro), and from there across *Untere Augartenstraße* into *Rembrandtstraße* 30 to Anny Moldauer, who has four pieces of the training material in her bag when she is in the official process of delivering the groceries for the unemployed nanny Wilhelmine Mayer. The unemployed nanny had bad luck. To her own detriment, at the end of July she appeared in the store of Berl Peisach, barber from Lemberg, born in 1870, Jewish, married. But just two days before, a police raid had been carried out there. Unfortunately, Ms. Mayer was taken along. Even though Eugenie Bindel, Bindel's wife, secretly hurried to carry 1869 copies of *Rote Fahne* to her neighbor Anna B. and to leave them with her during the raid, Ms. B. gave the package to us voluntarily when she heard the accusations made against the Bindels.

Franziska Weiser, on the other hand, Bindel's unemployed lodger, now homeless, previously Polish, ran to Charlotte Ruhig, née Feiglstock, with a package wrapped in a blanket. Ruhig burned the printed materials. The blanket was saved. Anny Moldauer received the training material and the package from a certain Paul, and she knows this Paul through Ernst Blaukopf (a fugitive, by the way) whom she has known for years.

Nine...ten.... I can't bear it any longer. The whip always whistles against the same blood-streaked place. Next to me women who have been half beaten to death practice knee bends, half dead and knee bends. Their boots kick to death anyone who can't get up. I won't remain lying down (not yet). Nine...ten.... I can't bear it any longer. I want to write about love. This is a love story. I am writing about Steffi out of love for Hans. I will write about Steffi's love for Hans. There is no sense in remaining silent about our love any longer.

Four years of work, the most intense conversations. Anni H. had hidden weapons. We had not gotten far beyond Franz Mehring and other writings when the building of the new organization occurred. Then the leaders were arrested. We lived in one household for exactly fifteen months and eleven days. Then they also knocked at our door or rang the bell. They came to our place in the evening. It was the beginning of the end. For us it was the end. On March 6, 1938, the leaders sent out the word to give up.

Not so for those who really believed in Austria. Without regard to posterity, for them what counted was: *The struggle continues, people of Austria.* It was beautiful and dangerous, but they knew that. And in the factories, the camps, in the army above all, in the occupied territories (France, for example) the Austrian resistance fought. (You're not alone, Steffi. Don't give up.)

We didn't go out alone. We usually went in pairs. If somebody had made an acquaintance, we let our comrade walk ahead with her soldier, a little ahead in the cinema, at the city train station, in the park, on the long streets. It was dangerous. It probably didn't always have the appearance of danger. Besides that, the soldiers were happy to be able to talk to a nice girl, to go to a café.

Conversations about the war, the situation on the fronts and at home. The contact with the soldiers occurred as if spontaneously. The girls made contact directly, on the bus, in the subway, in front of a store window or a monument. The idea came from Austrian and German antifascists. Many girls joined in, who had left their homeland for so-called racial reasons. This was the first contact of these *girls* with the workers' movement. They were young and very pretty, those girls. Even if it didn't seem especially costly, what they did was very daring. A little conversation, a flirt, even on a mission of peace against the overpowering force of war, a walk in the woods, a trip from Lille to Brussels and the return with heavy bags that didn't even have false bottoms, an invitation to a dance party could be disastrous.

Millions of pamphlets were distributed. Perhaps a hundred or more soldiers were moved to desert. Flyers, tracts. (Turn around! Don't walk alone! Take a second person along!) The soldier's newspaper printed on tissue paper (appears monthly, printed every two weeks under the threat of mortal danger) produced and distributed. Distributed in Paris, in Antwerp, Arras, Bordeaux, Liège, Lille, Marseille, Nancy, Nîmes, and Rouen. Distributed and carefully hidden, toothpaste tubes, condoms, bags and suitcases with false bottoms, always traveling, good on their feet and in danger.

Ten, eleven. April 8, 1938, a key date. The score of Steffi's song bears the date of April 8th, the song to the sleeper, the song to the dreamer *in some mother's womb ...Can we afford to have children?* This question, treated expressly in an illegal publication, was asked not only by Ernst Blaukopf's friends. Hans and Steffi Kunke undoubtedly asked themselves that, even if only secretly, even if they perhaps did not talk about it so openly. So Steffi Jelinek, whose married name was Kunke, wrote her song to the unborn dreamer. So the teacher's assistant—a figure of speech, perhaps a dirty trick, Steffi was

230

fully qualified—so Steffi wrote wonderful fairy tales in Ravensbrück, for the children in the camp. Unfortunately they have been lost. Then she went to Auschwitz.

But before that Steffi was arrested. She was already familiar with that. Two years earlier, she had already had the honor of being arrested. But it's different this time. Somehow she had indulged in the illusion that our Nazis would not become so bad, especially since there were some members of the defense alliance among them. They only hoped that in that manner they would be able to get revenge on Dollfuss sooner. At least that's what it says in Hans Kunke's report to the leaders in Brunn. Of course Hans repeated the general opinion.

On April 8th they made music together once more. A song was written. Hans, don't be sad. Hans, get to work. Let's make music, if nothing else. The work for the Party has been suspended, at least as far as the leaders are concerned. We have nothing to reproach ourselves with, except perhaps that Hans is a Jew. He didn't even think of that anymore. Most of the Jews like Hans had not thought about it anymore until they were forcibly reminded of it. (Austria's anti-Semitism is no greater than that of other countries, is it, Comrade?) So there is no reason for panic. On April 8th, or perhaps one or two days later, they knocked at the door. It doesn't matter how, it doesn't matter whether they pounded, rumbled, crashed, broke the door down, or very politely knocked. She already knew the way, no sentimentalities. The nondenominational Kunke is shoved into a car as a communist and a Jew. He is also still wearing his glasses, but not for much longer. The intellectual. That's dangerous. The designation intellectual can now mean the death sentence. Off through the middle of them. No you don't. Your wife will be taken separately. We still want to have a word with her. Now it is up to her. And Hans with his round spectacles, Hans with his beautiful eyes, Hans with the leather coat. Hans, our years together! Hans, our work! Hans...our life...Hans!

Eleven...twelve.... Up the steps, from the confinement cell through the door and up the steps. The fingerprinting room, the interrogation room, and the second decisive question. It no longer mattered, not for Steffi. But for those of us who are thinking of Steffi, in images, piecemeal, for us that question, too, Steffi's answer in particular is decisive. Do you want to...? (And that is followed by the beastly question in some irrelevant formulation, more or less impertinent.) Steffi's answer has been preserved for us, the answer given by so many at that time: *I'll share the fate of my husband.*

I'll share..., a figure of speech, an abstract formulation. It means: It will happen to me, befall me, swallow and destroy me. I'll share the status of a victim, the person sentenced to death. I'll share....

Steffi, the block leader, received twenty-five blows with the staff or the rod. She was carried away unconscious. She was taken to the punishment block. In the language of the camp it was the closest thing to the gas chamber. Punishment block meant: destruction through work. And yet there was another block that suffered under the same conditions, and that was the Jewish block, block number eleven.

From the point of view of traffic engineering, this camp was in a favorable location, one kilometer from Fürstenberg on the railroad line from Berlin to Neustrelitz, on the east shore of Schwedt Lake, which separated the camp from Fürstenberg. To the north and northeast

232

there was forest. On the south, the Havel, which flows through Schwedt Lake, formed a natural border. In addition there was the four-meter-high wall, with high-voltage wires on top, outside, a double chain of sentry posts. Later, machine-gun bunkers were added. The camouflage was good. No passer-by suspected that there was a camp in the hollow. No scream from those being tortured penetrated to the outside.

During the period from November 1938 to the middle of April 1939, fourteen housing barracks, two hospital barracks, and a wooden building with laundry and kitchen facilities were built by five hundred prisoners from the Sachsenhausen camp.

On May 18, 1939, the women from the Lichtenburg Fortress arrived. Their numerical series was adopted and continued beginning with number 1415. Then the villas of the SS were built. The Jewish prisoners and the prisoners from the punishment block were especially well suited for that. So Käthe had to carry out the most difficult kind of road work and load bricks onto boats on the Havel River. She wrote a poem about that, "Little Red Brick." And on Sundays she sang the old freedom songs with the prisoners. And the women from the political block came secretly and sang along. While working outside, Käthe and Steffi were able to exchange glances, (perhaps) exchange secret messages, and on the camp street the political prisoners put bread and sausage in their pockets.

In the storage room for personal effects, we clothed the old woman anew from head to toe. She wept so. We swiped sacks of clothing from the storage room and dressed the old women and the children. It was autumn. They were being deported. We suspected, but we did not know for certain that it was a deportation to death. (And the nice winter coat was wasted).

We did not walk alone. We always walked in twos, always cheerful and pretty. Only pleasant-looking and confident *girls* were suitable. They had to be fearless, if not daring (and were sure they would escape). As human beings they had to be secure in their personal integrity and moral strength. (Trude's moral strength.)

We asked: When are you leaving? We asked: Where are you going? We could immediately tell by listening if somebody came from home, from Austria. I'm going to Innsbruck. I live there. Yes, I'll take a greeting home with me, a kiss, perhaps a toothpaste tube, we'll see. (Sometimes a familiar face from Vienna appeared, but from the other side. Composure, just maintain your composure and a cheerful face.) (Trude's cheerful face.)

Steffi and Käthe were able to give each other hope, exchange glances, until November 1940. Then Steffi learned that her husband was dead. On October 30, 1940, Steffi's husband ran across the sentry line. It isn't known if Steffi's husband was still wearing his glasses. Comrades, forgive me! I can't stand it. He ran across the sentry line to be shot. He was small and not strong. *A small, weak man with a big heart.* One night he told his comrades in Buchenwald that he couldn't stand it any longer. (He could no longer carry the heavy stones.) Farewell and forgive me. A shot, a machine-gun salvo from the sentry line. Perhaps he was lonely. Perhaps he thought that he was easing Steffi's situation. (I'll share ....) Steffi, who received twenty-five blows on the Saturday before Pentecost, becomes a widow on the day of the Feast of Jesus Christ the King. She wanted it that way. I'll share.... With the Jewish intellectuals, she builds the Ravensbrück camp, at least the villas of the SS. It began on the streetcar, that is, for Steffi. Hans's

234

question. She gave the real answer in 1938. "I'll share
...," she said. And she shared the stones and the bloody
fingers, the wooden shoes, the bloody foot rags....

Was it an Austrian? Was he happy to be able to talk
normally for once, to escape from the drill and the
banging noises, to talk normally about his cares and his
homeland? A person had to be careful, and yet not too
careful. Soldiers were found who rebelled against the
Prussian drill, who brought weapons for the partisans,
who cautiously carried out anti-Nazi agitation, even
some who joined the *maquis*, the underground of the
French resistance movement.

There is no point in counting anymore. Steffi is
unconscious. We will spare ourselves the report about
those prisoners who did not count any longer because
they were already dead when they left *Alexanderplatz* in
Berlin. Of course the journey leads from Lichtenburg
Fortress through the *Alexanderplatz* station in Berlin.
The numbers used in Lichtenburg were retained so that
there would be no confusion in counting. An encounter
with a fellow prisoner months later was an encounter
with a mummy. When we arrived at Ravensbrück, there
were women there who had been confined since 1933.
The women were already old. The ten years had given
them the appearance of old women. The clothing was
made of canvas. Added to it was the colored, so-called
corner, a triangular piece of cloth that was intended to
create a hierarchy, to destroy the solidarity of the
prisoners. There were also heavy wooden shoes that
were too large, with sail cloth uppers. After two days of
working outside, their feet were raw. The camp was
covered with black cinders. There were infected, deep
holes in their feet. There were no bandages. Prisoner
doctors tried to bandage them with paper bindings. Many

died of the infection in their feet. It look a long time for us to succeed in bringing Käthe into the block from working outside. It took a long time and required hard, conspiring struggles to save Käthe from the work outside. Inside she had to knit. We knitted for her. Käthe had to build a complete bed. We built it for her. Somebody (a chain of abraded hands of solidarity) swiped paper. Käthe's sociological study of the asocial prisoners: Not the people, the circumstances are to blame. It is futile to describe ninety-two thousand kinds of death. But it is important to call to mind the countless small acts of help, under circumstances where the justice of the stronger prevailed.

We know nothing about Leibisch and Berta. We know nothing about Peisach and Eugenie. We know that Kurt and Ernst fought with weapons. And Trude Weisler, Ernst Blaukopf's wife, goes with the girls to the movies, to the bistro, for a walk in the woods. Trude Blaukopf met a Tyrolean. Everything is perfect. Tomorrow he will take the material. (Trude's fresh skin, Trude's cheerful laughter, Trude's young, strong body.)

In the spring, thanks to camp solidarity, Steffi was put in with Rosa Jochmann in the political block. She was already a skeleton. She became the block secretary. Her eyes often stared so feverishly into emptiness. She dreamed, if only for seconds. She wrote her most beautiful fairy tales and poems. They were all tendentious, and for that reason, after Rosie's arrest, unfortunately they all had to be destroyed.

The poems were biased. Steffi's poems were tendentious. Even Käthe's play was tendentious. (And who remembers the funny secret message from the Vienna district court: It will rain keys. The doors will open. We will leave. Women, do not despair!) The play was entitled *Tipsy, Tipsy*, written by Käthe and the communist Dr. Hertha Breuer. (Do you remember the Lichtenburg Fortress?) The preparations took weeks. *Tipsy, Tipsy* was perhaps the refrain of a satirical song. Roll call was the magic word for raising the dead. Aluminum jewelry made from toothpaste tubes, straw skirts, and a charming bride and groom. (They were all sent to the gas chamber.) *We Are Alive, Friends* was the name of the play, the name of the spirit among the shaven heads of the women, a spirit that was hard to believe and could not be killed. Women, much less the material. And thus the counter-piece, the mask, lay ready in Käthe's closet. (What a luxury for a woman sentenced to death!) It humiliated the Jews and recognized only the SS. It was actually a satire, but they didn't notice that. They fell for it. Otherwise we would all have been sent to the gas chamber immediately. The original was destroyed after the performance. Surely Steffi was there at the evening performance. Surely she went over there with Rosa. Even the celebrations in the camp were tendentious. For May first, for the twelfth of November (yes, Käthe believed in Austria), Käthe organized tendentious celebrations to save the women. Käthe, tell us about the French Revolution. And shortly before her death, Käthe, the child of the *court and trial lawyer*, the granddaughter of Bohemian industrialists and Romanian bankers, is still pursuing the establishment of equality. She passes on the precious legacy of the working class to her comrades. Skeletons with their hair shaved off and miserable creatures hear from her lips the story of the French Revolution that is familiar to all of them, told over and over again. Because nobody can tell it like Käthe, the story of the man of 1848, her father (at least according to his year of birth), brought from the library on *Ru-*

237

dolfsplatz and given directly to the heirs, Ravensbrück, the camp street, on Sunday, between roll calls. And they can then pass it on. That is nothing compared with the commune. And we, those of us in the dungeons of the Austrian fascists, do you remember, Sisters, how we made the chain? No, our commune mother doesn't come out of her cell.... Of course, Käthe's example also stimulated Steffi to write, if you can call it writing, with the acute shortage of paper, where possession of a pencil lead was both a privilege and a death sentence. (Refugees in Mauthausen were each equipped with a fountain pen by the international camp committee.) So Käthe's poem, "To My Brothers," was memorized by a young communist woman and preserved for us.

Meanwhile, Ernst and Kurt Blaukopf, the sons of Leibisch and Berta, take up weapons against the German occupation forces in France. They fight in the French resistance. And Trude, Ernst's wife, is in the so-called girls' group, a division of the French resistance. They move the soldiers to leave the role of animals fattened for the slaughter. Many of the girls have a long road from Spain behind them and a long road through the camps in Germany ahead of them. *Turn around! Don't walk alone! Don't shoot at the French!* One day Trude was arrested. She was not there anymore. (You know, of course, Trude with the fresh skin, with the cheerful laugh, etc.) The soldier with whom Trude had made an appointment simply walked on when I asked him. (Shouldn't that be something to think about?) The news had been packed into the tube in vain. Our comrade had gone to the appointment at the barracks in vain. *If you go to Innsbruck, don't forget Trude!* Things almost went wrong. The soldier had enough. He didn't want any news. He walked past. Finally our comrade noticed the strange accent of the man she was talking to. She retreated inconspicuously, reproaching herself. I was just supposed to say hello, namely from Trude. Does she lie buried next to Ernst Blaukopf (Ivry, September 28, 1943), or did she wind up in a camp?

If so, it was after Käthe's departure. Her blue eyes were on us. Käthe, sitting in the truck in the bitter cold. *Waving, she disappeared forever.* Käthe, who probably suspected everything, perhaps not everything, but much of it. Käthe was not spared anything, not even being selected out, naked, as was customary. (Which doctorate do you have? That will surely help you.) Then the farewell in the Jewish block, with a delay because the truck could not get through the banks of snow, the snow that becomes a deciding force on the eastern front, by the tons, soft, delaying snow. Finally the morning came, and two weeks later, as agreed, under the prisoner number of a Viennese Jewish woman named Buckowitz, Käthe's last secret message: *Everything fine to this point...traveling through Dessau....* And the warm clothes, shawl, canes, glasses, false teeth, everything that we had given them to take along came back. Waving, Käthe disappeared forever.

Soon afterward it was Steffi's turn. Soon it was Steffi's turn. In the spring of 1942, shortly after Käthe's death (just beyond Dessau in a railroad car), Steffi was sent to Auschwitz to build the camp. Steffi knew that she would not come out alive, and that she would carry stones again, dig up the earth, drag rollers. The dirt and the cold in wooden shoes that were too heavy. A last message: *Comrades, hell is here.* In Ravensbrück they learned from Steffi what Auschwitz was, namely, hell. As always, Steffi was in the new camp as one of the first, this time in Auschwitz, the third one. She didn't

239

come out again.

Soon typhoid, black typhoid, also overcame Steffi. The green of the woods around Mauer, the hills in autumn, the fever, the pain, the inimitable green. Don't give up, Steffi. The garden, the question, the apartment of the conspirators, the apartment in the green country-side, containers beyond the hills, roll call, red flags, *Tipsy, Tipsy*, burying the weapons. Anni H., little friend, the inimitable green of the Vienna Woods and the red evening shadows of the Mauer hill...cover...my eyes....

TONSCHI

ANTONIE MÜCK
Divorced Ludsky, née Pospichal
Worker from Vienna
Born: June 4, 1912
Arrested: June 17, 1941
Condemned: August 27, 1942, together with
nine comrades-in-arms from Viennese factories
Beheaded: November 10, 1942

Dear Parents, I am sitting in my cell. The day has come. For weeks, and today especially, I have been with you in my thoughts. Dear Parents, I am sitting in my cell. In front of me lies a pale sheet of paper for my last letter, the one for my life, the letter before my death. Dear Parents, I have lived to be thirty—thirty years, four months, and six days old. Today my last day has come. Dear Parents, Seff, my Erika, Brother and Sisters, People, the day has come and I am quite calm. The time of anxiety, fear, despair, hope is past. Gone is the time of questions: What do they know already? Were the others arrested? How many of us? Who confessed? Who lost their nerve? Who is dead now? Gone is the anxiety about the extent of the punishment and the question: If it is capital punishment, will the war be over before it is my turn? Dear Parents, I am quite calm. The day has come. I wish for nothing but the time to write a long letter to Erika, a letter that conveys everything to her, one that contains my life, my experiences, my beliefs, our struggle, and our hope that all this, the night of fascism, will soon be over, and that Austria will be free in a peaceful world.

Dear Parents, I sit in my cell. I have lived to be thirty—thirty years and some weeks and days. Time rushes on. It drips from the walls. It rustles in the straw. It seeps from the graves, trickles through the years, turns to dust on my lips, scintillates on a February day. Dear Parents, time, the poor people's gold, whispers in our songs, roars in our writings, thunders across the abyss, for time is with us. Parents, Brother and Sisters, People, time does not heal wounds. It lacks the time for that. It streams, flows, steps out, runs onward, rolls away, pulls things along, lifts them up, carries them further, slipping away, moving. It is a stream of blood, emerging from me, driving life out, throwing life out, bringing it forth. Time, time flows out of me, a whirling waterfall, unstoppable, power, unspeakable, red!

Dear Parents, you have no idea of what we know. It is better, Mother, that you don't know. But the letter to Erika, I must start writing it, the letter that wants the most powerful comrade-in-arms for itself, time! A letter that conquers time, becomes time itself, becomes history, power, nation, sent out to embrace my daughter, to embed her in the womb of time, to bed her down in the womb called time, a letter that begins before us with the line of working ancestors, reaches out beyond us, a letter of safe conduct for days to come, for future legions of peace.

Dear Parents, I want Seff to forgive me for everything he has had to endure because of me. I'm sure it was a lot. Seff, my dear, I won't write to you. We know each other well. No words are necessary. Seff, when you were there with me on the Prater meadows, Seff, I say with me, even if the others are there. Your shoulders, your skin, the fragrance of the summers from 1938 to 1940. Seff, I'm not writing to you. We're strong. We saw the sun. We were ready. The harder days came. Seff, your good, now chapped hands. The red scarf against your bare skin. It looked good on you. You were the most confident swimmer of us all. The laughter about the startled policeman on horseback. We met secretly, Seff, with our eyes, Seff, when the fires were burning and the mosquitoes flitted in Lobau. Rubber rafts, launched near Langenlebarn, Seff. Do you still remember, *Brothers, to the Sun, to the Sun*? It burned on our backs and before we got to Vienna it was already cool.

Seff, my dear, I'm not writing to you. No words are

necessary. You know, we are deeply united in these walls that are wet with tears and oppressive with heartache. I told the priest that I no longer need any comfort. "Let's talk about something else. Let's talk about the future," I said. Seff, we understood each other without words. Please forgive me. Seff, we're simple people. You know we haven't read as much as others were permitted to. And even though we obtained printed material for the literature shelf, education still remained a question of social class. And as much as I tried to learn in school, I only sorted out the tatters and rags of education for the paper at *Bunzel und Biach*, where our female comrade became so infected, you remember, for the paper that the enemy of the working class now uses for his lies. Even though at the end we produced our own newspaper in Stadlau, for me the fight for peace was simultaneously a struggle for my right and yours and that of our children to education. So don't leave Erika. When I am gone, she will only have you.

Dear Parents, I sit in my cell with a narrow, pale sheet of paper in front of me. Thank you for your love and loyalty, for the photograph, the familiar figures, the beautiful table arrangement, the festive atmosphere. Mother, you always knew how to give your children a good home. At 7:00 p.m., Mother, it will all be over. Mother, there were so many of us. You know, I wanted so much to study. Don't be sad. You still have so many other children and Poldi, who will also be safe with you someday. I met a young woman here. Her boy friend was a soldier. He deserted, and she tried to hide him. In the prison on *Schiffamtsgasse* we had it easy. Solitary confinement was good training for us. We were never alone. Father, just think, almost all of us are women from our movement, each of us from the Party. Father,

I would like to make a sketch for you, the right angle of the cells around the inner courtyard, with the steps leading up the far wall. Fortunately, the barred door to the stairway creaked, so the felt-soled boots were no good to the gestapo official at all. Grete Jost on the one side, Grete Schütte on the other, and Poldi Kowarik and Hedy Urach, our central-committee member, on the side across from us—they drum: *They're coming! They're coming!* For we stand at the window. There is a plank bed and the washboard, a wooden board for laundry, on the edge of the bed and leaned against the wall. With toes clamped around the edge of the leaning board, I can just reach the window with the tip of my nose, and we give each other signals in sign language. One of us gives entire lectures that way. If a new woman comes and weeps and screams, then it gets on our nerves. It is as if we were on the edge of a knife. Our toes are as if they were on the edge of a knife, a knife and a guillotine. When one of them screams for days, we know that she's not a member of the Party, or that she hasn't been one for very long. It takes a lot of patience and time to train a woman who is frightened like that. The walls are both a hindrance and a help with it. When the South American woman on the outside left is set free by her consul—because the gestapo is already trying to secure a hiding place for their unavoidable end—after Grete gives me the sign, I pass the word along, and when she walks through the courtyard and reaches the gate, we shout in chorus from all the windows: "Until we see each other again in freedom!" We are still proud of the shout that we raised together.

Dear Parents, thank you for your love and loyalty. I can't tell you how often I looked at the picture each day, at least once a day, at least in my mind. Father, you have aged in recent weeks. Mother, you should take care of yourself more. Erika, Child, what will happen to you in school? I was not able to give you what I always wanted to. My child, the bicycle belongs to you, everything else to your father, my husband, Josef Mück. He can do with it as he thinks best. Just don't forsake Erika, don't forsake her.

Sisters, Friends, forgive me, if I was not always as I should have been. Please don't hold anything against me. It was that horrible early shift, the smell in the rag warehouse, the dust where Anni already became infected, the endless bending in the draft and cold. When I rode my bicycle from the *Am Riss* housing development every day, and the fog rose over Aspern from the edge of the field, the shadows hastily fled from the allotment gardens. Here and there a bicycle glided over the country road, toward the mill pond or up to the Kaisermühlen dam. Then I often had the vision of a special roll call. A May proclamation like before the year 1934. The fog almost conceals the suspension bridge and permits no view of the city center, the tower of St. Stephen's Cathedral. Sisters, during the long nights in these cold walls, legions emerged from the fog, enslaved, in chains, comrades. They appeared from all continents, black, yellow, and other peoples that we have never seen. Standing silently on the bridge, they stretched out their chained hands with their fists balled. Mute faces call and call to me and I don't hear anything. I ride across the bridge. Fists in chains seem to pull me from the bicycle. I push on the pedals and ride on, to the commercial wharf, to the rag warehouse, the place where I work.

There the men of the gestapo are waiting for me, and this time they really do drag me from the bicycle, and the trial begins immediately. Then I go through the jails of Vienna. Almost every night the same dream, and I feel their calls more plainly and their urging more urgently, but I can't hear them. All the months I spent in prison, I firmly hoped I would escape with my life. When the death sentence came, I understood what my comrades were shouting to me, that they were calling me to them.

Poldi, Brother, you are surely with our parents once again. Look at Erika's grades and give her something for her A's. Remember me fondly. Don't be sad, and think of me sometimes. But the most important thing is Erika. I could not be with her anymore, and when she was a little girl, I didn't have much time for her then either. Brother, it is important for her to learn the truth about us, so that she can spread our ideas. She can probably do it better and more convincingly than we could, if she has the opportunity for further education. When the war is over, she should go to school, she should make an effort, should help prevent such working conditions. She should learn a trade and fight to insure that the tragedy of the war is never forgotten, nor those who contrived it. Fight so that such a thing never happens again, I beg of you.

Dear Parents, I sit in my cell with a pale, colorless sheet of paper in front of me. The day has come. At 7:00 p.m. it will all be over. We are very calm here. I talked to the priest, told him my dream. We talked about the future. Monsignore Köck is a decent man. He promised me that he would convey my last will to you, even if I did not want to discuss religious things with him. Dear Parents, I sit in my cell. I would have liked to go on living. I tried to give my best. Surely betrayal was a factor. How could it happen that they destroyed our group? Those of us who had to work will now fortunately escape with their lives. Dear Parents, who will write the stories of the individuals in the *Schiffamtsgasse* prison? Who will write the story of the cells on the fifth floor? All political prisoners, all sentenced to death, even those who hope for clemency. Dear Parents, I sit in my cell, and I think about the families of the comrades who heard the death sentence with me: *...to death, and disgraced for life*. Dear parents, it feels good to be in disgrace in these times, but I think of the families, of the tears and sacrifices, of all the money that you spent for me in vain.

Dear Parents, I think of Max Schädler and Andreas Morth, who picked up the printed materials at my place, the ones that I got from "Bartele." Alfred Svobodnik, Johann Hojdn, and Alfred Stelzhammer, Franz Stelzel, too, the child is still young, he did the copy editing. I think of Felix Pfeiffer who made the stencils, of Corporal Josef Leeb, and the leather worker Franz Mitterndorfer.

Dear Parents, the hall had blood-red cloth hanging on the walls, so that we would be afraid. You were not permitted to be there, and our tactic was: Save yourselves. Save yourselves and reserve your energy for the struggle. We entered the hall. It was like a stage play, not a good one. The judge screamed like a desperate man when a comrade answered too softly because of weakness. Dear Parents, I am happy that nobody from home was there. You would not have forgotten the sight for the rest of your lives. Dear Parents, we could hardly recognize each other anymore, pale, emaciated, and disfigured by blows. Dear Parents, they were afraid of our writings on poor paper, hand-printed secretly at night in the gardens. These apparently so highly educat-

251

ed people rebuke our writings with blood, with death. Parents, they fear a child of the working class who can write. Dear Parents, at the mechanic Franz Stelzel's place they found the *Mercedes Superba* and the radio that the city leaders provided. At the machinist Johann Hojdn's place the phonograph records—*Internationale, Marseillaise, The Socialist March, Brothers, to the Sun.* What bothered them most was the letter of a young worker to a Nazi comrade. The tract was found at the tanner Alfred Goldhammer's place.

Dear Parents, it was a blue August day. They probably lay on the beach at Gänsehäufl until late in the day. Just a piece of grass from there, if we just had a blade of it. It all went very quickly, the slamming of doors, the pounding of hammers. The judge shrieked. We denied as best we could, but our deaths had already been decided. So I did not return to *Schiffamtsgasse.*

Now it is gray November and the rooks inhabit the fields around Vienna. If only we could fly east with them in the spring and return with the Red Army.

Seff, I won't write to you. There is no more time. It shriveled up, it crouches in front of me, a mountain from the paper factory. Seff, just to ride a bicycle once more through the Prater in the fall with you and Erika, to see the different shades of green, the glowing yellow, the deep-red blackberry bushes, and the red of the mountain-ash berry in the bushes, and then the blossoming reeds. I was already saving my money. My comrade from Kaisermühlen knew of a child's bicycle for me, but it was not supposed to be. So Erika will get my bicycle, and everything else belongs to you.

Dear Parents, Brother and Sisters, Friends, People, time, the poor man's gold, lies before me as a bundle of rags. It steals away, creeps out of my sight, slips out of my hands. In front of me is a poor, pale sheet of paper. They will see me die fearlessly. It is better to die on your feet than to live on your knees. Time, time, I see it arise, our time, from rags and rubble. I see millions marching on streets of gold, brothers, sisters, to the sun, to freedom in the peaceful world.

Dear Erika,

I'm sending you many, many greetings and kisses. Dear Erika, I haven't forgotten your A's. I said I would give you ten pfennigs for every one you get. For that reason I will give you the forty marks that I still have, and for every A from now on Uncle Poldi or one of your aunts will give you the money. So that is why I am telling you to be very good, and see that you get many A's. Then you will also have money again. Good-by, my dear little mouse.

The agonizing hour was every evening at 5:45 p.m., the hour when those who had been condemned to death were led into the so-called poor-sinner's cell. Pastor Köck was always with them then. He also knew that his presence meant strength and comfort for the dying in their last hour. He himself returned as a completely broken man after every execution. He often told me about the deaths of our male and female comrades. One example was little Toni Mück. When Pastor Köck came to her cell, she said: "Pastor, I need no spiritual comfort, for what I have experienced in these walls, which are wet with tears and oppressive with heartache—these walls have made me forget how to pray. Let's talk about something else, about the better and more beautiful future for which we have to die."

(And) as the state's attorney read the indictment

253

again aloud, Toni began to sing the *Internationale*.

(Dear H., forgive me, but you know, I have to get it off my chest. That plain, quiet girl who sang only love songs to her homeland in her cell, who loved her homeland and perhaps, God knows, didn't do much for the Party, died as a great heroine and as an example for many of us.)

Anna

Translator's Note: I wish to express my appreciation to Beth Bjorklund for her preliminary work and her significant contributions to the translation of this book.

L.A.B.

AFTERWORD

Since 1945, one especially significant focus of creative literature and non-fiction written in German-speaking countries has been the treatment of a diverse and complex set of problems and unresolved questions related to the Nazi experience and the specific roles played by individuals and religious, social, ethnic, and political groups during the period of German fascism. The spectrum of writings dealing with these issues is extremely broad. In addition to poetry, plays, novels, novellas, and short stories, it includes first-hand accounts written by survivors of concentration camps, as exemplified in Margareta Glas-Larsson's *I Want to Speak* (1981, English translation 1991), lengthy historical documentations written from a variety of viewpoints, and collections of biographical sketches and case histories of individuals who participated in resistance activities, including such works as the two-volume *Deutsche Widerstandskämpfer 1933-1945* (German Resistance Fighters 1933-1945), edited by Luise Kraushaar (1970), and the more recent volume, *The Conscience in Revolt: Portraits of the German Resistance 1933-1945*, edited by Annedore Leber (1994).

Although the accumulated mass of factual materials gathered by historians and other researchers sheds important light on the external details of what transpired during and following Hitler's rise to power, some of the most valuable insight into the impact of Nazism on the *inner* lives of individuals has been presented in fictional accounts dealing with historically documented victims of the German tragedy. In 1959, for example, the East

German writer Stephan Hermlin published a slender volume entitled *Die erste Reihe* (The Front Line), containing thirty short stories based on the lives of young Germans who perished in the struggle against Nazi oppression. In addition to portraying specific events experienced by his chosen characters, Hermlin succeeds in conveying their feelings, an intimate contact with the atmosphere of the times, and a sense of the relationship between the victims of fascism and human beings facing similar social and political problems in the contemporary world.

What Marie-Thérèse Kerschbaumer accomplishes with the seven "reports" of *The Female Name for Resistance* parallels in some respects the results of Hermlin's attempt to let the reader participate, in a deeply personal way, in the lives of historical figures whose experiences might otherwise have little or no impact on modern life. Like Hermlin, through the eyes of her protagonists or observers of their actions, sufferings, heroism, humanity, and destruction, Kerschbaumer provides almost direct contact with timeless struggles to maintain human dignity, improve the basic circumstances of life, establish validity and constructive purpose for fundamental interpersonal relationships, and define the inherent worth of the individual. But it would be false to assume that she simply sheds additional light on these problems with illustrations from the lives of other people who were destroyed by the Nazis, or that the essence of her contribution lies primarily in the illumination of the specifically Austrian rather than the general German encounter with fascism. Kerschbaumer's narratives differ from Hermlin's brief sketches not only in their depth and intensity, but also in their substance, their perspective, and the kind of literary experience they offer the reader.

The unusual power of Kerschbaumer's stories arises at least in part from the successful manner in which she penetrates the respective inner worlds of her central characters. Intimate feelings and important elements of personal reaction to situations, events, relationships, and the consequences of decisions and actions are conveyed to the audience in a variety of ways. In some of the accounts, the author permits the protagonists to speak directly through dialogues, letters, and reflections about past, present, and future conditions and circumstances. In others, external figures analyze and interpret deeds, thoughts, dreams, remembered comments, and other memories of personal contacts with the figures in question. The synthesis of ongoing mental associations pertaining to experiences on a variety of levels, with the raising of questions about behaviors, attitudes, and motivations, and the calculated guiding of the reader through carefully selected trains of thought toward sometimes jarring conclusions leads to an almost vicarious participation in the world of the women to whom the author introduces us.

On the other hand, Kerschbaumer's unique treatment of her broader substance is especially meaningful in elevating her literary message above the level of observations about events and people viewed in a limited geographical and historical context. The effectiveness of the author's communication of significant ideas results in large measure from her ability to project descriptions of individual lives into the higher dimension of general human experience. To be sure, beyond the simple fact of the protagonists' nationality, the stories are imbued with the distinct flavor of things Austrian, including the country's multi-ethnic society, the relationship of its inhabitants to the physical landscape, and the molding forces of a specific religious and cultural heritage. On a broader scale, however, the Austrian Nazi experience is carefully integrated into the whole of human history. In the section developed around the lives of Helene and Elise Richter, for example, in the course of the dialogue the two sisters relate their personal fates to matters far removed from themselves, including the evolution of man as a living organism differentiated from other species, early European history, and the situation in modern Israel. Similarly, by portraying postwar attitudes toward the remnant of a people, the author exposes the extermination of Austrian Gypsies as just one link in a historical chain that extends into the present; and the timeless, boundless nature of the horrors experienced by the nun Restituta, including the failure of society to punish the perpetrators, is underscored through questions raised about atrocities perpetrated by American soldiers in Vietnam.

Even the purely female perspective suggested by the title of the collection sets these particular portrayals apart from works such as Hermlin's vignettes about German resistance fighters. Not unexpectedly, less than a third of Hermlin's stories have women as main characters.

Women's problems have received more serious treatment in Austrian literature since 1975, but by transforming material from the lives of selected victims of Nazism into broader statements about the more general problem of male tyranny over women, Kerschbaumer has added a powerful dimension to women's literature as a whole. The way she approaches her creative task permits her to use the stories of figures like Stefanie Kunke, Antonie Mück, and the poet Alma Johanna König to raise forceful and important questions about female roles in society, in a new and compelling way.

For all of that, the true meaning of these seven accounts cannot be measured in terms of their content and message alone. They are also especially valuable as literary works of art.

Kerschbaumer's creative approach is particularly interesting. One device she uses to move her stories into the realm of universal experience is a process of interpretation of known facts, combined with the examination of possibilities, to yield suggestions of how things not necessarily were but might have been. The manner in which she presents her material clearly defines the relationship of these narratives to significant trends in postwar Austrian literature. Her literary method involves various forms of the experimentation with language that was fostered by the *Wiener Gruppe*, a group of writers who had profound influence on Austrian letters from 1956 to 1964. Kerschbaumer employs lengthy arrays of participles, adjectives, verbs, and nouns to emphasize the diversity of available alternatives for interpreting her data. She also repeats key phrases and sentences as leitmotifs that focus the reader's attention on specific ideas. Peculiar narrative structures occur in which there are long passages comprised of such things as vocatives, one-word sentences, phrases, and partial sentences without verbs. Ideas are thrust upon the reader in forms ranging from discourse, through dialogue, to indirect interrogation. As a result, the reader is compelled to participate in the evaluation of evidence and assess whether the portrayed feelings, utterances, relationships, and intimations are valid, while at the same time drawing conclusions about their meaning for his/her own life.

In addition to claiming their rightful place as significant works of contemporary Austrian literature, Kerschbaumer's stories also reflect the influence of the broader

German literary heritage. Direct mention of works by Theodor Fontane, Conrad Ferdinand Meyer, and Johann Wolfgang von Goethe is not simply incidental to the presentation of Kerschbaumer's own material, but rather something of an acknowledgment of her indebtedness to other writers for some of her ideas. One of the most interesting examples of a visible relationship to earlier literature occurs in the final story of the collection. There, Toni Mück describes a dream in which "future legions of peace" representing the whole world emerge from a fog, enslaved and in chains, and symbolically raise their fists to proclaim their determination to be free. In some respects at least, her vision and reaction to it are reminiscent of the title figure's dream and subsequent waking vision of a future in which the people of the Low Countries shake off the shackles of tyranny, in the final scene of Goethe's *Egmont.*

If nothing else, in its own way each of the accounts in this volume forces the reader to respond to the allegation—made by various figures representing the contemporary world—that nobody is interested in what happened to these women anymore. The thinking reader will recognize that the allegation is false, and that Kerschbaumer's "reports" are powerful documents of the timeless problem of man's inhumanity to man, or, better said: man's inhumanity to woman.

Lowell A. Bangerter, February 1995